**Praise fo**
  *I S*
**but My**

"Sarah Shankman hits a mother lode in this story. . . . [A] rich, spirited funfest . . . as earthy as the music it celebrates—packed with vividly alive characters, ribald dialogue, and suspenseful incident."

—*Kirkus Reviews*

"The title is enough to get you to open Sarah Shankman's book, and her bouncy country heroine, Shelby Kay Tate, is enough to make you stick with *I STILL MISS MY MAN BUT MY AIM IS GETTING BETTER*."

—Wormwood Scrubbs, *Des Moines Register*

"Set your boots next to the easy chair and kick back. . . . This is a romp through country music . . . [with] lots of froth and laughs."

—Roberta Alexander, *Time Out Travel* (Walnut Creek, CA)

"Ms. Shankman shows an appealing affection for her characters, even the minor ones. . . . In Ms. Shankman's world people are sometimes wrongheaded, sometimes short-tempered, always befuddled by a kaleidoscope world, but they mean well and the things they do can be pretty dang funny."

—A. Barton Hinkle, *Richmond Times-Dispatch* (VA)

# SARAH SHANKMAN

# i still miss my man but my aim is getting better

POCKET STAR BOOKS

New York   London   Toronto   Sydney   Tokyo   Singapore

"I STILL MISS MY MAN" Copyright 1995 New Street Songs (SESAC)/Stan Webb Music (SESAC)/Sarah Shankman. Words and Music by: Kenya Walker/Stan Webb/Sarah Shankman.

"BIG LEGGED WOMAN" published by "Frankie Staton Music Publishing Company." Copyright 1995. Words or Lyrics written by Frankie Staton.

"TURN YOUR FAITH ON" by Angela Kaset. Copyright 1994 Coburn Music, Inc.

This book is a work of fiction. Names, characters, places and incidents are products of the author's imagination or are used fictitiously. Any resemblance to actual events or locales or persons, living or dead, is entirely coincidental.

A Pocket Star Book published by
POCKET BOOKS, a division of Simon & Schuster Inc.
1230 Avenue of the Americas, New York, NY 10020

ISBN 0-671-89750-0

First Pocket Books paperback printing July 1997

10  9  8  7  6  5  4  3  2  1

POCKET STAR BOOKS and colophon are registered trademarks of Simon & Schuster Inc.

Front cover illustration by Tristan Elwell

Printed in the U.S.A.

*For Harvey Klinger*

# Acknowledgments

None of this would have been possible without Kenya Walker, Nashville songwriter, who was led by *her* guardian angel to find me on her very first flight to New York City. Kenya opened her heart, her music, and her life.

Also in Nashville: Dianne Petty, a godsister any songwriter would be blessed to have, who fed me and told me tales. Stan Webb, Angela Kaset, Karen Taylor-Good, and Frankie Staton are all superb songwriters and peerless guides to their special world. Pat Halper walked me through the business of music publishing. Ronny Light, producer, took me backstage. Jerry Atnip, art director, was a location scout extraordinaire. John Howard opened the first doors. Riqué *is* local color and the Sunset Grill my favorite hangout—especially with Nancy Saturn.

The Nashville Metropolitan Police Department was superbly helpful. Especially, Jim Stephens and Suzanne Stephens. Thanks also to Nancy Felder, Tommy Jacobs, and Daniel Baker. Lee England, of the Sheriff's Department, provided the grand tour of lockup.

Finally, much gratitude, as always, to those at Pocket Books, both in New York and in the field, who make it all possible. Thanks to Don Tapert, who started me down the road, to Lenora Robinson for the dumplings, and to Ruth Sandler, for the soap.

i still
miss
my
man
but my
aim is
getting
better

# 1

TUESDAY, ELEVEN-THIRTY, A BRIGHT SPRING MORNING, Shelby Kay Tate, already late, races down a sidewalk, speeding past a row of little shops.

She's just finished working the breakfast shift at Sweet Willie's, her day job. In an hour she has a songwriting date back at her apartment. Now she's headed for the cleaners to pick up the outfit she's wearing Thursday night.

*The Big Night.* Fifty-six-and-one-half hours from now, Shelby and her friends Lynn and Althea will be playing out, performing their own songs at a songwriters' night at the Sutler, a funky club out on Franklin Pike.

One more chance to set the world on fire.

Or Nashville, anyway.

Now, as Shelby lopes past the gift shop where she buys greeting cards, a tiny crystal star, hanging from a slender gold chain, snags her eye.

Shelby stops.

Is this star the perfect magic charm for a girl from Star, Mississippi? Thursday night barreling down on her? Needing all the help she can get?

A little bell tinkles as Shelby enters the shop.

Shelby Kay Tate. Thirty-two. Average height. About forty pounds too heavy, much of that in her overblown chest. Wild drifts of red-brown curls. Creamy valentine of a face. Nice straight nose. Mahogany eyes, a circle of gold around the left iris.

She's standing, dangling the little star. Watching the way rainbows of light bounce from it. Singing to herself, *Put the pedal to the metal, let the rubber hit the road,* a line from one of her songs.

Shelby's played for an audience four or five times in the year she's been in Nashville. But *this* writers' night is the one she'd been hoping for, praying for.

This could be her big break.

The chief honcho of A&R from Liberty Records, Chris Cassel, has put a couple of Shelby's songs on hold for a new album with superstar C.T. Maguire. And Chris's still looking for more. He's promised to be at the Sutler show, front and center.

Shelby stares at the fragment of crystal, asks, Do you have the power to make the man pick my songs?

She can see herself up on the Sutler's stage, belting one clear through the back wall, the star shining just above her cleavage. Hollering, ripping the feelings from deep down inside her. Janis Joplin does the country blues. Moaning low over her keyboard like she's gonna lay a big wet one on it. Screaming those desperate notes: Her lover's just driven off, left her on the side of a lonesome road, it's midnight and starting to rain.

Can you *please* help me, little star? She swings the

crystal from side to side, squeezes her eyes tight for a long moment, wishing hard.

Opens them and catches a flash of yellow over her shoulder.

Shelby turns, but the golden-haired man she's glimpsed is already edging out of the frame of the plate-glass window.

She freezes.

A drumroll.

*Leroy.*

Leroy in Nashville?

That's the *last* thing she'd wish for.

The man was the right size: five-ten, skinny. Shoulders hiked up toward his ears. Long hair slicked tight, but the curls fighting their way free.

Shelby didn't see his face.

Is it almost-handsome like Leroy's?

Does the man have Leroy's strange ice-blue eyes, so pale, you catch the right angle, you think you might see clear through to the back of his head?

*Leroy Mabry. Her ex.*

Nawh. Unh-uh.

She's been dreaming about Leroy recently. Hot dreams. Maybe this glimmer of gold is just a little flashback.

A sudden zigzag of heat lightning.

In her dreams . . .

*She and Leroy, newlyweds, jump out of his truck. Run like quicksilver through the Crossroads Club's parking lot on the south side of Jackson, Mississippi.*

*They're laughing, their teeth shining under the street-lamp. Shelby's all dressed up in a gold skirt and a short black velvet jacket. Leroy sports gray dress pants and a white shirt buttoned up to his Adam's apple, his blond curls swirled back like Jerry Lee Lewis's.*

*The Crossroads's main room is low and dark and smoky. A mirrored ball sends arrows of light bouncing off the dancers' faces, onto the hardwood. A black band swings up on the stage. The lead singer hugs the mike to his blue-spangled chest. Then throws it out, grabs it back, moaning, shaking, punching his pelvis. That microphone is a down and dirty slut, he just can't get enough of her. Shelby's hot to join the man on the stage. Show him her licks.*

*But Leroy says, Here. Hands her a shot of tequila, a lime, a beer. Then they hit the floor buzzing. Grab hands, twirl, pop at the ends of their arms like perch on the line.*

*They bump shoulders. Hips. Rub back-to-back, butt-to-butt.*

*Then they tuuuurn for the slow nasty.*

*When their hipbones touch, sparks fly.*

*Leroy is pistol-hard against Shelby's thighs of gold.*

*She isn't thinking about singing now. Doesn't even hear the band. Her mind is tapioca.*

*Leroy's tongue is gliding ever-so-slowly across her soft throat. He nuzzles her earlobe, whispers wet things.*

*Leroy's fingers search, find what he's looking for.*

*Then they race, headlong, out to his truck. Too hot to stop for anything. Slide onto that slick vinyl seat.*

Standing now in the gift shop, Shelby asks herself, Leroy's truck isn't out there now on Twenty-first Avenue, is it?

She carefully sets down the crystal star, thanks Betty behind the counter of Gordon's Gifts, then hits the sidewalk at a good clip.

Shelby runs first one way, then the other. She

brushes by a young woman about her age with a little boy in tow. The woman gives her a funny look.

Hillsboro Village is a sweet little throwback to the fifties, a single-story strip of semi-hip but still old-fashioned stores in one of Nashville's nicer neighborhoods. Chunky white girls don't gallop down its sidewalks, not unless they've been shoplifting.

Then she sees it. An old green pickup making a left turn up the street. It *looks* like Leroy's, but she can't tell from here if it carries Mississippi tags.

And what the hell would Leroy be doing in Nashville anyway?

The last time she saw him was six months ago. A high-ceilinged courtroom in Brandon, Mississippi, the county seat, an old walrus of a judge rumbling through the final shutdown of their nine-year-old marriage.

Leroy shaking his head No the whole time.

*Hadn't they promised to love one another until death them did part?*

*He had. And he would.*

*I've changed, Leroy.*

*Well, I haven't.*

Standing there on the sidewalk, considering maybe that's Leroy she's just seen, probably, ninety percent it was him, Shelby feels crazy.

She thinks, I don't have *time* for Leroy, a million things to do between now and Thursday, not the least of which is finishing that last song for C.T. I'm in a *hurry* here.

Her blood is hurrying, too. Racing. Roaring around inside her. Shelby feels like she's stuck her finger in a light socket.

And it's an awful sensation, except for that tiny part of it that feels good.

# 2.

GODDAM LEROY. LEROY ON HER MIND, SHELBY COMpletely forgot to pick up her big green shirt from the cleaners. Just jumped in her ancient blue Toyota, pointed it toward the Natchez Trace Apartments and home. Then *slightly* rear-ended a station wagon trying to make a left off Twenty-first. Spent twenty minutes talking the old lady driver out of calling the cops. Barely had time to change out of her greasy restaurant clothes, straighten up her apartment a little, there's Chuck rolling in the door.

Chuck McGivern. One of her best friends and a favorite writing partner. Her twelve-thirty writing date.

Sitting on her blue velvet sofa now. Strumming on his guitar. Watching her bounce around her tiny kitchen, making coffee.

"You seem upset," he says.

"Well, I'm not."

"Don't try to con a con man, Shelby."

"Wouldn't think of it."

"Sure, sure. But I'm telling you, forget it, 'cause whatever's on your mind, it's gonna come out, sooner or later. Give it up, let's see if we can't use it in this song." Chuck hits a chord. Then modulates it into a minor key.

Chuck McGivern is a songwriter's songwriter. He's had scores of cuts and several hits so big that drunks think they can remember all the words.

Shelby holds firm. "Nothing to tell. You ready for this coffee?"

"Is it your momma?"

"Nope. Talked to her yesterday. Mamaw's fine, too."

"Good. How 'bout Lynn? Y'all have a fight?"

"What are you talking about?"

"Talking about Leroy, I expect."

Shelby knocks her coffee over.

"Yep," says Chuck. Tapping his noggin. "Leave it to an ex-cop every time."

"What do *you* know about Leroy?"

"Not much. You won't hardly ever talk about him. Pisses me off, too. Depriving us of all that good material. I keep telling you, ain't nothing like an ex-spouse for songwriting. You can't make up that kind of dirt."

"I don't want to write about Leroy. Don't want anything to do with him. Don't have *time* for Leroy."

Then her dam bursts.

"Now, now. It was just a shock seeing him after all this time. Unexpected like." Chuck has Shelby snuggled up next to him on the sofa. Wiping her tears. Giving her a big old squeeze now and then.

Shelby thinks this could be dangerous.

Look at the man. Sweet as a peach cobbler in his new yellow-and-white-checked Western shirt, jeans,

7

cowboy boots. Six feet, strong and muscular, with a gut, but he carries it well. Sandy hair beginning to thin, but what do you expect, the man's fifty-three years old.

Chuck has been kinder to Shelby than any man in her whole life, and she's crazy about him.

In fact, there've been nights, all by herself on this very sofa, she's rationalized her way around the fact that he's married to Joyce. After a couple of beers, she starts asking herself, So what?

But even if Joyce were run over by a truck, there'd still be the Music City rules: You can write together, or you can do the wild thing, but not both.

Chuck says, "Why don't you go ahead and let your hair down about Leroy? I bet it'll make you feel a whole lot better."

"I wouldn't even know where to start."

"How about the beginning?"

"So, I was twenty, still living at home in Star, Mississippi, when we met. Population five hundred seventy-five. Most boring little burg in the entire universe."

Chuck laughs. "That's 'cause you ain't never lived in Jasper, Alabama."

"Don't want to, either. Anyway, I was playing piano and directing the choir for Star's Baptists. Taking some classes at the community college, keeping books for my stepdaddy, Dwayne's, garage.

"Now, I'd started writing songs back when I was a kid, soon after Mamaw set me down in front of the piano. Played by ear from the very beginning. She showed me some chords, that was it. Playing and singing and writing, they came natural as breathing.

"And in the back of my mind, I always thought, one day, I'll get on a bus, take off for Nashville, see if I can do any good.

"Then one night, Dwayne brings Leroy home for supper. New guy working in the garage. I hadn't dated much. And, you know, when you're that young, it's easy to mistake lust for love."

"Ain't that the truth."

"So we got married, moved into a double-wide mobile home on the edge of Momma's property. First year was good. Hell, what am I saying? It was great. We hardly ever got out of bed. Then things kinda cooled off. I was wanting to write more, Leroy said No, I needed to get myself a real job."

"Bet he didn't give a rip about your making music, did he?"

"Sure didn't. I think it made him uneasy, like he knew from the beginning that it was something separate from him, something he couldn't touch.

"So, anyway, I got this job in Jackson working for the Yellow Pages. Sales service. Eight hours a day of folks saying, *Well, what do you think? All caps or upper and lower? Is that box around it extra?*

"Five-thirty, I'd fly out to the parking lot, twenty-two miles and thirty-four minutes of songwriting freedom. Singing while I was dodging eighteen-wheelers, scribbling like a crazy woman on legal pads. It's a miracle I wasn't a piece of roadkill.

"Sometimes I'd be so close to finishing a verse, I'd just cruise on by the Star exit, park somewhere, make up a story when I got home: A wreck, Leroy. Rubberneckers from here to yonder, traffic backed up for half a mile . . .

"One time I was pulled over in front of a boarded-up Esso station, beating out the rhythm on my dash, so lost in Songland I didn't see Leroy until he stuck his face right in my window. I screamed, and he hollered, *I been behind you for five miles, wanting to see what kind of wreck you was gonna run up on tonight,*

9

*couldn't get home to have my dinner hot on the table. I felt guilty as if he'd caught me with a lover."*

"Same thing, idn't it? Lots of ways?"

"Yeah, well, and he just never let up on it: Who'd I think I was, anyway? Miss High and Mighty. Just wasting my time on pie in the sky."

Chuck says, "Tough enough, anyway, ain't it, sweet pea, writing songs? I still have days I think I ought to give it up, go back full-time to my landscaping business. For sure, us insecure songwriters don't need anybody like Leroy joining in on that chorus."

"That's the Lord's truth. So, anyway, we fought. Fought about my writing. Never had enough money. Bloom was off the rose. Funny though, the sex was still good, when we got around to it. Most of the time, we were too tired. Or Leroy was too drunk."

"That, too?"

"Oh, yeah. I mean, he always drank, from the beginning, but then, all you guys do, don't you?"

" 'Fraid it's part of being a good old boy."

"Yeah, well, it caught up with Leroy bad. He was a mess. Looks went to hell, too. Though that didn't keep him from picking up the occasional floozie."

Chuck counts off Leroy's transgressions on his fingers. "That's drinking and catting around and squashing your ambition. He hit you, too?"

"Never. Not once. He had, I'd been gone long before I was." Shelby laughs. "Maybe he didn't do me any favor in that category, now that I think about it. He'd knocked me around, I'd been over here writing years ago, already have myself a bunch of cuts."

"So what made you finally leave?"

"Oh, God. You're gonna love it. It's a great country song."

Chuck strummed a couple of chords. "Well, let's hear it."

"You know the part about how I'd heard Lynn talk at a songwriting workshop I'd sneaked off to in Jackson. That was almost two years earlier. She moved my heart. It was like something just burst inside me, a voice in my head hollering, Yes! Yes! Yes! I knew then I had to do this songwriting thing for real or die.

"So, anyway, I kept in touch with Lynn, and I was writing writing writing all the time like a crazy person.

"One weekend I lied, I told Leroy I was going to take Mamaw to visit her sister Margie over near Birmingham. Mamaw covered for me, and I came over here to Nashville for the first time. Lynn took me everywhere: Opryland, the old Ryman Auditorium, the Bluebird, Music Row.

"After that, I guess I was just a time bomb ticking, the least little thing could've set me off.

"Then one night, a year ago, Leroy and I are over at Momma's for dinner, and Dwayne and Leroy really get into the whiskey. Both of 'em could get real ugly when they were drinking, and the next thing you know, Leroy's yelling at me about wasting my time songwriting, and I'm yelling at him, and Dwayne's yelling at Momma and me both. Then Dwayne up and drops a full bottle of Old Crow right down in the middle of Momma's three-layer walnut cake. Cake goes ballistic. It's everywhere. Momma's crying. Leroy's laughing his head off. I tell 'em both to get the hell out."

"God, don't you love families?"

"They're what God gave us before He invented talk shows. Anyway, Momma and I clean up the mess. Then I go on home to that damned double-wide mobile home that I purdee hated by this time, go to bed. Mad. And alone.

"The next morning, I get up, Leroy's not home. I go about my business, getting ready for work. I'm out the front door, and there in the yard, pulled up in my flowerbed, is Leroy's truck.

"He's piled up in the front seat, naked as a jaybird, and he's got company. Also naked. Also yellow-haired like him, but female. Both of them snoring."

"That must have been a pretty sight."

"Well, I'll tell you it was. 'Cause I saw them, the message was clear as a bell. *Time to go.* I turned around, went back in the house, phoned in my resignation to the Yellow Pages, packed up, had my car loaded, the two of them were still asleep. I slapped on the hood of that truck, said *Bye, Leroy!* I was gone."

Chuck leans back and roars. "I always knew you were crazy, woman."

"Yeah, well, like I said, I'm still sorry it took me so long."

Chuck grabs both their coffee cups, refills them, sits back down. "Let me ask you this. Say Leroy walks up to your door right now." Chuck leans over and knocks three times on her coffee table. "Now, what're the first words out of his mouth?"

"Shelby, I want you to come on back to Star."

"That's it? You sure? He's still burning?"

"Pestering Momma to death, whining and moaning how much he loves me. Says she can't go to the Piggly-Wiggly, he'll sneak up behind her, beg for my address."

"Ain't he found himself no other women?"

"Lots, according to Momma. But she told me just the other day he'd been thrown over by Tinker Bradshaw, a little redhead I knew in high school. I didn't know Tinker had that much sense. Took *me* nine years."

"Well," says Chuck, "whyever he's here, I don't like the looks of it. If that was him in Hillsboro Village, it's no accident. He's tailing you, you can count on it.

That's not good, Shelby. He comes around here, you get right on the horn, punch nine-one-one."

"Don't be silly. Just because I don't want to see Leroy, doesn't mean it's an emergency."

*Unless,* she thinks, *I get it confused with my horny dreams, start taking my clothes off. Then I'll dial for sure, see if they'll send over a shrink, pronto.*

Chuck says, "Listen up. You even sniff that old boy, you call, say your ex-husband is stalking you, the cops'll be over in a red-hot minute. Nashville police are *very* serious about this domestic violence business."

*"What* domestic violence? I told you, Leroy never raised a hand to me."

"And we want to keep it that way."

"Yes, sir, boss." She laughs. "You know I'm gonna feel awfully silly, those sirens screaming, pulling up in the parking lot, Leroy's saying he wanted me to be the first to know he's getting hitched again, hopes it won't hurt my feelings. Or maybe he won the ten million dollars from the Publishers Clearing House, wants to give me a chunk of it."

At that, Chuck reaches over and grabs up his guitar. "You start coming up with that kind of creative bull-shit, I think it's time we got down to some serious songwriting."

"You're right." Shelby looks at her watch. "I've only got an hour and a half left now, all our jawing. Lynn's coming over at two-thirty, then I've got to be back at Willie's at five, filling in for somebody, dinner shift."

"Well, let's get to it, girl."

"Okay. But hold on just a minute, Chuck. All that coffee, I need to go pee."

The bathroom of Shelby's little one-bedroom apartment is down a hallway lined with posters of Janis

Joplin, K.T. Oslin, Mary Chapin Carpenter, Reba, k.d. lang, Patsy Cline, Elvis—Shelby's own Hall of Fame. A refreshing change from the stuffed heads of poor dead animals Leroy had shot.

Now, coming out, zipping up, Shelby reaches up under her big turquoise sweater and jerks on her bra. It won't stop riding up. The booger's elastic is shot. She could concentrate a lot better if she took the damned thing off.

A minute later, standing in her bedroom, naked to the waist, she calls to Chuck, "You know that thing you're always saying about how the most serious problem in country music today is finding a rhyme for *truck* that ain't dirty or stupid—other than, of course, young'uns thinking they can use their craft more than their spirit?"

"Unh-huh."

"Well, I was thinking about Leroy's old green pickup and—" Shelby slides open the second drawer of a yellow-enameled chest of drawers.

It's then that she sees the thing nestled up inside the right cup of her black lace bustier.

Now, Momma'd always said Shelby's scream was a snake-strangler.

# 3

AT FIFTY-THREE, CHUCK STILL HAS THE MOVES. He comes flying into the bedroom at a slight diagonal, his big body crouched, the pistol in his left hand pulled in close. He sweeps the room right to left, back and forth.

"Where is he?" Chuck's eyes are wild, rolling.

"Would you look at this!" Shelby grabs up the thing from her drawer and sticks it in his face.

Chuck steps back, narrowing his eyes, trying to focus. Finally he gets it. Sputters, "A piece of fried chicken? What the hell, woman?"

"A chicken breast that Leroy Mabry plopped right in here!" With two fingers, Shelby holds up the long-line bra. Jabs at it.

His adrenaline slowing down, backing up, disbelief stepping into its place, Chuck lowers the gun he'd pulled from his briefcase. "You're hollering about fried chicken in your underwear? Jimminie Christmas, Shelby, have you gone nuts?"

15

No. She shakes her head. She knows exactly what she's talking about. "Leroy did this. No doubt about it. Leroy's been here."

"Hon, you want to sit down? You need a glass of water?"

"I do not, and do not patronize me. I've not gone stupid. I'm telling you, Leroy has been grubbing around in my dresser drawers. I *hate* that. Jesus."

Chuck sticks the gun in his belt, snug up against his gut. Leans back on his heels. Shelby can see him, Southern sheriff in some car commercial. Chevrolet. Ford. One of those.

"Tell me, Shelby," he says, "how do you put this chicken together with Leroy?"

She doesn't care at all for his tone. "Chicken *breast*, Chuck. Leroy always was a major boob man."

Shelby glances down at her own chest for illustration, and only then realizes she's still naked to the waist.

"Good Lord have mercy, McGivern! Thanks a lot!"

She grabs for her sweater, hugs it to her the best she can.

Oh, boy. *Now* she's pissed.

Pissed at Leroy.

Pissed at Chuck.

And, suddenly, very turned on.

For with the exception of a couple of one-nighters in the past year, Shelby's been lonely too long.

Chuck says, "I guess you'd rather I'd have said to the mother-raper, which is who I thought was in here, Oh, excuse me, I'll just come back when Shelby's decent."

"No, but you could have said *something*."

Or you could have just grabbed me, she thinks. Just reached out and grabbed me. Gathered me up. Pulled me back and looked straight into my eyes. Said, Shelby, I want you. *Need* you, baby. Bad.

But what Chuck's saying is, "You want to stand here and argue about it, or you want to put your sweater back on?"

He turns sideways, away from her. But he's sneaking looks. She can feel his eyes on her chest.

She thinks, Come on, Chuck. Make your move, son. Put your hands where your green eyes are. Smoking peepers. Melting bedroom orbs. And a ruby red mouth so soft and warm, I can just feel it.

Sweat's pouring down Shelby's forehead. Dripping through her lashes. She raises one hand to wipe her brow, her breasts swing free.

See, Chuck? See *that,* son?

Chuck sits down on the corner of her bed. Leans back on his elbows. Gives her his crooked grin. The grin of a man who knows exactly how sexy he is.

Lynn once told Shelby that, years ago, when Chuck was working at a mill, he'd get off work, there'd be three or four cars waiting for him out in the parking lot, women flashing their headlights. *Pick me.* Was that how he met Joyce?

Pick *me,* now, darling, Shelby thinks. She turns. The turquoise sweater is still in her hands. Then one hand. Now on the floor.

She says, "Leroy was wild for my boobs. Couldn't keep his hands off them. Always making awful jokes about chickens. White meat." She picks up the piece of fried chicken. Dangles it, closer and closer to Chuck's mouth. "No doubt about it, darling. This is Leroy's calling card. Leroy's here in Nashville. Been right here. In my bedroom." She purrs out those last words.

Chuck's gaze is a barn-burner.

"Come here, woman," he groans, reaching up.

Palms turned toward him, fingers beckoning. "Come on, Shelby. Come on, baby."

Lord, she prays, You better give me a sign here quick.

She waits, a nanosecond. Hears nothing but the pounding of her own love-starved heart.

Shelby falls, tumbles into Chuck's open arms. He catches her, holds her tight.

Oh, Lord, Lord, Lord. It's been *so* long.

He presses his hands against her cheeks. "Baby, baby," he whispers over and over, looking at her like she was the only one. Ever. Forever.

She devours the lie, doesn't give a damn. Swallows it whole.

Chuck lowers his mouth to hers. Their tongues start flirting. Fluking.

Shelby needs more flesh. More heat. More muscle. More bone. She needs this big man all over her. She reaches for the buttons on his shirt.

Then her front door slams, and a woman calls, "Hey, Chuck? It's me, Joyce. Where y'all at?"

# 4

OFFICER JEFF WAYNE CAPSHEW HAS HAD A BAD DAY from the get-go.

At six A.M., he was buckling on his service revolver, thinking, I bet she didn't buy any coffee, when she, Danielle, struggled up off her pillow and glared at him.

"This is it, Jeff Wayne," she said. "Marry me or move out."

Her timing sucked. The day before, Jeff Wayne had put in a righteous seven-to-three patrol with the Nashville Metro P.D. followed by eight hours guarding a women's clinic, pro bono, the star in his crown for the week.

"Tell me this," he said, staring down at her. "Did you get to the Krogers' like you said?"

"I know it was my turn, but I had a *real* busy day." Danielle stuck out her bottom lip. She thought it made her look like that blonde in the jeans ad, but it didn't. "Mary Sue has the flu, and I had to pick up her step class on top of my own. But, anyway—" The Queen of the Aerobics Instructors sat up, her big rosy nipples daring him to cross her. "Don't try to change the subject. It's put up or shut up, Jeff Wayne."

She was still yelling when he slammed out the door, late, didn't have time to stop at the Dunkin' Donuts. He got to the barracks, the coffee maker had just shorted out and died. Then the lieutenant ordered him to report NOW to the big old limestone capitol downtown. Jeff Wayne stood around half the day behind a barricade, caught a glimpse of the President in his limo. Which was more of a thrill than he'd thought it would be, but still didn't make up for his morning.

He'd just escaped Operation Baby-sit, was cruising down Demonbreun toward some emergency rations at the Burger King, when he passed his friend Jerome Bible pulling out of the firehouse. In his Suburban, just off duty. Come on over to Sweet Willie's with me, said Jerome.

Jeff Wayne's regular meat-and-three is the Elliston Soda Shop. But Sweet Willie's is good, too.

Roast chicken, fried chicken, chicken and dumplings, meat loaf, liver and onions for the meat. Choice of three vegetables: fried okra, candied yams, green beans with fatback, black-eyed peas, macaroni and cheese, corn, cottage cheese, pineapple rings, Jell-O.

Dessert: sweet potato pie, pecan pie, banana pudding.

Decor: smoky pine-paneling with signed photos of country stars, politicians, visiting Indian chiefs. Red Leatherette booths around the perimeter. Beige Formica tables in the middle. Chrome chairs.

The main difference between Sweet Willie's and the Elliston is that the waitresses at Elliston are about a hundred-and-three. Sweet Willie's caters to the music trade, hires young songwriters to say "How kin I hep you?" Many of them awfully pretty.

Jeff Wayne and Jerome have claimed a booth.

"Move out?" Jeff Wayne's saying, running a hand back through his golden waves. "Marry her or move out? The woman's nuts. I don't want to marry her. Don't plan on moving out, either. It's *my* house."

"I thought so." Jerome carefully adds dollops of cream to his coffee until he and it are the same shade of dark brown. "Though there is a lot to be said for the institution of holy matrimony."

"Easy for you, man. You've got Althea."

"She is something, isn't she?" Jerome grins. "But Danielle, now she's a good-looking woman."

"Yep. Danielle is a fox. Natural blonde, body by Jane Fonda, and a killer face."

"Sounds like you writing up her rap sheet, 'stead of praising Mother Nature for her bounty." Jerome's peeling the paper off a straw, trying not to light up because he knows Jeff Wayne doesn't like the smoke. "Uh-oh. She ain't regressed to that Abbie shit again, has she?"

Abbies are famous in Nashville. Coeds at the Absolute University—the college of the fundamentalist Absolute Church of the Holy Spirit—they are said to give the best head east of the Rockies, but won't do the Big One before the preacher says, You may kiss the bride. It had taken a few months for Jeff Wayne to convince Danielle that she was getting shortchanged.

"Nope," says Jeff Wayne. "Everything's tip-top in the bedroom."

"Well, what else? She starving you to death? As I remember, the girl doesn't even know how to roast marshmallows."

"No, but that's cool. You know I'm a culinary genius. Better than any fireman."

SARAH SHANKMAN

"Watch your mouth, Goldo. You're treading on sacred ground."

*Goldo Cop.* That was Jeff Wayne's fair hair plus his build. Not blown up like Schwarzenegger, but there'd been many a perp who'd given second thought to throwing down with the big man.

Jeff Wayne says, "You and Althea come over for supper this weekend, I'll treat you to some real grub." Then, getting back to Danielle, "Let me ask you, Jerome. Does Althea ever *bore* you? I mean, do y'all have stuff to talk about, most of the time?"

Jerome laughs. "You know Althea. The woman could jaw from now till Judgment, she'd be barely warmed up."

"Yeah, but that's not it. Do you ever just get sick of being around her? Does she *bore* you?"

Jerome pushes his linebacker shoulders back into the booth's red Leatherette, his fingertips on the edge of the tabletop. "Nope, she never does. You know, I was thinking, just the other day, the difference between Althea and all those other women I was with is, even four years down the pike, I hang on her every word. There's something about Althea that *delights* me. Like a puppy would, or a child, 'cept I don't mean this in no childish way. I like what's inside Althea. The way she expresses herself. I like watching her eyes. . . ."

Jeff Wayne gives his empty coffee cup a twirl. "Yeah, I was afraid you were going to say something like that."

Then their waitress sashays up, her hands full. Wanda, says her name tag. Cute face. Bright blue eyes. Her punk hairdo is an amazing platinum, black roots out about an inch.

"Here's y'all's burgers. One rare and one burnt to a crisp. Now is there anything else I can get you?"

Jerome thanks Wanda kindly, is about to tell Jeff
Wayne about this funny thing that happened yesterday
at the First National, where he moonlights security
three shifts a week. But it's just then that the two-way
on Jeff Wayne's belt starts jabbering about a domestic
disturbance on Acklen Avenue at the Natchez Trace
Apartments, a neighbor's called it in.

"I can wrap up that burger if you can wait a minute," Wanda says to Jeff Wayne, but she's talking to
his back.

Jerome says, "You know what? Could you take that
back to the chef, ask him to fire it till the E. coli's
well done, *then* wrap it? Thank you kindly, Wanda."

# 5

JEFF WAYNE CAPSHEW HAS BEEN A PATROLMAN WITH the Metro Police for ten years, long enough for him to know that a domestic disturbance is his least favorite kind of call. For one thing, these at-home dustups can be more dangerous than your average armed robbery, in which, at least, you have a pretty clear fix on the perp's intentions.

This kind of home-destruction dispute, you can never tell when one of the parties involved is going to have a change of heart midswing and decide the root of the problem is the Law.

It isn't the least bit unusual for a police officer to find himself on the receiving end of brooms, baseball bats, bowling balls, or pool cues. Cast-iron skillets are of particular danger in a region famous for its fried chicken and mustard greens. If somebody jerks up a red-hot panful of one of those and throws it at you, you'd wish they'd had a pistol.

Besides which, with the President in town, Jeff

Wayne finds himself rolling up to the Natchez Trace
Apartments with no backup. He's been here before.
The complex is red brick, two stories, great big U
going back from a parking lot. Efficiencies and one-
bedrooms, in a good neighborhood near Music Row,
but run-down, on the shabby side.

He knocks on the door of 114A. It's opened by a
roundish white woman with an amazing mop of dark
red-brown hair.

Shelby's startled. The man standing in front of her
bears such an astonishing resemblance to Leroy before
the booze started eating at him—except that he's
much taller, a *big* man, and he's wearing a police uniform—it takes her breath away.

"Yes?" she finally manages.

"Ma'am, I'm Officer Capshew, Metro Police." He
shows her his ID. "One of your neighbors reported
a disturbance."

"Oh. Sure. I mean, I guess we were pretty loud.
Somebody would."

"May I come in?"

Shelby turns, looking back over her shoulder at her
tiny living room.

Normally, she's proud of what she's done with it:
the old dinette set, little tables she's dragged home
from garage sales, painted flat-white, fixed up.
Sponged the walls a soft blue. The navy sofa, somebody with more money than sense had just left it on
the street.

But the place is a mess now.

The good news is Joyce skipped her electric piano.
But she's done one hell of a job on the TV. Threw
Shelby's Jim Beam Elvis right through the screen.
There's broken glass all over the blue shag. At last
the King was empty, the place doesn't reek of booze.

Next Joyce swept the coffee table clean. Knocked all Shelby's silver-framed photos to the floor. Momma and Mamaw, squinting into the sun on a trip they'd taken to Biloxi, are lying atop Shelby's daddy. He's at the beach, too, near Da Nang, wearing fatigues. Right before his Huey went down, burned him to a crisp. Now the glass from the picture frame is sticking in his knee.

Country music stars grin up from magazines skidded across the carpet.

Joyce had started on the kitchen cabinets, tossing cans of tuna, mushroom soup, tomatoes, peas, when Chuck got hold of her.

Now Shelby turns back to Officer Capshew, starts to offer him her hand, and then that doesn't seem to be the right thing to do, somehow, so she just points at herself. "I'm Shelby Kay Tate. This disaster area is my apartment. And that over there's Mr. and Mrs. McGivern. Chuck and Joyce."

Joyce is sitting on the sofa, and Chuck's leaning over her, pat, pat, patting at her shoulder.

Joyce, her head in her hands, shrugs him off. She's a tiny woman, barely five feet, probably ninety-five pounds in her jeans, matchstick arms in a peach-colored polo shirt. Bright gold ponytails stick from each side of her head. Joyce is about fifty, way too old, thinks Shelby, to be wearing her hair like that.

Chuck holds his hand out to the policeman like the two of them had just met at a barbecue, maybe, or a Sounds game out at the ballpark. "Good to meet you," he says.

"You want to sit down?" Shelby points the cop toward the one easy chair, an afghan thrown across it. She's somewhere between humiliation and humble, but then, too, she needs to get this over with. She's got a lot to do. "I guess you want to know what happened?"

"Well, that would be good."

"Nothing good about it," Shelby says, looking him square in the eye. "What we have here is a terrible misunderstanding."

Joyce lifts her face and wails.

Shelby continues. "Chuck and I were in here writing. Songs. We're songwriters. And I went in the bedroom to change. I'd just come in from my waitressing job and hadn't had time. I opened a chest of drawers, reached in for a brassiere, there was this piece of fried chicken my ex-husband had left in my black lace bustier."

Joyce snorts.

"Well, I screamed," Shelby picks up the pace. "It was a shock, realizing Leroy'd been here and all. Broke in my apartment, I guess. Chuck came running in from the living room, to my rescue. It was just about then Joyce here walked in. Came straight back to the bedroom and found us in what *looked like* a compromising position. Seeing that I was still naked to the waist."

And there it is. The same story that Shelby told Joyce when Chuck sat on her to make her stop screaming and breaking things. The story that's almost completely true. The story Shelby's sticking to.

Officer Capshew looks as if he's considering it. Maybe leafing through the pages of a Victoria's Secret catalog in his mind, trying to find the bustier she's mentioned.

"Well, ma'am—" he begins.

But Joyce is talking now, pointing at Shelby. "She's lying. It wasn't going to be but a minute, they'd've both been buck naked. Rutting like dogs. Oh, Jesus!

What am I gonna do?" Joyce's mouth crumples up on her, and she starts in crying again.

Officer Capshew looks uncomfortable. Shelby thinks maybe he'd be more at ease with a straight-ahead knifing or shooting, the blood and guts providing something to focus on other than people's hurt feelings.

"Joyce, hon, I wish you'd listen to reason," Chuck says. "We tried to explain to you what was going on, you went and had yourself this hissy fit . . ."

*"We?"* Joyce says. Putting considerable heat into it. Sucking up hard into her nose. *"We,* as in you and this heifer? Like thirty-three years of *us* don't mean a thing? Hell, I don't have to put up with this. No way." Joyce shoulders her big purse and is headed for the front door before anyone can grab her. "Can't nobody make me sit around listening to these two fornicators. Not even the law."

# 6

BY THE TIME SHELBY AND CHUCK AND OFFICER JEFF
Wayne Capshew catch up with her, Joyce McGivern
has slammed her shiny black van into the rear of Jeff
Wayne's white Nashville Metro PD cruiser.

Both taillights are gone, and the trunk is pretty well
smashed. Her van doesn't bear a scratch. It's not clear
if you could say the same about Joyce, who's slumped
facedown over her steering wheel.

Chuck jumps up on the van's running board. Struggles to get her door open. "Joyce!" he's yelling at the
window, "Darlin'? Are you okay?"

Jeff Wayne runs around to the passenger door.
It's locked.

Shelby stands off to one side. She feels really awful
about this whole thing, but, the truth is, it's getting
*way* out of hand. She sneaks a peek at her watch. It's
two. Lynn'll be here in half an hour, they're doing
their three-by-three—walking three miles three times
a week.

Jeff Wayne's reaching inside his car to call for an EMS vehicle and the fire department when Joyce suddenly sits up, rolls down her window, and spits. Straight into Chuck's face.

"Hold on a minute," Jeff Wayne says to the dispatcher.

"I hate your guts," says Joyce. "You've ruined my life."

"Now, darlin' ..." The big man wiping his eyes.

"Don't be darlin'in' me. Go darlin' that hussy over yonder." She points out her window at Shelby.

Shelby turns, sticks her nose up in the air. Then she notices a small crowd of tenants, Vandy students, passersby who don't have anywhere special to be, early afternoon on a weekday, beginning to gather in the parking lot. This kind of publicity, she can do without.

"I'm sorry about your car," Joyce hollers at Jeff Wayne, who tells the dispatcher to disregard his call. "I didn't mean to do it. I guess I didn't look before I backed up."

"That's okay, ma'am. As long as you're not hurt." Jeff Wayne walks up to the van, but not so close she can spit on him, too. "We'll let the insurance companies worry about the vehicles. But in the meantime, could you step out of your van? Let's get a handle on what happened here before you really hurt yourself."

Shelby thinks he sounds like he's taken some sensitivity training. She can't get over how much he looks like Leroy. But he's probably an awful lot smarter. Not someone who'd think that breaking into her apartment, leaving a piece of fried chicken in her underwear, would be the way to worm his way back into her heart.

Joyce holds tight to the steering wheel. She isn't getting out. "I ain't got nothing to say to that strumpet."

"Joyce." Shelby steps up to the van. She knows the woman has good reason to be upset, but Shelby's running out of patience. Fast. "Now, I already told you what happened. Which didn't stop you from going right ahead and trashing my apartment. But now, you need to get a grip."

"*I* don't need to do anything."

Shelby sighs. Starts explaining the whole thing over again, real fast, to Joyce. When she gets to the part about Leroy and the fried chicken, Joyce shakes her ponytails and says, "Oh, he wouldn't do that."

"I beg your pardon," Shelby says. "Since when do you have opinions on Leroy's behavior?"

"Since day before yesterday," says Joyce. "Since he came by and had supper with me."

Shelby and Chuck both do double takes just like the ones you see in the movies.

"He *what?*" says Chuck.

Joyce shrugs. "I don't know why you think that's so strange. He says he's here in Nashville to try to talk *her* into coming back home. Though why he'd want to is beyond me. But, *anyway,* he said he'd come by Shelby's a couple of mornings ago, was about to knock, he heard the two of you in her living room. Having a little too much fun."

"Jesus!" Chuck says. "Sunday? We were *writing*. Just like today."

"Don't take the Lord's name in vain," Joyce sniffs. "You would've been better off in church in the first place. Anyway, Leroy said he started to barge on in, then thought better of it. Thought he'd come call on me."

"How'd he know you even exist, Joyce? Much less where we live?" asks Chuck.

Joyce ignores him. "Walked right up on the front porch, knocked, explained how he'd come to warn me. I invited him in. We had supper, cheese enchilada TV dinners, he told me all about y'all."

"You *fed* a total stranger?" says Chuck. "He could have been a serial killer."

Joyce gives him a hard look. "So I came over here today to see what you were *really* up to. Well, you can see what I found." She sniffs, then leans forward and switches on her ignition. Says to Jeff Wayne, "Anything she claims about Leroy, I'd say, consider the source." Guns the engine. "She's a cheating whore, you'll pardon my French. And, Leroy, well, I feel sorry for him. He's way too good for her, ought to find him somebody else." Then Joyce peels out, rubber burning in her wake.

A while later, at the Burger King over on Hillsboro, Jeff Wayne, biting into emergency rations, the first food he's had all day, finds he can't shake Shelby Kay Tate's face.

Which is strange, his personal taste not running to hefty ladies.

But there'd been this music in her voice. And he hadn't been able to take his eyes off her eyes, the way they lit up when she talked. That golden ring around the iris of the left one seemed to draw him in. . . .

What does that *mean?* he asks himself.

Then something flutters against Jeff Wayne's cheek. He brushes at it. Looks around. Are there moths in the Burger King? Butterflies?

Must be his imagination. Or low blood sugar. He really needed some chow. Like this hamburger and fries. Officer Jeff Wayne Capshew reaches over, grabs for the ketchup.

His hand, strong and steady as an oak—which is why she chose him as her agent in the first place—passes straight through Patsy Angel, who smiles, then goes right on about her angeling business.

# 7

SHELBY HAS JUST FINISHED PICKING UP THE PIECES OF Elvis off her carpet when Lynn Hildebrandt taps on her door. Lynn takes one look, says, "Let's hit the road."

Ten minutes later they're striding down Sixteenth Avenue South, headed for the Church of Country Music. Which is what they call Music Row.

"When I'm feeling low, fresh out of inspiration," Lynn had said when she brought her here on Shelby's first visit to Nashville, "I walk up and down these streets. Just call out the famous names. I remind myself, some of these people know *my* name too. I'm part of this. I belong."

The Row doesn't look like much. It used to be an ordinary residential neighborhood. Sixteenth and Seventeenth Avenues South, the alley between, from Broadway to Edgewood, old two-story houses, World War II bungalows. Even now it's mostly that, with the occasional new brick office building and the shiny ASCAP tower tossed in.

But the signs out front tell the story. Ernest Tubb Record Shops HQ. Chet Atkins's office. And there's Owen Bradley's office, the man who'd produced Patsy Cline. Ronnie Milsap, Mel Tillis, Rosanne Cash all have offices here. The Country Music Hall of Fame is down on Division, near the tourist gift shops. Sony Tree Publishing, Warner Chappell, RCA, Atlantic Records, Warner Bros., Billboard Magazine. BMI, ASCAP, SESAC—the rights organizations that collect royalties for songwriters. Recording studios, booking agencies, music lawyers, tape duplicators. It has to do with the country music industry, it's here.

Strolling past Capitol Records, Shelby's saying, "Well, the good news is I didn't get down and roll around in the dirt with Joyce. And didn't use the F-word, not once."

Lynn says, "That's very ladylike. Considering she'd dragged your business outside. Might as well have charged admission, sold hot dogs."

"Jesus, what was I thinking about? Doing it with Chuck? Married *and* my best writing partner. Except for you, of course."

"Hey, give yourself a break. People have done much worse. Don't you ever watch daytime TV?"

Shelby goes on, "Like I didn't know the music business is nothing but a bunch of bubbas upholding the double standard. And I don't *ever* meet anybody else. Even Sweet Willie's is lousy with music men."

"That's the truth. I tell you, I don't know what I'd do in this town if I didn't have George."

"Hell," Shelby snorts. "Something happened to him, some bald-headed dude in plaid golf pants'd be squiring you to the Belle Meade Country Club in a New York minute."

Lynn Hildebrandt, a long lanky blonde with a strong resemblance to the young Lauren Bacall, lives the other half of her life with her entertainment-lawyer husband in the tony West End.

"But, anyway," Shelby says, "after Chuck and Joyce left, the cop went back to my apartment looking for signs of a break-in. And you know what? He said it looked like somebody jimmied the bedroom window. Said even if I'd left it open, Leroy just climbed in, it's still breaking and entering."

"What's he like?"

"Who?"

"The cop."

*"I* don't know, Lynn. Nice. Big. But, hey—" Shelby turns, walking backward, facing her. "—you wanta hear something funny? He looks so much like Leroy, he could be his brother. Giant economy-size version." Shelby bows up an arm, making a muscle.

"You're kidding."

"I am not. When I first opened that door and saw him, I like to have fainted."

"Well, hon, *he's* not in the music business. What's his name? Is he married?"

"Officer Jeff Wayne Capshew, I don't know his marital status, and the *last* thing I need is somebody who reminds me of Leroy Mabry. I'm telling you, Lynn, all I want Leroy to do is go on back to Star. I'm too busy for this."

"Are they going to investigate? See if it really was Leroy?"

"Officer Capshew said they could take fingerprints and all, but I said the same thing I said to Chuck. *Of course* it's Leroy, but he's not going to hurt me, so forget it. I've got bigger things on my mind. You know, I still haven't finished that song I want to do Thursday for Chris...."

"If a song's meant to be, it'll be, you know that. I

just can't believe you're not more concerned about this Leroy business."

"Look, Lynn, this tracking Leroy's doing—lurking around my place, calling on Joyce, that gift shop thing—it's just exactly like Leroy deer hunting. The man doesn't have a lot of imagination. He's doing what he knows how to do."

"Exactly. Except you're the deer. You gonna wait around for him to take you down with a twelve-gauge?"

"That's not it at all. Look, Leroy's not real good at communication. He probably figures at this point he can't walk up to me and talk any more than he could talk to a doe."

"That's nuts. You're nuts, too, you ask me."

"What I'm *really* pissed off about is screwing up my writing thing with Chuck. You think Joyce is ever going to let him come near me again?"

"Missing the point here, girlfriend."

Shelby stops, points Lynn toward a blue log cabin. Music Mill Publishers. "Do you see that big yellow banner there? Congratulating Tony Haselden on his latest hit?"

"I'm not blind, Shelby."

*"That's"* what concerns me. That's what I want, seeing my name up on a flag just like that one. Knowing that I write the songs that touch so many people's hearts they just can't help themselves, have to race out and buy them, send my music straight to the top of the charts. And nothing Leroy Mabry did or does or can do means doodly-squat to me unless he gets in the way of that."

Lynn shakes her head. "All I can say is, if you're not concerned . . ."

"What I'm concerned about is that this mess about Chuck and me is already flying around up and down the Row. I bet there are people inside that Music Mill this very minute laughing their butts off, somebody sent them an E-mail about us."

At that, Lynn's face lights up. "Well, now, that's not all bad. Let's look at this a different way. That fried-chicken-in-the-black-lace-bustier? Honey, if that's not pure Nashville, I don't know what is."

"So what you're saying is maybe Leroy's come here to give my career a jump-start? This chicken thing is just the beginning of a big publicity campaign he's planned for our writers' night, gonna make you and me and Althea famous? He'll do a couple more stunts, make the papers, they'll be standing ten-deep to catch us Wild Women at the Sutler Thursday night?"

"Now I think you've gone too far."

8

BACK ONCE MORE IN SHELBY'S PARKING LOT, LYNN leans out the window of her old boat of a black Mercedes. "You're sure you're gonna be okay?"

"I told you. I've got to work dinner tonight, fill in for LouLou, she's sick. I'm not sitting staring at my busted TV, if that's what you think."

"Tell Willie her favorite niece sends her a big one. And you remember, if you need me, just pick up the phone."

Shelby starts up her concrete walk. She has an hour and a half before she has to leave to go sling hash. Ninety minutes to empty her mind of everything but working on her song for C.T. McGuire.

*I didn't know that gun was loaded. When I pointed it at you.*

It's a song with attitude. About a woman, has been done wrong by her man, isn't putting up with it anymore.

*I didn't know that was the trigger, until I heard the boom.*

Shelby'd had her momma in mind when she started the song, Momma giving what-for to that good-for-nothing Dwayne she'd married after Daddy died. But Shelby hadn't meant for the action to be so blatant. Where had that gun come from? The focus was off the woman and onto the gun. That wasn't right. Maybe she ought to junk it, start over.

Shelby opens her screen door of 114A, shoves her key into the lock.

The door swings open.

"Hi, there," says Leroy. "How you doing, girl?"

Shelby stands for a long minute, trying to take it in: Leroy on her navy velvet sofa, smoking a Camel. Dangling one of her glasses. Her ice. Her bourbon.

*"You* looking awfully good," he says. Giving her his gummy grin. "Looks like you had yourself a little party here." He points his chin toward the smashed TV. The scattered magazines. Cans of chili, garbanzo beans rolling around.

Look at Leroy.

The man's puny. Always skinny anyway, he's lost weight. His arms are ropy. His old white T-shirt gapes at the neck.

How old is he? Six years older than her, that makes him thirty-eight. But he looks much older. Lots worse than six months ago, back in that courtroom.

Shelby raises a hand. Brushes at her hair, damp from her walk with Lynn. As if she cares how she looks to him. It's definitely a reflex action. This isn't the man she's been seeing in her dreams.

No doubt about it, Leroy's lost his starshine.

Or maybe it's her eyes that have changed.

His are still that spooky ice blue.

"What are you doing here?" she asks, moving into the room. *Her* living room.

"Hey, it's a free country. You ain't the only one they let past the Nashville city limits."

"You know what I mean."

"Well, howd'ya like that? Ain't seen your husband in all this time, you'd think you could at least say, Hi there, Leroy. How ya been?"

Shelby crosses in front of him, into the kitchen. She runs water in the sink until it's cool. She drinks long, her throat working. Then sets the glass down carefully on the counter.

Why the hell had she come on in? She could have just turned tail, run.

But she wants this over with. Now. Wants him gone. Gone back to Star.

She says, "Leroy, why would you call yourself my husband? We're divorced, you know that. And I sure don't appreciate your barging in. So why don't you just drink up, be on your way?"

His grin bounces to the floor. "*You* got a divorce. I didn't."

"Yeah, well, the way the state of Mississippi looks at it, we both did."

He knocks back the bourbon in his hand. "Don't mean nothing. Divorce is just a word."

"Oh, yeah? Well, here's another one. G-I-T. And another. O-U-T. You need any more?"

Leroy stands, both hands open in front of him. Eyes down, head turned. Uh-oh. Here comes his Jesus-on-the-cross routine. She's seen it lots of times before.

"I'm sorry, Shelby," he begins. "Listen, already this thing's gone all wrong. I didn't come over here to make you mad. Honest. I came to beg you to come on back home."

"You could have saved yourself the gas."

"Shelby, darlin'." He reaches out.

"Please don't. Just go, Leroy."

# SARAH SHANKMAN

He throws his hands up over his ears. "I don't want to hear there ain't no chance for us again. You can't *know* how sorry my life has been. You left. Dwayne fired me. I can't hardly find enough work to keep body and soul together. Don't hardly want to anyway, without you."

He reaches out again, but she backs away, keeping the coffee table between them.

He says, "I know I done wrong. The drinking and the women and you wanting to make your music and me not—well, hell, I don't need to remind you of all my bad points."

He's lost another tooth. And that tiny black hole makes her feel sorry for him. Damnit. She hears herself saying, "Listen, if you need a few dollars, I can help you out a little. Then you have to go. I've got work to do."

She starts straightening up. Picking up the country music magazines. Lorrie Morgan grins at her. A woman who'd for sure known the misery of a drinking man. Hers died of cirrhosis, left her with a family to raise. At least Shelby hadn't made *that* mistake.

Leroy's saying, "Come on back to Star, pudding. Honor those vows we made." His mouth's trembling at the corners. Tears sparkle. "I'm looking at you, it's like that very first time. Dwayne brought me over to your momma's house. You remember that?"

"Ancient history, Leroy. I'm not that girl anymore."

"But you are! Nothing's changed."

"Everything's changed."

"Okay, okay, I tell you what. You want to live in Nashville, here I am." He throws his hands wide. Under his nails, black crescents of grease. "I can get me a job. There's room enough for both of us here in this apartment, we get rid of some of this stuff. I don't see a blessed thing I remember anyway."

"You remember Mamaw's little yellow chest-of-drawers, don't you, Leroy? The one you left the fried chicken in?"

He grins. "You liked that, huh? I thought you would. A little reminder—me in your pretty places."

"That's it. You're out of here." She marches over to the door, sets her hand on the knob.

"You throwing me out?"

"Afraid so."

That's when he grabs her by the shoulders.

She stares at him. Just like you'd stare down a German shepherd. Or are you supposed to look away?

He says, "I miss you, baby." Then loosens his grip. Kneads her shoulders. "I'm trying to tell you how lonesome I've been without you."

"And I'm real sorry about that. But we're over and done with. You need to find somebody new, Leroy. Somebody to love you."

His fingers tighten again. "Oh yeah? Like you found that Chuck?"

She stays cool. Keeps her voice neutral. "Chuck's only a writing partner, not that it's any of your business. And why'd you go out to his house anyway? You shouldn't have done that, riled up Joyce. You can't go around sticking your nose in my business."

"You was sharing it with the whole neighborhood a while ago. Police, too." His tone is smug.

"Oh, yeah? Where were *you,* hiding in the bushes? This whole thing is stupid, Leroy. Go on home."

His hands slide down her arms. Then his fingers grip hard. Bruises tomorrow, for sure, she thinks.

"You telling me you don't miss me? Not one little bit?"

"Correcto. Now get your hands off me." She tries to pull free.

It's a dumb move. He jerks her toward him, then slams her hard up against the door.

"You bastard! Stop this!"

Leroy shoves up against her, lowers his mouth to her throat.

"Don't!"

"Shut up, Shelby. Come on, now. Be sweet to your daddy." He's rocking against her.

"Lee. Roy. No."

"Come on, Shelby. I know you've been missing me. Just got your head turned in the big city." Punctuating each word with his pelvis. "But we can fix that." He kisses her hard.

She twists away, but he's all over her. Hot lips. Teeth. Tongue. Shoving her harder against the door. Forcing a knee between her legs.

"How does that feel, huh? Dudn't it feel good? Long time, huh, girl?"

"Let me go!" She's getting louder.

He shoves a hand up under her sweater, grabbing at her.

"Stop it, goddamnit!" She's hollering now. And praying for rescue.

He pulls her down. Slides atop her. Straddles her on the blue shag. He's jerking down her black tights.

"You're gonna rape me, Leroy?" she gasps. "Jesus!"

"Shut up." Rooting now. Rocking. "You know you want me, baby. Jesus, you smell so good."

He reaches for his fly. She pushes up, straining to roll him off, but it's no go. He's jerking at her panties.

Shelby belts a scream out of the park. Puts a lot of spin on it. Nosy neighbors, where are you now that I need you?

Leroy whaps her one across the mouth. It hurts like hell.

"GODDAMN YOU!" she yells.

"Ms. Tate? Shelby? Is that you?" The voice is only a prayer away. Just outside her front door.

"Yes, pleeease! Jesus!"

After Officer Jeff Wayne Capshew, angel-sent, backs up and gets a running start, it only takes one good tackle to bring down that door.

# 9

THEY'VE TAKEN LEROY'S PICTURE AND HIS FINGER-
prints, and now a huge black sheriff's deputy is frisk-
ing him.

"Got any cigarettes or smoking materials anywhere
on your person?" he barks.

Leroy tries to explain how they already did all that
on the police side of the Criminal Justice Center before they sent him over here, but the man doesn't
want to hear it.

"The cops, they don't have to live with you like us
sheriffs do. Now, strip and bend over."

After that they give Leroy his bright orange two-
piece uniform, move him along.

Another deputy hands him one receipt for his
clothes and another for his valuables: wallet, money,
the keys to his truck, the watch Shelby gave him for
an anniversary. Leroy never can remember which one.

"You sobered up enough to understand the charges
against you?" That's the officer behind the desk in a

room filled with hundreds of hanging black garment bags. They look like dead bodies, give Leroy the creeps.

Leroy says he understands, but he didn't mean to hurt Shelby. Didn't mean to do anything but try to get her to come back home.

The officer nods, says, "Here's a list of bail bondsmen you can call. Use the phone over there on the wall."

None of them wants to talk to Leroy. The first three moneymen hang up the minute he says he's from Mississippi. Finally one takes the time to explain that it'll cost him five hundred dollars cash to cover the ten percent fee on his five-thousand-dollar bond. But he's going to need a local property owner to sign for the other ninety percent.

In case he skips.

"I wouldn't do that," says Leroy, "I got to get this thing straightened out. Make Shelby understand." But the man's already gone.

So here Leroy sits with his aching head, all by his lonesome in a rear cellblock. Wondering if his second-cousin Chris Cassel—the only person he knows in Nashville other than Shelby—will come to his rescue. And if he will, is he a Davidson County property owner?

He's left a message on Chris's answering machine. Hasn't talked to the man in over ten years. Hasn't even spoken of him, thought of him. But, boy, he's thinking of Chris now.

Leroy is scared shitless. He can't believe that Shelby marched right up to that judge, *happy* to rat on him.

He bets she's sorry.

'Cause she *knows* him. Leroy. He'd just had a few too many. Things got out of hand. Wasn't his fault.

Anyway, he'd been sleeping in his truck a couple of days, wasn't himself.

Leroy stares at the sign behind the officer out at the desk. *No, I can't call your mother. No, I cannot give you a cigarette. No, I don't want to hear how the other guy did it. No, I can't let you out.*

The officer says that Leroy has to wait here for classification, which means they have to check to see if he's a sex offender or a homosexual or a serial killer or hates black people.

Jesus, no, Leroy says. He doesn't want to be locked up with none of them, either. Leroy doesn't want to be locked up with nobody.

They give him a meal of tacos and corn and beans and applesauce, which helps his head some. Then an officer about Leroy's height, but otherwise the spit and image of Abe Lincoln, tells Leroy to come on. To pick up the gray plastic tub holding the two sheets, pillowcase, toothbrush, toothpaste they issued him. He takes Leroy onto an elevator, punches Four. Says, "No special unit for you, Mabry. Looks like you kept your nose clean back in Mississippi."

"I could've told you that," says Leroy. "So what's on Four?"

"Your basic felons. Badasses been beating up on their wives, robbing, killing people. You gonna be right at home, Mabry."

Leroy and Abe stand outside the barred door that opens into Cellblock C. Leroy's breathing hard, trying to get a grip. His stomach is full of bumper cars.

He's staring in at twenty-two five-by-ten cells marching down the right and left of a large rectangle.

Goddamn. This is a real jail. Filled with real damn

criminals. *Mean*-looking suckers he's about to be locked in with any second.

A bunch of them are hanging around five or six wooden benches in the center of the open space in the middle of the cellblock. They're watching a TV hanging from the ceiling. A basketball game's blaring.

Abe slides the door open, and every mother's son of them stops and stares at Leroy with ice-cube eyes.

Leroy doesn't know where to look. But he knows he needs to decide real quick because he isn't going to get a second chance. He's seen movies about prison. Terrible things happen to skinny white guys like him. He stares back at a couple of them—one black, one white.

Somebody says something he can't make out, and they all laugh. A real greasy sound.

"This here's yours." Abe points toward a cell on the right. Second one in from the hallway. The barred door opens.

Leroy looks in at a double bunk, a stainless-steel toilet without a seat, a steel sink on top of it.

"And this's Mac McKenzie. Your cell mate."

A short white man lies stretched out in the bottom bunk, a whistling snore ruffling his red lips.

Leroy is relieved. At least the guy isn't some huge black mother just waiting for lights out to get a head-lock on him. But still . . .

"Do you have one I could be in by myself?" Leroy asks.

Abe laughs. "Ain't a hotel, Mabry. We did you a favor, putting you in with Mac." He gives Leroy a grin, then saunters out of the cellblock, sliding the door behind him with a *ka-chunk* that make Leroy's bowels seize up.

He really is locked in here. Really.

Leroy stands, paralyzed, gripping his gray plastic

tub. He just can't believe it. How has this happened to him? He's staring at Mac, unfocused.

Then Mac opens his eyes and sits up. Not with a jerk, as if he's really been asleep, but like he's been playing possum. He stands, and the two of them are close enough to tango in the tiny cell.

Mac sticks out his hand.

# 10

MAC MCKENZIE LOOKS LIKE SOME KIND OF ELF. FIVE-
foot-three. Late fifties. Scrawny arms and legs. Big old
watermelon of a gut poking out from under the shirt
of his orange two-piece prison suit. Hair a frizzy
faded-red and silver. Cut in a shag—short on the top
and sides, shoulder length in back. Yellowed-white
mustache like a banana slug. Mud-brown eyes.

"My goodness gracious," he says, pumping Leroy's
hand. "Would you look what we have here?"

Then Mac stretches his thin lips into a smile so wide
it looks like it hurts. His voice is lower than you'd
expect from such a small man. And raspy. His teeth
are tiny tombstones: flawlessly white and clearly not
his own.

"Company, by God! Just as I was thinking how
lovely it would be to have someone to talk to. None
of the other residents knows how to carry on a con-
ver-*sa*-tion." He puts a funny spin on the word.
"Nothing even resembling a nice chat."

Out in the middle of the room, someone cuts a loud fart. Laughter, then someone says, "Chat that."

Mac ignores them. "Have you never been incarcerated?" he asks Leroy.

Has he been in jail? Is that what the man means? "Drunk tank a couple of times, back home. But I don't remember much about it."

Leroy is uncomfortable, standing close enough to smell this man. Something rank coming off him, like rotten vegetables. But the only places to sit are the seatless toilet or the bunks. The bottom one is Mac's. It seems rude to climb up top, look down on him.

Mac says, "And pray tell the cause of your present detainment?"

"What?"

"Why are you joining us in this ninth circle of hell? Did you run over a tiny tot? Pull a knife in a barroom brawl?"

"I don't want to talk about it."

Mac flops back down on his bunk, clasps his hands behind his head. His stomach stands tall. "Come on, now. Tell Mac what you're in for. Holding up a liquor store?" Then he laughs and his belly dances. "No no no. If it were something like that, you'd be strutting. Unless, of course, it went wrong. Let's say the clerk you robbed turned out to be the brother of the girl you raped out in the parking lot after your senior prom."

"I didn't even go to my damned senior prom. What are you talking about?"

Mac closes one eye and pins him with the other. "I was only postulating, son. Teasing, if you will."

"Yeah, well, I don't like to be teased. Listen, mister, all I want you to do is scoot over a little bit. Let me climb up on my bunk here. I'm going to sleep."

Leroy raises one foot, and then, as if a sudden storm had blown in on him, bursts into tears. He free-falls back to ground level.

"Well, well! What have we here?" Mac sits up again and pats his bunk in invitation. "Sit yourself down, lay your burden on your Uncle Mac."

But Leroy is way too upset to sit. Upset with Shelby, upset with himself—squalling in the middle of all these mother-rapers. Why, he hasn't cried since he was about ten, his old man backed over his dog, said it was Leroy's own fault for letting her out.

"I just wanted Shelby to come back home," he blubbers, struggling for control. "One thing led to another and . . ."

Mac smiles and insists again that Leroy sit beside him. When Leroy does, he gives him a manly one-armed hug.

"Listen, son. With Mac McKenzie, you're dealing with an old hand. I've been incarcerated more times than you have fingers and toes. Believe you me, I know the system inside out. You just tell Mac McKenzie exactly what it is you did, we'll figure you out a plan." He taps himself on his sunken chest.

"Mac McKenzie, Esquire, yes sirree. Jack of all your criminal trades." Mac leans closer. His rasp drops to a whisper. "I've been in some tights, son, I shudder to mention, but I got away with my tough hide every time. I used my wiles. My criminal bean. I'm a regular Nashville outlaw, that's what I am. And a righteous jailhouse lawyer, too.

"Yes sirree bob, I've seen some fancy lawyering in my day. Didn't hold a candle to me. Take that lawyer looking after Jerry Lee. We were locked up together down in DeSoto County, Mississippi, myself and Jerry Lee. Now, there was a boy who needed himself some fancy legal footwork. I told him, I did, I said, Jerry

Lee, son, you can't keep your hands off the lily-white necks of those women you keep marrying, you should stop marrying."

Leroy's lost. "I don't know what the heck you're talking about, mister." Wipes his nose on his sleeve.

"Jerry Lee Lewis, son! What other one is there? DeSoto County, Mississippi, just south of Memphis, he owns a ranch over there. That was when the IRS sicced the local cops on him. Charged him with narcotics possession. But he didn't stay locked up any time at all. Arresting Jerry Lee in DeSoto County, that was like arresting Elvis in Memphis. It wasn't something anybody wanted to do.

"Do you know you look a lot like him? Jerry Lee, that is. In miniature, of course. People ever tell you that?"

*Now* he's pushed the right button. Leroy sits up straighter and lifts his chin. "Yeah, there's been some. You really *met* Jerry Lee?"

Leroy doesn't know anybody who's ever met anybody that famous, except for his aunt Nancy, who'd once seen Billy Graham in person. He'd kissed her Bible. She wouldn't ever let anybody touch it after that.

"Of course I've met him. We're comrades-in-arms. But how could you doubt me? Now listen up, and listen up hard. Mac McKenzie would steal the gold out of a dead woman's teeth, leave her children crying of hunger, tear up her house for the scrap, but he would never, ever lie to you. Now do you believe that?"

"Yes, sir," says Leroy. He's finding himself drawn to Mac, like maybe he's the secret long-lost uncle Leroy had always dreamed would come and rescue him from his old man.

Mac's pointing a tiny finger in Leroy's face. "Lying,

Leroy. Lying's the worst thing in the world. My sainted mother taught me that." He smiles at the mention of her.

"My ma was a lady of the evening from Liverpool. Same place the Beatles grew up. In fact, she went to school with John Lennon's mom. And my da was a Mississippi riverboat captain, lived in Memphis, played a mean steel guitar."

"Well, I'll be." The news momentarily rips Leroy out of his own grief.

"You believe that, I'll tell you another one." Mac cackles.

Now Leroy is confused.

Mac's face grows serious again. "Actually, that's the God's truth. The truth and nothing but the truth, so help me God. Tell you what, I'll confess to the events that brought me to this place and time." He punches a finger into the mattress of his bunk. "Then you show me yours." He laughs, then gives Leroy a wink. "Don't be so tetchy, boy. You need to learn to take a joke."

Mac's rasping voice is so tamped-down now—like the sound one spider leg makes, rubbing against another—Leroy has to lean forward. "It would have been the largest heist in the history of Nashville, Tennessee. The First National, right there at Grand where Broadway turns into Hillsboro, they cash checks for Vanderbilt Medical and Baptist Hospital both. Ten million would have been the haul, yesterday being Super Payday, the both of them."

"No shit. What happened?"

"The problem with this kind of job is, you can't do it by yourself, and the good old days are gone. It's impossible to find anyone you can depend on anymore. He blew it."

"Your partner? That's rough."

Mac spreads his hands wide. "I chose him. I accept the responsibility. Good news is, what they're holding me on is simple weapons possession. I hadn't made my move when the police come lathering in. I was just standing there. An innocent bystander, as it were."

"With a gun?" Leroy whispers.

"Of course not! That would be a different story entirely. My Smith & Wesson was still in my belt. Hammerless snubnose .38. Belonged to my dad. The riverboat captain."

"Then how come they locked you up?"

"A man with my record, it doesn't look good, I'm marking time in a financial institution with a gun, a robbery attempt is in progress, even if I'm not doing a thing.

"But I'm not worried about me. Let's get back to you, son. Raise your right hand. Tell me the truth about the events that brought us here together. And don't be shy. Whatever you did, it was all part of God's plan to bring us together."

What does *that* mean? Leroy squirms.

"Oh, smoking Jehosaphat, I wish you could see your expression. Leroy, Leroy, son, I'll tell you in straight language, I'm no queer. That isn't the kind of togetherness I'm talking about. What I'm saying is, there is such a thing as Destiny with a capital D. And the second I laid eyes on you, I knew it as well as I know my own name." He hooks his forefingers together in an X. "You and me. Kismet. Meant to be. Riding down the road together. Like Butch Cassidy and the Sundance Kid. What we've got here, son, is a natural-born friendship."

Well. Isn't that something? Leroy is amazed. Could it be this easy?

But, for sure, he could use a friend.

This past year, he's had more loss in that department than he can bear. Shelby. Then Dwayne, her
stepdaddy, firing him from the garage, won't even
speak to him again. Like it was *his* fault Shelby's ma
had thrown him out right after Shelby had up and left,
like following Shelby's example. Dwayne had been as
close to a real good friend as Leroy had ever had.

Suddenly Leroy finds himself blurting it all out. The
whole thing. Shelby leaving him, moving over here to
Nashville. How he tried to get her to come on back.
Her only response the divorce papers.

How miserable he'd been. How lonesome. How he
hadn't known what a treasure Shelby was until she
was gone. How he'd gone kind of wacko. Stole her
letters out of her ma's mailbox, copied down all the
names of the people in those letters. Had them on a
little card in his wallet. Along with their phone numbers, addresses he got from information. Information'd give you all kinds of stuff, you asked them
nicely.

Then Leroy explained about Shelby and Chuck and
Joyce and his losing it big time at Shelby's apartment.
That cop busting down the door.

And here he is.

He's run down, is waiting for Mac to say something.
But Mac's head has fallen over to one side. The man
is sleeping? While he's pouring out his heart? That
really burns his butt.

He pokes hard at Mac. "You ain't listening to a
damned word I say."

Mac sits up. "That is absolutely untrue. You see,
Leroy, what I have is an analytical mind. It grasps
onto the salient details just like one of those pit bulls.
Doesn't let go. Then it worms its way"—Mac waves
a bony forefinger back and forth—"through all the

underbrush, you know, like the hors d'oeuvres, sort of the emotional whoop-de-doo, ends up with a synthesization of the big picture."

"What?"

"Man don't know *what* he's talking about," says a deep voice from out in front of the TV.

Mac says, "It is my analysis that you've happened upon your ex-wife with her tit in a wringer. So to speak. Which I think you ought to be able to use in court to your advantage."

"Huh?"

"Leroy, Leroy. You just explain to the judge how she was doing this married man, his wife caught them, you witnessed the commotion out in the parking lot, heard all the disgusting details, were so overcome with grief at her behaving like this, the only woman you'd ever loved, you went to talk with her, things got away from you."

Leroy says, "Well, that's kind of the truth, except Shelby explained how she wasn't really doing Chuck. It was just a mistake, her in the middle of changing her clothes when she found the fried chicken I'd left, screamed, Chuck came in to see about her, then Joyce was mistook."

"Leroy." Mac shakes his head sadly. "I guess you have an explanation for the cop, too. That the same one you'd seen earlier came back and knocked the door down, dragged you in, had you arrested."

"What are you saying?"

"Well, why'd he come back? Isn't it plain as the nose on your face? He's her lover, too."

"No no no. You got it all wrong. Shelby ain't doing nobody. Neither one. I couldn't live if I thought that."

"Ummmmmm, maybe." Mac pauses, his eyes dancing behind narrow slits. Inside his head, the possibilities for mischief whirl. Combinations. Permutations. Eenie. Meenie. Minie. Moe. Then three cherries roll up.

He says to Leroy, "Forget Chuck. It's the cop. The cop's the one in her drawers."

A volcano explodes in Leroy's gut. A hot bright yellowness scalds his throat. "No," he croaks. "Don't say that."

Then Leroy draws a long ragged breath. Ever since Shelby left him, these kinds of dark thoughts have tried to worm their way into his brain. Destroy it. Maggot thoughts.

Seeing another man in Shelby's sweet places. Places that belong to him and him alone. Another man burglarizing what belongs to him. Stealing. Pillaging. Like Leroy's nothing. Can't defend his own.

Is no kind of man.

That was why Leroy had come up with his Grand Plan. The thing that he knew would bring Shelby back to him.

He wouldn't have to worry anymore.

Except he hadn't had time to explain it to her.

Okay, he'd had a little too much to drink, getting up his nerve. Things had gotten screwed up. But he'd just been trying to make Shelby understand.

Then that big cop had knocked down the door. Burst in on them. Their private business. Sacred, what went on between man and wife. No one's business.

Blue uniform. Gun. Nightstick. Thought he was something, snapping those cuffs. Oh, he could still see that cop. He was burned forever on Leroy's retina.

Mac is talking again. "Did you ever strike Shelby with your hands before?"

"No."

"You didn't even just slap her around a tiny bit, I

mean, when she deserved it? When she got on your nerves?"

"No, sir."

"That's good. Now, equally important, do you think she'll lie and say you did?"

"What do you mean? She better not!"

"Now, that's not the tone you want to be taking, Leroy. Sounds like a threat, do you see what I mean? The picture you want to paint here is that you were simply overcome with missing her. Were even willing to forgive her messing around, behaving like a whore. Your love was overflowing. Sap rising. She wanted you too, or so it seemed to you. Maybe you were mistaken. Misread her signals. It can happen, in the passion of the moment.

"Maybe she did whisper, *No, not now.* You didn't hear her. Or you thought she didn't really mean it. Either way, you're ever so sorry. Tell the judge that. That's it. No problem, Leroy."

"I don't know."

"I'm telling you, here's the plan. You give me Shelby's address, I'll go and talk with her. I'll wager she doesn't want to see you in jail any more than you want to be here. She'll drop the charges."

"How are you gonna go and talk to her? You're in jail, same as me."

"Yes, but this little bird is going to fly the coop on bail any minute, which is faster than your kin'll come through for you." Mac stands, draws himself to his full five-foot-three, raises one hand. *"And,* when you do get out, it is of paramount importance that you don't race over to Shelby's in an attempt to patch things up with her."

"But . . ."

"Forget it, son. You're simply going to bollocks things up. Infuriate her all over again. Besides, she's most undoubtedly thrown a peace bond on you. You come within a block of her, they'll toss you back in the slammer so fast it will make your head swim.

"But if *I* call on her as a go-between, and tell her how sorry you are, you promise never to do it again, how much you love her, I'm sure she'll back off. In fact, I guarantee it."

"Why?" Leroy asks.

"Why what?"

"Why would you want to help me out?"

"Son"—Mac spreads his arms wide, which makes his belly even more prominent—"they must grow some awfully mean folks over in Mississippi, don't know how to offer a helping hand. Stranger or friend, it's a star in your crown, doing what you can. I figure I'm rather behind on stars my ownself, need to do some catching up."

That makes sense to Leroy, who grew up in the Church of the Nazarene and heard, every single day of his young life, folks talking about doing unto others, helping your neighbor out, extending the right hand of Christian fellowship.

There sure hasn't been much of that in his life recently. It's been more like dog-eat-dog.

So it touches his heart that here, in this place, with him at his lowest ebb, a sophisticated man of the world like Mac McKenzie would offer to help out.

*To be his friend.*

And it's not ten minutes after Leroy gives up Shelby's address and phone number that, sure enough, the jailer, Abe, says, "McKenzie, grab your stuff."

# 11

FIVE-FIFTEEN, SHELBY ROLLS HER CAR INTO AN EM-
ployee parking spot at the back of Sweet Willie's.
Late, but Good Lord have mercy! If a day can be
tougher than this one, she doesn't want to know
about it.

Down at the Metro Center, in between booking
Leroy, waiting to go before the night court judge, and
telling her story to him, she'd asked Jeff Wayne a
couple of times, "What were you doing back at my
apartment? I mean, I'm real happy you were there.
But why . . . ?"

"I just had this feeling," he said, "that I needed to
be there. *You* needed me to be there." Then he
shrugged. Looked off. Like he was trying to make
sense out of it himself. Then he'd looked back, concentrating on that gold ring in her eye like it was
hypnotizing.

Now she tilts her rearview mirror, stares at herself.
Well, she's looked worse. This isn't *too* bad,

considering. Racing around all day. Working the morning shift. Then Chuck. Joyce. The cop. Her three-mile walk. Leroy. Lord! Rolling around on the floor with him didn't help one bit.

Her lip doesn't look real good where he smacked her. Leroy, what a fool. What the hell did he think he was doing? Well, he'll have plenty of time to figure it out in the pokey.

She pulls her lip gloss from her bag. Gentles a little on. Some blush. A swipe at her hair. There now.

The gold ring in her left eye flashes. Mamaw'd always said that ring made her special. Chosen. Her salvation. She'd know it when the time came. Well, if that circle helped save her butt from drunk old Leroy, she's grateful.

She salutes herself in the mirror. Shelby Kay Tate— waitress, songwriter, survivor—reporting for work.

Just in the door, Willie Johnstone, proprietor of Sweet Willie's, says to her, "Baby, didn't you get my message?" Poking her pencil sideways into her inky chignon.

"What message?"

"I called your machine, told you LouLou said she was feeling better, could work her shift after all. I'm sorry you came on in."

"No, no. Hey, listen, I'll just go home. I can use the rest." But she's already thinking, maybe do a little work on that last song for C.T. Maguire.

Willie's blue eyes squint behind rhinestone cat-glasses. "Who busted you in the lip?" Then the phone rings, and she puts Shelby on hold like a scarlet-nailed traffic cop.

"Well, praise the Lord. How *you* doing, baby?" Willie says into the receiver. "Yes, indeedy. I'd be proud to. Uh-huh. Turnip, mustard, and collards, we got all three. Or you can have them mixed. How about some black-eyed peas, a little bit of candied yam on the side? All righty. I've got some of your favorite pecan pie. Banana pudding, too. You want a little of both? Cornsticks or biscuits? He sure is. Baby, I couldn't get Teedell out of the kitchen unless I shot him, and then I'd have to shoot myself. Yep. And where are you? Unh-huh. Got it. No, no problem at all. Well, I can't tell you how good it is to hear from you again, baby. I will. I do. And you do the same."

"Shelby?" Willie has the strangest look on her face. "Can you do me a really big favor, run this special order over to East Nashville? I know it's way out of your way, baby, but I tell you what. You do this, I'll pay you for the whole shift."

"Yes, ma'am!" says Shelby, grabbing the ticket out of her hand and stepping back to the kitchen. "Ordering out."

Twenty minutes later Shelby stands ringing the bell of a big yellow Victorian house. Proud of herself, because she didn't get lost driving here from Willie's.

Nashville's main arteries radiate out from the state capitol downtown like a big spiderweb, then the interstates go round and round. Not only is there no grid, only wiggles and diagonals, but also many streets change names every ten blocks. Shelby, who loves to drive, is constantly finding herself lost *and* in the wrong lane. On some four-lane, headed for Chattanooga or the Gulf Coast, when she just wants to go to Tower Records.

But here she is, 301 Greenwood Avenue, East Nashville, exactly like Willie's ticket says. A neighborhood just over the Cumberland River from downtown, was once the Place to Live. Went to seed, now youngsters were buying the big old houses, restoring them to glory.

And this one is a dilly. Two stories and a turret, a pale buttery yellow. Lots of carpenter Gothic trim running around it like white eyelet. Wide wraparound front porch, rocking chairs. A fenced-in front yard with a slide, a jungle gym, a small fort, a wading pool, a pile of red and yellow plastic toys.

So where is this Ann King? Shelby stares at the name on the delivery slip, punches the bell for the third time.

Come on, girl. Your supper's getting cold.

Finally somebody yells, "Hold your horses!" Footsteps. Then the front door slams open.

There stands a short round white woman, pushing seventy. A headful of curls—also short, round, and white. Bright blue eyes, huge behind silver-framed lenses, blazing at Shelby.

Shelby's surprised. She's expecting a younger woman, momma to the kids the front yard implies. "Are you Miz King? You order from Sweet Willie's?"

"Yeah. About an hour ago. Could've starved to death. Knew it was a mistake from the get-go."

Shelby takes in the old bat's red basketball shoes, zippered navy blue jumpsuit. Half-moons of sweat in the pits.

Then she holds out the brown paper bag.

Thinking, take it, lady, let me get on home. I've had a hard enough day. Don't need you to be the cherry on my cowpat.

But, on the other hand, looking at the old woman, she thinks about Mamaw. Another old grump. She smiles, says, "Sorry it took so long. You want to grab this before it gets cold?"

The lady snatches the bag, wheels, takes off back

down the hall. Barely misses tripping over an ancient dark Siamese.

"Nadine, goddamnit!" she snaps. Then says to Shelby, "Just a minute, let me get you your money."

"Ma'am? Ma'am? It's no charge, compliments of Willie."

No use. Not only is she mean as a snake, she's deaf, too. Shelby noticed two hearing aids.

Shelby leans down and pets the cat rubbing up against her legs. Finds the sweet spot under her chin. Shelby misses having animals, but doesn't have time to take care of them here in Nashville.

Says to the cat, "Hey, Nadine. Does the old bitch beat you? Why don't you jump up in her bed, middle of the night, suck her breath out?" The cat purrs. "You know, she reminds me of somebody, Nadine. I mean, somebody other than my mamaw. You have any idea who that is?"

Nadine says, *Murph.*

Shelby says, "Well, hell, let's go find her. Get this over with."

The interior of the house is plain and simple as a Shaker box. The center hallway and double parlors are painted a soft cream. An overstuffed beige sofa, a couple of striped easy chairs, an old upright piano. A few sturdy pieces of Mission oak sit on wide bare polished floorboards. Brass-and-wood ceiling fans move the evening air.

Shelby comes around a dogleg in the hallway, nearly smacks into the old woman.

She's lowered the zipper of her navy jumpsuit and is fiddling with an envelope safety-pinned to her bra. Nudges out a dank handful of green bills. Says, "How much do I owe you?"

"I was trying to tell you, Willie said it was on the house."

"Don't be stupid."

"No, ma'am, I'm not. Willie said not to take one red cent. Said to tell you it was awfully good to hear from you again."

Whoever you are, Shelby thinks. Who are you, Ann King, you huffy old broad?

"Oh yeah? She did, huh? Well, that's nice. Now tell me, sis, what do you do when you're not delivering Meals-on-Wheels?"

Shelby steps back. Does generosity rub this old biddy the wrong way? She can't take nothing from nobody without getting all stiff-necked about it?

Shelby's seen it lots of times before. She throws her mind back. Once in particular, she'll never forget it. . . .

A long time ago, she must have been about six, Mamaw had carried her along, she and some of the other ladies from the Star Baptist were delivering Thanksgiving turkeys to the needy. They'd already been by three or four other houses, and then they'd driven down a long rutted road through a cotton field toward a little falling-down shotgun shack. When they pulled up, three bony mongrels ran out, snapped at the tires. Shelby, in her favorite orange-and-brown plaid corduroy dress, white lace around the collar, had stared at the house. "There ain't nobody home," she'd said. Looking harder, she'd seen eight eyes, four sets of two in close stair steps, staring out from a window, one broken pane covered with a piece of cardboard. "Why don't they come on out?" she'd asked. Mamaw had said for her to hush. Then Shelby heard a woman crying, "Please, Olan, it's the ladies from the church. The kids were counting on it." But nobody came out on the tumbledown porch. "We could leave it on the steps," one of the church ladies whispered. "The

dogs'd eat it," said Mamaw. Then the torn screen door
flew open, banged against the front of the house. A
man walked out backward, his stringy bare back
bowed forward in his ragged overalls. His neck,
crisped brown from stooping and picking, was lined
as a roadmap. And even though they couldn't see his
face, still he held one hand up over it. The other, he
flapped out to the side. "Git on," he shouted, most of
the sound blowing back toward his family. But there
was enough of it coming their way, that Shelby and
three ladies in the car could make it out. "Please go.
Don't shame me like this."

Is Ann King like that old man? Too proud to let
anyone do her a favor? Can't see charity as a virtue?
Whatever, she sure as hell finds it difficult to say
thank you.

Shelby takes another look at the old woman's face.
That's devil-light dancing in her eyes. Shelby says,
"What do I do when I'm not delivering chicken-and-
dumplings as a special favor to folks too lazy to come
in and get it themselves? Folks so uppity they don't
care that Willie doesn't even *do* deliveries, say, Bring
it on, anyway? Well, Miz King, I'll tell you. When I'm
not doing that, waiting tables, or having my ex-
husband slapped in the pokey, I do a little
songwriting."

The old woman laughs, throwing her head back so
far Shelby can see all her gold.

She's heard that laugh before. Where?

The old lady says, "Do a little songwriting, do you?
Well, ain't that something? And your ex, he's the one
popped you one in the kisser?"

"Yep, sure is."

"And you had him locked up? Well, that's all
right." Then she's off again, heading deeper into the

interior. Calling over her shoulder, "Come on then, Miss Songwriter, help me eat this supper."

"No, ma'am," Shelby yells after her. "I can't do that. I've got to get on home. I've had a real long day."

But hollering is useless. If she isn't looking straight at you, the old lady can't hear zip.

Miz King's kitchen is large and square, black-and-white-tiled, last remodeled in the fifties, from the look of it.

"You want a glass of iced tea?" The old lady drops the bag of dinner on a big golden oak table. Nadine, who's trailed along, too, eyes the distance from the floor to the table's edge.

"No, thank you, ma'am, as I was saying, I've got to get going. I've had a real hard day. What with one thing and another."

"Sit down. And stop ma'aming me."

"Yes'm." Shelby sits. Who *is* it this Ann King reminds her of?

Shelby looks around, searching for a clue. Six high chairs against one wall. "You have a lot of grandkids?"

"Yep. As a matter of fact I do. Seven, no, I guess it's eight. I lose track. Never see 'em. They're mostly grown away."

"So who're the high chairs for?"

"I do day care for the neighborhood teenagers' babies, girls want to stay in school. State program pays me and my friend Reola, she comes in and helps."

"You don't say."

"You think I'm too ornery to work with little kids?"

Shelby grins. "Nawh. My mamaw's mean as you. Toughened me up. Gave me some grit."

Miz King is lobbing good china plates and fine sil-

verware onto the table. "Cain't stand to eat out of
paper plates. Never could, not since I got away from
home. Grew up sitting on the floor, eating off tin.
Always swore, no matter what else I had to do without, I was going to eat pretty. But you didn't come
over here to hear my sad tale."

"Oh, yeah." Shelby leans back. Hands behind her
head. Beginning to warm up to this old lady. "I'd
love to."

"Love to steal it, you mean. Songwriters ain't to be
trusted. I've seen your kind before."

She deals Shelby a plate piled high with Teedell's
golden chicken and dumplings, greens, yams, peas. Nadine's already licking at her chicken in a saucer on
the floor.

"You know many songwriters?" Shelby asks.

Ann sits. Picks up her fork. Says, "Thank you,
Jesus, for this food." Then, without missing a beat,
"Now who in Nashville don't know songwriters? Half
the folks I know dream of making the charts. Lawyers,
doctors, hairdressers, schoolteachers, electricians,
they're all plunking away. How you doing with it so
far?"

"Can't complain."

"Tell me. From the start. Tell me your songwriting story."

"You sure?"

The old lady nods.

"Well, I left my husband and drove over here from
a little town in Mississippi about a year ago, a shoe
box beside me in my Toyota filled with work tapes of
my three best songs. Recorded one side only and labeled with the titles, my name, address, and phone
number on the cassette in a clear plastic cover with
the lyric sheet neatly typed and rubber-banded to the

bottom. That's how *The Songwriter's & Musician's Guide to Nashville* said the pros did it."

"And?"

"I've kept body and soul together so far."

"How long did you walk up and down the Row dropping off those tapes before you got any notice?"

"I've been real lucky." Shelby knocks on the golden oak table. "Luckier than most. I'll tell you, there's some women in this business have been awfully nice to me."

A measured look from those baby blues. "Why do you think that is?"

"Beats me, but I'm sure grateful for it. I came over here because of the encouragement of my friend Lynn I met at a songwriter's workshop in Jackson. But after I started looking around at all the talent, I thought, Boy, Leroy's right—that's my ex—I'm flat crazy. Gonna starve to death.

"Then I'd only been in town a couple of weeks, and I'd signed up to play at an open mike night at Douglas Corner, when who should show up but this executive from SESAC. That's a rights organization. Collects royalties for writers. But they help new writers along, too. Kind of grow them, you know what I mean?"

"Unh-huh. And then what?"

"Well, it was like a miracle, that evening. Dianne Petty, that was the executive's name, she walked up to me after I'd done my two little songs, said she wanted me to come around to her office and see her. The next thing I knew she'd fixed me up with some co-writers. And Lynn, who I write with too, got me the job waiting tables at her aunt Willie's place." Shelby stops. "You know Willie, of course."

"Haven't seen her in a coon's age. Go on." The old lady waves her fork.

"It was Willie who helped me along the next step.

Served up a tape of mine to Selma Phillips of Bandit Music along with her chicken-fried steak."

"And she signed you to a writing contract." Ann slaps the right leg of her blue jumpsuit. "Kind of like Lana Turner getting discovered at Schwab's Drugstore."

Shelby isn't sure what she means. Says, *I guess,* to be polite.

"How many cuts you had made?"

"A couple of songs on independent labels. Nothing else, really, to speak of. But Wynonna has one on hold, Trisha another. And C.T. McGuire has two. She's going into the studio soon."

"Yeah, but that don't pay you a cent, does it, them artists reserving 'em, *thinking* about 'em?"

"Nope, don't mean a thing till the record's released. Miz King, it sounds like you been in the business yourself."

The old lady pushes back from the table and heads for the stove, sidestepping her question. "You want some coffee? I'm making some. Why don't you go on back in the living room and warm up the piano? Nadine and I'll be in there in a minute, you can put on a little show for us. Nadine's a *fine* judge of a good song."

"I'd love to, but I can't. Maybe another time. Really, I'm bushed. I need to get on home."

"Songwriter ain't *never* too tired to show off. Besides, if Willie didn't think you'd keep me decent company, she wouldn't have sent you over here in the first place. Now, go on. Don't make me tell you again."

The old upright is well tuned. Shelby starts noodling with the song she's trying to finish for C.T. The song she was thinking about when she opened her door, walked smack into Leroy.

*Just like the times you didn't know*
*How bad you beat me up*
*When you threw me down and took my love*
*When you got whiskey drunk*

Well, those are sure as hell prophetic words, aren't they? She didn't know how much when she wrote them.

Shelby plunks out the melody. Fingers dancing around the notes. The way she works, first the words, then the music.

"Don't let me stop you." Ann is carrying a silver tray with two coffee cups. Smoking a little cigar tucked into the corner of her mouth.

"Hell, this song's a mess," says Shelby. "I'm trying to finish it for a writers' night, Thursday. Maybe I ought to give it up."

"Let's give her a listen."

"Okay. But I'm warning you. The title's the only part that works. 'I Still Miss My Man, but My Aim Is Getting Better.'"

Ann laughs.

Shelby sings . . .

*I didn't know that gun was loaded*
*When I pointed it at you*
*I didn't know that was the trigger*
*Until I heard the boom*
*Just like the times you didn't know*
*How bad you beat me up*
*When you threw me down and took my love*
*When you got whiskey drunk*

"And the chorus . . ."

*I do miss you*
*But I don't want to*
*Thank God my missing you*
*Is almost through*
*I've got a shaking in my hands*
*I'm being steady as I can*
*Yeah, I still miss my man*
*But my aim is getting better*

"I've got a start on the second verse, but . . ." Shelby shakes her head. "I don't know."

Ann sits staring at her, big blue eyes swimming behind her lenses.

So she hates it, thinks Shelby. Well, she's not that crazy about it herself. The drinking, raping, shooting—it's all too direct. She likes the conceit of the title, but she's got to work on a more subtle way to get the message across.

"That Willie," the old lady says. "I pick up the phone and call, she sends *you.*"

Shelby doesn't need this. "Well, damn, Miz King. I didn't think the song would *offend* you." Half-standing. Fully pooped. She's outta here.

"The *song?* Hell, the song's got possibilities. Sit your butt back down. Here, scoot over."

At that, the old woman's shoving Shelby halfway off the bench. She leans over, spreads her arms.

Shelby's melody ripples out of her right hand like a brook. Crescendos of chords crash like rapids out of her left. The woman's a *hell* of a pianist. Crazy chords jangle in the air. Opening up whirling worlds of possibility.

"Okay." The old lady stops. "What have we got? Let's concentrate on the chorus. Now, as a hook, I'd say the title kicks ass. But you need to chuck those first two lines. Do it like this. Speed it up." Ann half-sings, half-speaks while she plays . . .

> *Damn these shaking hands*
> *For messing up my plans*
> *Yeah, I still miss my man*
> *But my aim is getting better*

Shelby sits back. "How long *you* been writing?"

The old lady shakes her head, fingers still dancing, flirting with the notion of moving the song into a minor key.

"Come on. Who the hell *are* you? *Ann King?* It doesn't ring a bell."

"You're way too young. I ain't written anything for years. And I ain't *that* good."

"One hell of a lot better than me."

The old woman throws her head back. Her laughter fills the room. "And you think that's saying something?"

"Yes, ma'am, it is. I'm not as good as I'm going to be, but I'm one hell of a lot better than a poke in the eye with a sharp stick."

"Nothing I like better than a woman who knows her own worth. Ain't that true, Nadine?"

Nadine says, *Mrink.*

Shelby says, "So, listen, you gonna help me finish this thing?"

"Oh, I don't know." The old woman trails a finger along the keys.

"What do you mean? What kind of songwriter are you, anyway? I *need* this song for Thursday night. Forty-eight hours. I don't have much time."

The old lady laughs. *So* familiar, that sound. But

Shelby doesn't have time for guessing games. She's got a song to write.

"Listen," Shelby says. "You've got the feel for this one. Won't you help me out here?"

"I don't know. Maybe I . . ."

"Great! How about tomorrow afternoon? I'm doing a demo, then I've got rehearsal. I could be here five, five-thirty. What time are you through with the kiddies?"

"Does it even cross your mind I might have something better to do?"

"No, ma'am. A song hanging in the balance, I can't believe that you would."


Shelby gone, the old lady tidies up the kitchen, then takes Nadine upstairs. Cat and woman tuck into a high brass bed, then the woman reaches over and picks up the guitar her friend Patsy gave her so long ago. She begins playing one of her own songs, one both she and Patsy loved.

She sings in a different voice than the one she'd used downstairs. No half-voice here. And while it isn't the voice of her girlhood, the voice that packed them in, made them give up their applause, the sound is still pure and clear. When she hits a high note, glaciers four thousand miles away shift, melt.

She sings full-out, exactly like she did when she and Patsy shared a stage. Her big sound is shameless. Naked. Holds nothing back.

She can do that, here. In her bedroom up the stairs, she is safe. No one can hear her, except Nadine.

Or so the woman thinks.

But this night that truth doesn't hold.

For Mac McKenzie—who's been tailing Shelby since he got out of jail, picked up his car—now creeps out of his hidey-hole on the service porch behind the kitchen.

He stands at the bottom of the stairs listening. Openmouthed at the sound.

Saying, Well, I'll be damned. Be *god*damned. Ann? Ann *King?* So that's what she's called herself, all these years. What a piece of luck! I must be living right!

Mac listens for a long while. Finally the music slows. Then stops. The lights switch off upstairs. The house is dark and still.

Then, cauldron of toad and newt aboil, the possibilities for mischief bubbling in his rotten brain, Mac tiptoes back out the way he's come.

Nadine awakens briefly. Yawns. Stretches *ever* so long. Then she lowers her chin again to the lilac-sprigged bed cover and returns to her dream of s-l-o-w mice and their sweet little bones.

# 12

WEDNESDAY MORNING, BRIGHT AND EARLY, LEROY steps through the swinging glass doors of the Metro Police toward Second Avenue and freedom.

The officer said his cousin Chris would be waiting for him. Leroy hadn't seen Chris in such a long time, he isn't sure he'll recognize him.

Then, right on cue, someone calls, "Leroy! Leroy! Over here!"

Leroy whirls. A small crowd of people, none of them looking too happy, is lumped up on the sidewalk. A hefty woman in a two-piece purple jogging suit reaches down and slaps a little girl tugging at her leg. Says, "Wondra, I've got enough on my mind without messing with you."

"Leeeeeroy!" the voice calls again.

Leroy pushes through the stew of people and finally spies a hand waving from the passenger window of a red 1972 Cadillac Coupe de Ville. The hand is all he can make out, the driver hidden in the car's dark interior.

The hand waggles again. "Leroy, come on! Get in!"

Leroy opens the door. "Chris, I can't tell you how much—"

Someone from behind him says, "Leroy? Boy, is that you?"

He turns and sees the tall lanky frame of Chris Cassel heading toward him. Chris's hair's thinning, but Leroy'd know him anywhere. He still has that hitch in his get-along, fell out of a tree at their granny's when they were kids.

"Chris?" Leroy's backing out of the Cadillac when Mac floors it. It's all Leroy can do to tumble in and hold on.

It's a hop, skip, and a jump from the Metro Police and the Courthouse to the Cumberland River Bridge. After that, Mac and Leroy leapfrog 65-24 to 24-40 to 24 South. Low-cost single housing, strip malls, and fast-food huts as far as the eye can see.

Mac is driving with his window open. His long grizzled hair blows out the back of a brown felt muleskinner's hat. He keeps turning to Leroy with a smile.

Mac is absolutely joyful. And why shouldn't he be? He's free.

White, in a part of the country where that still means something, by God.

And alive.

Very much alive, which is something, in his opinion, that too many people take for granted. Alive with possibilities. Absolutely squirming with them.

Lookahere.

Here's Leroy. Leroy Mabry, himself. The man's like a gift wrapped in gold under the Christmas tree.

Then there's Shelby, the ramifications and permutations of whom he has only begun to sniff out.

And the one and the only, oh, let's call her ANN KING!!!!!!!

Lordy, lordy. His cup overfloweth. Where to begin? So many goodies.

Well, let's start with Leroy, right here.

Mac gives Leroy his brightest whitest smile. His TV preacher grin. Lays a generous dollop of sincerity into his voice. Sugarcoats it with a little Jimmy Swaggart. Says, "What do you want, son? Just tell Mac your heart's desire. Talk to me."

They're passing a Shoney's. Leroy thinks, Well, I'd like me some scrambled eggs, grits, sausage, bacon, biscuits, pancakes, and sweet rolls from the breakfast bar. But he knows that's not what Mac means.

So he says, "Like I told you, I want Shelby to come on back."

"Yes, sir, yes, sir, indeedy." Mac's drumming on the wheel. "But after that? What's your yearning? Black? White? Dead? Alive? Animal? Vegetable? Mineral?"

"Well, I can't say, precisely."

"And that's *precisely* why you don't have it. You got to name the thing, then concentrate on making it yours. *That,* my boy, is one of my fundamental operating principles."

"Oh, I don't know about that, Mac."

One of the things Leroy's daddy'd knocked into his head: You say things out loud, folks start pushing ahead, trying to get there first.

But, on the other hand, Leroy doesn't want Mac believing he'd never even thought about improving himself.

"There is my Grand Plan," he drawls.

"Ahhhh." Mac stomps it, passes an eighteen-wheeler, his Caddy showing *that* big old son of a bitch. "Let's hear it, Leroy."

"You sure?"

"Positively."

"Well, it all started a couple of weeks ago. I was having a few at the Magnolia Lounge in Star out by the highway. 'Stand By Your Man' was playing on the jukebox, and I was feeling lower than a snake's belly."

"Because Shelby hadn't stood by you at all."

"Exactly! So there I am crying in my beer. Not really crying, but you know what I mean. This old fellow sitting next to me at the bar says, 'I used to drive her bus.' I didn't know what he was talking about. Then he says, 'That woman singing on that record, Tammy Wynette, I drove her bus. Sure did.' "

"Well, isn't that something?"

"Just wait. The next thing I know, the geezer's telling me all about country singers on the road doing three-, four-, five-, six-day runs. Most of their sleeping, eating, *everything's* done on a bus custom-rigged for music folks. Stars travel with a whole *entourage,* he called 'em. Jammed up together, closer than any family. He said that's why the bus is so important. *And* expensive, he said, lease for about ten thousand dollars a month. Even more."

Mac whistles long and low.

"That's what I said. And that's when I started thinking, Hell, a man who knew something about motor vehicles—and I do, being a mechanic licensed by the state of Mississippi and got a piece of paper to prove it—with some carpentry skills, which I also got my fair share of, could make himself a fortune. Get ahold of himself a couple of them music buses, lease 'em out. Besides which, I figured, it being the music business and all, it comes back full circle to Shelby."

Mac's eyes are spinning. "Leroy, Leroy. You've hit the nail right on the head. Nashville was created for people like you and me. The enterprising minority. Can see What Is."

Leroy nods. He likes Mac's enthusiasm.

Mac says, "Now, this city may not look like much to the untrained eye. Big, sure, but just a Big Old Country Town, really. New South Neutral. Bumpkin City Beige. A church every two feet. Lousy with insurance companies full of stiffs in brown suits. Not to mention the thumpers publishing all those kajillions of Bibles.

"But don't let that fool you, son." Mac raises a hand as theatrically as Oral Roberts in full sway. "That's to confuse the Yankees, send 'em sniveling on home. You grab ahold of Music City U.S.A., Nashville's a sugar tit. That's the What Is.

"The music business is Nashville's raison d'être. Its alpha and omega. Nashville's a Dream Center. Same as Hollywood, except this is a different business, and you don't have to travel as far. You've come to the perfect place, Leroy." Mac tips his flat muleskinner hat. "I think your Grand Plan, Nashville, it's a gathering of forces and energies in the same time frame and location. It's MAGIC, Leroy, your Grand Plan."

It sounds wonderful, Mac's saying it aloud like that. Like it's something real. Leroy is thrilled. Everything looks *glorious* out the window. That U-Haul office. That liquor store. That Dunkin' Donuts. *Magnificent.*

Mac winks. "To our new partnership."

"You really want to join in on this?"

Mac sniffs. "Let me reiterate what I told you yesterday, Leroy. Mac McKenzie don't lie, and Mac McKenzie don't ever say anything he don't mean. Besides, I seem to be fresh out of associates for the opportunities Lady Luck keeps throwing my way. And I sure wouldn't want to miss this one."

He leans closer, which is something Leroy wishes

he wouldn't do, actually. For all he's crazy about Mac, there's no getting around the fact the man's breath smells like pig farts.

Mac says, "The first thing I did, I got free last night, I went searching for my former partner." He spits the words from the corner of his mouth like beebees. "He'd already made bail. The one from the bank, you know what I mean. I fired his ass."

Leroy's heart leaps. Just the two of them. Can this be?

"The way I look at it, Leroy, you were sent as his replacement. A gift from God. He brought you and put you in my cell. And along with that comes the responsibility for my helping you realize your dreams. Yes, sirree bob, here's to us, Leroy Mabry, to our new partnership. MacKenzie and Mabry." Mac extends his right hand.

It's then that Leroy notices the long and curving nail on Mac's little finger.

He'd known an old black man back in Star with the same kind of nail. The old man, who sold burial insurance to colored people, said it was a sign he'd made it out of the fields. Didn't have to do stoop labor anymore.

Leroy grabs Mac's paw. "I'm right proud to be your partner." He's feeling a little teary, but he doesn't want Mac thinking he cries at the least little thing.

Leroy leans back, beaming as the roadside whizzes by. A gorgeous Kmart over there, its parking lot jammed. It's a wonderful feeling, being chosen. Except . . .

"I want you to know," he says to Mac, "I don't do stuff like bank robberies. Music buses is our business, right? I'm not planning on ever seeing the inside of a Nashville jail again."

Mac laughs, and the mud-colored eyes scrinch up

above the wide flat nose. Just as Leroy's thinking that Mac bears an awful strong resemblance to a copperhead when he laughs, Mac does something with his tongue, and his whole upper denture pops straight out. It hangs there for a long moment, then jumps back in.

"Haw!" Mac laughs at Leroy's amazement. "Ain't that a cute one? Well, Uncle Mac has more tricks up his sleeve than Carter's has pills. Don't ever let anybody tell you that isn't true." Then he reaches over and grabs Leroy's hand again and wrenches it. "Don't worry your pretty head about jail, son. Those boys in blue aren't going to get a whiff of us as we go about our appointed rounds here in the city of opportunity.

"Which reminds me, last night, after I finished with my late partner, I ventured by to see that wife of yours."

You could pick Leroy up off the floorboards, he's that flattened with amazement.

"Shelby? You saw Shelby?"

"Sure did."

"Well, how was she?"

"Looked fine as wine."

"What did she say? Did she say she'd drop the charges?"

"Not exactly."

"Well, what then?"

"I didn't precisely get to talk to her."

"She wouldn't let you in?"

"I didn't knock. I didn't want to disturb her. It didn't seem the opportune moment."

"What do you mean?"

"Chill, Leroy, chill. Our first duty is to begin cogitating on obtaining that first music bus, then building our way up to a fleet. We can't do that if you aren't concentrating. If you have your attentions spread out over matters that don't amount to a hill of beans."

"Just tell me why it didn't seem the right time to speak to her."

"It didn't seem appropriate because when I got there, there was a man hanging around her parking lot." Mac tweaks his yellowed mustache. "A man in uniform. *Not* in a patrol car, but I know a Metro Police officer uniform when I see one."

Okay, Leroy tells himself. It could be that they'd sent somebody to make sure that Shelby was okay. Except, if it was him, Leroy, they were worried about, they knew that he was still in jail. He says, "Maybe the cop was there for somebody else. There's lots of apartments."

"Could be," Mac agrees. "Except, now, tell me, Leroy, what did you say that policeman looked like? The one who came bursting into Shelby's apartment, interrupting you in the midst of your bid to win the return of her favors?"

Leroy answers slowly. "Blond hair just like me."

Waiting for Mac to start shaking his head no.

"Blue eyes, too."

Mac ought to be saying, No way.

"But a big guy."

Come on Mac, say, It wudn't him. Nunh-uh.

"Six-two, -three, maybe. Built."

Say, It was some other dude.

But Mac nods all the way. Like it's breaking his heart, but there's no way around it.

"I'm afraid it was precisely the same man, Leroy. The one I referred to yesterday as Shelby's lov—" Mac stops himself. "I know how upset you got, so I won't repeat the word."

They are pulling off at an exit. Pretty much out into

the sticks. Cheap motels just behind the right-of-way. Leroy has no idea where they are.

Doesn't care either. "Damnit!" He slaps the dash so hard he hurts his hand. "That son of a bitch, sniffing around her again."

"Now, Leroy, don't get yourself all riled." They pass a fancy-looking motel, a big sign advertising its Mexican restaurant. Then a Shoney's.

But Leroy isn't hungry anymore. "Damn it all to hell!" He smacks the dash again. "I've got to go see her. That's all there is to it."

"Leroy, son," Mac says, "now, I told you about that. You can't. You get within sniffing distance of Shelby, she'll call the cops, they'll throw your butt back in jail."

"I don't care. I've got to tell her. Explain to her."

"Promise me you won't."

Leroy stares out the window. The landscape has turned to shit.

"Leroy. Do you hear me? If you're gonna act like this, we can't go on. I can't have a partner who lets trifles bother him. Now, I promise you, I'll talk to Shelby real soon. I told you I would."

Leroy takes a long shuddering breath.

"Say it," says Mac. "Raise your right hand and say it."

"Okay. I promise."

"Promise what?"

"I'll stay away from Shelby."

"Good! Now, we're gonna stop by my place, pick up a few things, then we'll go get cracking on your bus. Let's do it, son. Stay concentrated. Chill. Breathe through your nose. Look at the big picture. Close your eyes for a minute and think about your bus."

Mac makes a sharp right and pulls up into the driveway of a motel. Big, white, rambling.

Leroy tries his best to get a grip. He shuts his eyes and imagines a long vehicle, metallic flake blue, gold detailing, and down in the righthand corner of a panel on the side, below a huge painting of a steel guitar, is his name. *Customizing by Leroy Mabry,* it says.

He can see himself in the driver's seat. Next to him, Shelby. On the other side of her, Mac, Mac the Magician, who's going to help him pull his heart's desires out of a hat.

Leroy exhales slowly. He's ready—ready, willing, and able—to do whatever is necessary.

Within reason, of course.

# 13

SHELBY ROLLS OVER AND FUMBLES FOR THE CLOCK. Nine-thirty. Praise the Lord. She's slept ten hours, hardly moved. Well, she needed it, after yesterday: Chuck, Joyce, Leroy.

*And* this very afternoon she's writing with her new writing partner, Ann King. Shelby stretches. Oh, that feels good.

So this morning, she'll ... Jesus mothering Christ. *This morning* she has a demo session at ten! In half an hour.

Didn't she set her alarm last night for eight-thirty? Didn't she?

Shelby stares at the clock. It's set, all right. But the alarm's off. She must have punched it in the night.

She bolts. Grabs underwear. Throws on her clothes running out the door.

When Selma Phillips gets hold of her, she's, well, she doesn't even want to think about it.

\* \* \*

Out in Shelby's parking lot, Officer Jeff Wayne Capshew is busy worrying about himself.

Jeff Wayne is a down-to-earth man from down-to-earth people who scratched a living from the Kentucky hills. They knew how to fix things when they broke, do without when there was nothing to fix. There was a gracious plenty of root-hog-or-die in the Capshew genes, plus two generations of straight-ahead law enforcement.

But ever since Jeff Wayne walked up to Apartment 114A of the Natchez Trace Apartments early yesterday afternoon and Shelby Kay Tate opened the door, he'd been acting like some kind of dingbrain who didn't know his butt from a stump.

And here he is again this morning, tailing Shelby's Toyota out of her parking lot when he ought to be doing his regular patrol. Shelby is heading east on Acklen, then over to Wedgewood, and on up to where the land rises toward the big hill where the TV tower is.

He can tell himself that he's providing Shelby with protection, her husband, Leroy, having made his bail this morning. Jeff Wayne checked on that first thing. But bodyguarding isn't among the services offered by the Metro Police, so who does he think he's kidding?

And how does he explain yesterday afternoon?

Running back by her place in his own car after he dropped the cruiser off at the barracks? What was it he thought he was going to ask her, anyway? What would he have said if she just answered her door, Leroy wasn't on top of her?

Then Jeff Wayne followed her from Leroy's booking at downtown HQ. Over to Sweet Willie's. Sat outside a house in East Nashville, listening to WSIX on his radio, and he doesn't even like country. Provided her with an escort from there, not that she knew it, making sure she got home safely.

What *is* the attraction, son?

It was like voodoo, she'd put a spell on him or something. It sure wasn't because Shelby was a babe. The woman could lose thirty, forty pounds, easy. Look at her. Then look at Danielle. No contest.

Danielle. Now there was a mess.

Last night when he finally rolled home, Danielle was waiting for him. Sitting in the kitchen surrounded by tons of coffee, must have been a couple of cases. A full pot perking in the Mister Coffee. Danielle wearing a big smile. Period.

Pink and pearly as the day she was born, perched in the altogether on the counter of his shiny yellow kitchen. Four-bedroom, three-bath, family room split-ranch, Cherry Hill development, just south of Percy Priest Lake.

Danielle's body always stopped Jeff Wayne cold. She was a long tall slender girl with a big chest just like those women you see in the girlie magazines but hardly ever in real life. And teaching her "Moving with the Spirit" Christian aerobics program had honed to near perfection what God had given her.

"You're late," she snapped.

"I don't want to talk about it, Danielle. I just want to take a shower, go to bed."

She followed him into the bathroom, jawing about all the girls she knew, their engagement rings, what their bridesmaids were wearing, where they were going on their honeymoons.

"Let's don't do this tonight," he said as he closed the door to the guest room, "tomorrow either," pulling the covers over his head. Jeff Wayne was one of those people who closed his eyes, counted to ten, good night.

He'd dreamed . . .

\*     \*     \*

*He was in the woods. The cabin he'd been dreaming of building was rising up against blue mountains. Everybody was pitching in—his brother Jack and a bunch of male cousins, uncles, too—laying the logs, lifting the heavy roof beams.*

*Interior walls going right up. And rising like smoke against the mountains was the mournful keen of bagpipes. His cousin Billy playing the old songs like he always did at family gatherings. The piney smell of fresh-cut two-by-sixes. Yard sloping down to the tear-shaped lake. His little green fishing boat bobbing up to the dock. He was in the boat, looking back up at the cabin, completed now. A woman standing in the doorway, waving. Shelby Tate. He could see that gold ring in her eye glowing at him. He called her name.*

He awakened to Danielle screaming, *Shelby who?* He vaulted, but Danielle was quick as a cat. Caught him on the shoulder with a bedside lamp.

"Who's this Shelby you're dreaming about, you son of a bitch?"

When she got riled Danielle had a bad mouth on her, especially for a dedicated Christian.

He grabbed his uniform and equipment, scrammed.

Now here he is, trailing half a block behind Shelby's beat-up old blue Toyota.

"Turn left, hoss," he says to himself when she makes a right. "Let her go." But he can't.

Something has happened to his free will. At least as far as Shelby Kay Tate is concerned.

# 14

BUD RILEY'S RECORDING STUDIO IS IN THE BASEMENT of an old wide-hipped brown-shingled house up by the TV tower. Selma's red BMW is parked out front. Bright as a traffic light. A stop sign. An F on your report card. What other associations can she make? Shelby asks herself, jumping out of her Toyota.

Fresh blood. There's one. Would it help to open a vein, say, See, Selma? See how sorry I am I overslept? Now if you'll just let me tell you about my simply awful hideous horrible day, but the good news is, I found this old woman who's gonna help me finish that last song for C.T., you'll be so proud. . . .

Sure. Sure. Shelby runs around the side of the house, throws herself down the steps to the studio. Flings open the door.

There she sits, Selma Phillips. Executive VP of Bandit Music. A study in *noir*. Wings of short dark hair back from her face. Black Armani suit. Gorgeous black pumps of something like unborn calf. She always

92

makes Shelby feel like a big old fat hog who just hitched her way out of the swamp.

Selma holds a cellular phone to her ear. Raises one perfectly manicured finger at Shelby. *I'll deal with you in a moment.*

"I am *so* sorry," Shelby mouths. Can't wait for Selma to get off the phone to start apologizing.

Bud, the studio owner and sound engineer, comes over and envelops Shelby in a big hug. A ginger-haired ox-wrestler of a man. Hams for hands. Hard to believe he's so at home in this roomful of thousand-buttoned, million-dialed recording consoles. "We've got a pot of fresh coffee, sugar. You want some?"

Shelby most certainly does. She pours herself a cup, then sits biting her bottom lip, staring at Selma, still on the phone.

She remembers their very first conversation. Selma sat Shelby down in her black-and-white office, gold and platinum records the only decoration on the walls, and said, You've got talent, but so do ten thousand other writers in this town. Songwriting's a business. You want to be an *artiste,* write when the inspiration hits you, pull that *temperamental* shit, there's the door. You want to be a songwriter, I'll give you a nine-hundred-dollars-a-month draw, you give me your quota, four songs a month that are good enough for me to spend the money to demo. You do writers' nights. You meet and greet and make nice with industry folks. You show up whenever I ask you to. On time, showered, shat, and shaved. Got it? Especially that on-time part?

Shelby got it loud and clear. But that didn't mean, every once in a while, she didn't screw up.

Now from over Shelby's shoulder, a high, disembodied voice calls, "Hellooooo. Is that the talented Miss Shelby Tate, herself?"

Shelby looks for the voice. Bud's studio is a pine-paneled version of a dozen of the low-budget kind she's been in before. The front room jammed with Bud's consoles, sofa, couple of stools at a high worktable, microwave, coffeepot, little fridge for the beer. A large soundproof window opens to the middle and third rooms. The middle holds a piano and a drum set, some music stands, six chairs. But no musicians today. They laid down their tracks a couple of days ago. In the smaller third room, demo singer Arlen Tapert waves through the glass from beneath a hanging microphone.

Then he slips off his headphones, comes out to the first room, takes her hands in his. Gives her a big toothy Jimmy Carter grin. "I sure do like your songs, young lady."

Shelby doesn't know what to think. Here she's kept one of the best demo singers in the business waiting, he's acting like *she's* the star.

"Thank you, so much," she burbles. "I'm thrilled to pieces to be working with you. And I'm *so* sorry I'm late. I wouldn't have kept you waiting for the world."

"Not at all. You just gave me and Bud here the chance to do a little catching up."

"And me the chance to wake up some people on the Coast," says Selma, joining them. She gives Shelby a quick tap on the shoulders that says: Do it again, you're dogmeat, now let's get on with the show.

"Arlen." Selma smiles at the singer. "I think we're going to start with 'I Wanta Drive.' You want to do a quick run-through, let us hear what you have in mind?"

# 15

THE GOODBUY INN IS A U OF THREE-STORY WHITE concrete block buildings with an empty pool in its middle. Mac wheels the Cadillac to its backside: four stories traipsing down a hill, facing I-24. Leroy wonders how Mac can sleep here, all the traffic noise zipping by.

"Come on in for a minute," says Mac, climbing out. "I need to pick up a few things."

The three flights of rusty metal stairs are covered in ragged green outdoor carpeting. As they climb, Mac nods and wishes top of the morning to three—nope, there's another one—four young strong-looking black men wearing loud shorts-and-shirt outfits and gold chains thick as a thumb. They seem to be hanging, just passing time on the long covered walkways that run the building's length.

"They live here, too?" Leroy asks Mac, who's huffing and puffing ahead of him.

"Sort of. The Goodbuy's their place of business."

Leroy thinks about that for a minute, decides he doesn't want to know.

Mac's unlocking a door. He calls, "Home sweet home, your Papa's back."

Leroy steps in, then reels back. The room is a dank cave, gassy with Mac's smell.

The mottled green carpet's a badlands map, marked with burns and spills. There's a snaggletoothed dresser, a three-legged chair. The thin orange bedspread is polka-dotted with blood and beer and semen. On the sticky bedside table: a half-empty bottle of Early Times, peanut-butter-and-cracker wrappers, Maalox, brown prescription vials.

Mac says, "Make yourself at home. I'll be back in three shakes of a lamb's tail." And is gone.

Jeeeesus. Leroy doesn't want to touch anything. Or, even worse, let it touch him. But he does have to take a leak.

A bad mistake. A shattered mirror, shower head ripped from the wall. Mildew. Rust. Rotten shards of a shower curtain. The bathroom door has taken three real bad hits. One to the head, two to the gut. But the cracked toilet flushes, surprise.

Back in the bedroom, Leroy stares at Mac's wardrobe hanging from four hooks screwed into the wall: a tan raincoat, two worn denim jackets, two pairs of Western pants, a pair of jeans, four shirts, a cowboy hat. A pair of black boots run-down at the heels.

Leroy was raised poor, but not like this. Even the Mississippi delta's colored lived better. This sure isn't what he'd pictured, listening to Mac.

But before he can get down to some serious cogitating about what this means, heeeere's Mac. The man himself, bustling back in, motormouthing. "Well, gracious goodness, Leroy, son. I wish you could see your face. You look like you just bit into a green persimmon." He waves a hand at the room. "Clever, don't you think, this shit hole, my protective coloration? The smart man conceals from his compadres how well-fixed he is, if you follow my drift. Do you understand what I'm saying, Leroy? This place is like a disguise? Well, never mind, we're out of here." Mac flailing clothes into a tattered brown suitcase. Along with a paperback copy of *The Firm*. A couple of girlie magazines. The bottle of Early Times, the drug vials. "Let's hit the road, Leroy."

"Where are we going?"

"Man down the way has the cash he's been owing me for quite a while." Mac pats his hip pocket. "See how things work out for the best if you just have faith. Now, come along." Shoves the suitcase into Leroy's hands. "Carry this, you don't mind."

And off he goes, clattering down the stairs with Leroy close behind. Mac hasn't exactly answered Leroy's question.

Down in the parking lot, Leroy looks for the red Caddy, but Mac's heading for a new dark turquoise Toyota Camry. Its motor's running, its doors are wide.

"Throw those things in the back," says Mac, sliding behind the wheel. "And hold the questions."

They peel out, the G-force socking Leroy's curly blond head back. He doesn't have a clue where they're going, but he knows he's headed *somewhere* fast.

# 16

DEMOS ARE THE SALES TOOL OF THE MUSIC BUSINESS. Music publishers send them to record producers, to singers, but primarily to record companies' artist-and-repertoire staff, whose job it is to find material.

Because Nashville is chock-full of little studios like Bud Riley's and jammed with great singers and good solid musicians, a song can be demo'ed for about three hundred dollars. Even less, if the songwriter records her own voice track.

But Shelby's voice is too big, too bluesy. If an artist hears such a strong take, she can't hear the song, can't hear *herself* doing it. And the point of a demo is to sell the song, not the singer.

Arlen Tapert—with his vanilla tenor, a perfect demo voice—is back in the third room. He's given them a couple of takes, and Selma's nodding her head. She likes what she hears.

Turns to Shelby. "What do *you* think?"

"I Wanta Drive" is one of those songs that wrote

itself, a gift. It came to Shelby, almost of a piece, a glorious afternoon about a month ago.

She was flying down the highway, on her way to Bell Buckle, Tennessee, where she and Lynn and Chuck were playing a benefit for the local fire department, when the first words came to her:

*I wanta drive. I wanta go. Put the pedal to the metal. Let the rubber hit the road.*

The song is about freedom. Cutting loose. A girl behind the wheel of her chariot, the windows down, her hair flying in the wind, letting the road take her where it will.

It has a hard, driving beat.

"Arlen," Shelby says into the backtalk, "I'd like to hear you *hit* those beats harder. Sock it to them on *Drive. Go. Ped*al. *Met*al. *Rub*ber. *Road.* I don't think I gave you a very good work tape, hon. I had a bad cold when I made it."

Arlen tries it once more.

"That's great," says Shelby, "you're punching 'em, but then get down and wallow around on 'em for a minute, those same beats."

"Do it for me, Shelby," says Arlen. "Let me hear it."

Shelby signals Bud to run the music track again. She steps up to the backtalk mike, takes a breath so deep that it knocks her back to age fifteen.

Her first driver's license is burning a hole in the pocket of her denim skirt. She's sliding behind the wheel of Momma's big Buick. Alone. Feeling the power of all those horses in her hands, rumbling below her feet, rolling beneath her butt.

"Eye-eye-eye-eye-eye-eyeeeeee." Shelby winds up on the first word, reaching back home to the Magnolia State, the heart of Dixie, for the sound. She's sucking it out of a Mississippi ditch, a dark line of water running between two cottonfields, full of black pickers, bent and scrabbling, hands bleeding, *grabbing* the crop in, saving it from the storm that's moving in like a freight train from the Gulf.

*"Eyeeeeee wanta driiiiiive."*

Shelby's *wheeling* that old boat of a Buick down a hot ribbon of asphalt. Heat's rising. She can smell the ozone from the lightning in the distance.

*"I wanta gooooooowa."*

The wind's whipping her hair. Whipping it. Whipping her cheeks. And that whipping feels like nothing she, young girl, has ever felt before. But she knows the feeling in her bones. Has been waiting for the feeling. Hoping for the feeling. Praying for that feeling that's soooooo good.

*"Put the pedal to the metal."*

Pushing the gas now. Goosing it with her toes. Playing with that thing, seeing just exactly how it goes. What it likes. How much oooooooowa oooooooowa oooooowa to put behind it.

*"Let the rubber hit the road."*

And there's your hard and your soft and your hot and your cold and your fast and your slow all coming together, coming together, rocking together, rolling together, faster and faster, watch 'em go, wheels of that old Buick roooooollllllling down the road.

Shelby finally squeezes the brakes on the last note, slows to stop. Opens her eyes.

It takes a second for her to make the trip back from Mississippi, back into the studio. Back to Selma and Bud and Arlen, all of them standing there, staring at her.

"Good Christ Almighty," Arlen finally says.

"Lord," breathes Bud.

"Shelby," says Selma, looking at her like she's never laid eyes on her before, "maybe you want to sing the whole thing through for Arlen one time. Why don't you go on back there and do it in the mike in the third room." Signaling to Bud, Roll and *record*, by God.

Shelby steps up to that mike, reaches back to her foremothers and her forefathers—Janis Joplin and Elvis and Patsy and Hank, Sr., Kitty Wells and Big Mama Thornton and Randy Newman—and *jumps* on that song.

Jumps on it with all four feet. Grabs it by the throat. Kicks the shit out it.

She's in the navel of the song. The gut. She *is* the song. She and that song are one thing, and that one thing is the entire universe pouring out of her throat.

And in these moments Shelby *is* her heart's desire. *Every* little beat of her heart.

Unh-wah. Unh-wah. Unh-wah.

She's doing what she was born to do.

Writing, oh yes, writing, that is one thing. That is a good thing. A noble thing. A tough-hard-ball-breaking-son-of-a-bitching thing. *Worth* the trip to Nashville.

And *enough* for lots of folks.

But writing the song and then singing it?

Lord, Lord, Lord. There is nothing sweeter in the universe. There's nothing else that feels so much like being at home.

Shelby's up on her tiptoes. Straining. Sweating. Pumping. Banging the beat with her heels on the floor.

*This* is right. *This* is good. *This* is the breath of her breath, the marrow of her bones.

And, Good God Almighty! This is the *magic*. This is the *moment*.

Yes, Lord, yes, Lord, yes. This is the *secret* hope Shelby wished for on that little star. The one she wasn't admitting to anyone. Afraid to say the words out loud.

Star bright, star light, crystal star twinkling on a chain of gold. Chain, chain, chain. Gold chain doing wheelies around the mahogany of her left eye, making circles, wrapping up her heart, her voice, gold chain chain chain of her soul.

Shelby Kay Tate. Songwriter. Singer. Star. Look at those words, up in lights.

Now ain't that what she wished for?

Ain't that what she, heart-of-hearts, now, tell the truth, girl, tell *all* of it, ain't that what she *really* wants?

# 17

MAC IS DRIVING LEROY THROUGH MUSIC ROW, POINT-
ing out the sights. Leroy can't see what all the hoo-
hah is about. He'd sort of like to stop at the George
Jones gift shop, but other than that the whole area is
just a bunch of old houses to him, some with signs
out front bearing semifamiliar names.

But he hasn't seen a single solitary music bus. That's
the only thing that will make the trip worthwhile.

"Okay," says Mac, "*I'll* show you something."

Mac hangs a left, then a right onto Fifteenth, another left, and the next thing Leroy knows, they're
climbing the hill he's noticed in the near distance. It's
crowned by a huge red TV tower.

The street narrows, shrinks to one bumpy lane.
Then a dirt track. Finally they're up top, snuggled in
beside the gigantic silver feet of the fenced-in tower.
NO TRESPASSING, it's posted. Mac cuts the engine,
climbs out, throws his arms wide.

"There she is," he crows at the panorama, proud as

if he'd toiled for six days and six nights, created it himself. "Nashville. Athens of the South. Spread out before you like a woman awaiting your embrace."

What the boys see is a handful of banking skyscrapers to the northeast; the rest of downtown is on a lower, older scale. The remainder of the metro area is one- and two-story, melding into suburbia in the distance. There's nothing special about Nashville's physiognomy—it could be one of a hundred other medium-sized American cities—unless, of course, you're from a tiny town like Star.

Mac slaps Leroy on the back. "It's all here, son, like I said. The land of milk and honey. The tit of opportunity. Waiting for you to suck."

Leroy sure hopes so. He hopes that Mac knows what he's talking about, thinking they can just jump in here and start up a business. A miracle business, that's going to bring him not only buckets of money, but Shelby. His woman. His center. Lost, oh lost.

"Isn't she grand, son? Isn't she just?" Mac pounds Leroy's shoulder. "So, what do you say? Let's go tear off a piece of her, okay? Are you ready? Are you pumped?"

Leroy yells, Yes!, slaps Mac a high five so hard his hand hurts, and they climb back into the dark turquoise Camry.

Leroy still hasn't asked about the car. He can tell Mac is holding that story close to his chest. Doesn't want to discuss it. Leroy can understand that. Sometimes there are things a man just doesn't want to talk about.

So they make their way down the bumpy one-lane trail, hang a sharp right, and begin to circle back the way they came.

Then, suddenly, Mac lurches the car over to the right. Slams on the brakes. Stops.

"What?" Leroy cries.

"Very carefully, now"—Mac's talking out of the side of his mouth like there's someone in the backseat trying to eavesdrop on their every word—"tell me what you see back there. No, no, *don't* turn around. Here." Mac jiggles the rearview mirror.

"Where?" Leroy doesn't know where to look.

"In front of that brown house with the porch, on the right. Do you see what I'm talking about?"

Leroy peers, hard. "Looks like a police car to me."

"That's right, Leroy. And who is in that police car?"

"Can't tell. Can't make him out."

"Well, I can," Mac snorts. "That, Leroy, is the same big blond police officer who I saw last night. The one who's been sniffing around your Shelby. The one who slapped the cuffs on you."

Leroy is halfway out the door when Mac snatches hold of his shirt and reels him back in like a bigmouth bass. Says, "Now, where do you think you're off to?"

"We're going to have it out. Get this thing straight. Right here. Right now." Leroy punctuates his words with his finger.

"Leroy, Leroy, Leroy." Mac shakes his head sadly, holding on tight to Leroy's collar. "That's not the way you do these things. You don't put yourself in the man's face."

"I don't?"

"What you want is for him to come to you, on *your* terms."

"I do?"

"Yes, indeedy. And I know exactly the thing to make that happen. Stick with Mac McKenzie, Esquire."

And with that Mac throws the car into Drive and tears out. They race on down the hill.

"Wheee!" Mac squeals like a kid at the bottom.

Then pulls right out into traffic. "Nothing ahead but gravy and good times, Leroy. Can you dig it?"

And they miss by inches a big silver music bus headed down toward Music Row. Its license plate begins with the letters LM, Leroy's initials.

Leroy takes that as a sign. A harbinger of Good. Better and Best waiting right around the next corner.

# 18

GAIL POWELL WAS ONE OF THE BRIGHTEST STARS EVER to light up Nashville.

Back in the fifties, when girl singers were nothing more than window dressing, she rode the long highways from one honky-tonk, fairground, small-town auditorium to the next. Singing the heartbreak songs.

Gail hung out with Dottie West, Jan Howard, Brenda Lee, and Loretta Lynn.

But it was Patsy Cline, five years her junior, but way ahead of her on the road to the top, who became Gail's best girlfriend and mentor.

Patsy gave Gail clothes, rhinestones, a place to sleep when she needed it, tips on how to wow an audience. They cried and laughed over the men in their lives. They prayed together, laughed together, and Patsy showed Gail, whom she called Peach, that an ambitious woman could be a star—just like a man.

Not that Gail didn't bring anything to the party. She had a startling, wonderful soprano, but it was her songwriting skills that Patsy most admired. The two of them spent many a late night on the road drinking bourbon, smoking cigarettes, and writing songs. You'll remember "Stranger," "Satin and Silk," and "Luray Moon."

Now, it was Patsy who convinced Owen Bradley, her producer at Decca Records and one of the architects of the swooning Nashville Sound, to take a listen to her good girlfriend. He liked what he heard and signed up Gail.

After that, with his guidance and promotion, she rose up the charts, right behind Patsy.

In 1961 Gail Powell went gold with "Me, Too." Finally, at thirty-four, after fifteen years of scraping, singing every two-bit dive from Menosha to Memphis, she became an overnight success.

Patsy, twenty-nine, crossed over into the pop charts and superstardom that same year with "I Fall to Pieces."

They had a blast on the road together. Sang and joked and cut up. There was many a time when the tiny blond blue-eyed Gail with the high silvery soprano opened for Patsy. They played the Opry together. Did benefits. They were country music's favorite high-flying girlfriends.

Then came early March 1963. Gail called Patsy about a show in Kansas City, a fund-raiser for the family of a deejay who'd been killed in a car wreck. Gail thought about not telling her at all. Patsy wasn't well yet from her own near-fatal smashup. And things were rocky in Patsy's marriage to the goodtiming Charlie Dick. But Gail knew her Patsy. Play hard, work harder, never say die, that was her motto.

Patsy was booked back-to-back into Birmingham and New Orleans before the Kansas City gig and arrived in KC dead tired and sick with the flu. But she rallied and, wearing a heavenly silver-and-white sequined gown, gave a heart-stopping performance.

The next morning after the show dawned stormy and bitterly cold. Patsy was anxious to get back to Nashville. Gail tried and tried to dissuade Patsy from flying home in the small plane piloted by her manager, Randy Hughes.

Please don't, Gail begged. Sure, it's a long drive, but it'll be safer than flying.

Oh, all right, Patsy finally agreed.

They got as far as loading Patsy's luggage into Gail's old Oldsmobile when at the last minute, Patsy changed her mind.

Nawh, Peach, she said. I can't. I 'preciate it, but I don't have the patience. I'm dying to see my babies, and if I fly, they'll be in my arms all that much sooner.

Gail tried again, but this time, she failed to make Patsy change her mind.

You know the Cline, said Patsy. Stubborn as they come. Tell you what, Peach, you want to do me a favor, carry this damned guitar back in your car. I don't know why I brought it in the first place. I'll pick it up from you later.

There never was a later, of course. The weather worsened, and Patsy's plane finally departed Kansas City the next afternoon. It hopped and skipped through the storm fronts, touching down and waiting for the weather in Little Rock and Dyersburg. Eighty-five miles west of Nashville, near Camden, Tennessee, it ran into dense rain and clouds—and out of luck.

The plane crashed, 6:20 P.M., March 5, 1963, instantly killing Randy Hughes, Hawkshaw Hawkins, Cowboy Copas.

And Patsy Cline.

Gail Powell died in the wreckage, too.

She'd arrived back at home to Franklin, Tennessee, near Nashville, late, after a sixteen-hour drive. When she didn't hear from Patsy, she assumed she was in bed with the flu, too sick to call.

But at the precise moment that Patsy's plane went down, Gail was seized by a terrible chill. When she heard that Patsy was gone, she ripped her telephone from the kitchen wall. Drew her shades. Bolted her locks.

Two days later, her friend Reola broke a window and let herself in. Gail sat in her dark living room. Smoking. Drinking. Patsy sang "Crazy" on the hi-fi, over and over.

Reola said, Come on now, you need to get yourself cleaned up.

Nope. No way, said Gail. Not going nowhere. Staying right here.

Gail had already called Owen Bradley, her manager, told them she was through. She was over and out of the music business. Didn't have the heart for it anymore.

She tortured herself with the question, Why hadn't she tried harder to stop Patsy?

And how could she ever sing another note if Patsy couldn't?

With that, Gail disappeared. Vanished into thin air. Becoming—in a city and an industry famous for its tragic legends—one of the most enduring.

And, oh, the stories they told. Some said Gail Powell'd slit her wrists in the bathroom of a Birmingham hotel. Others were certain she'd joined a convent. But then someone swore he'd spotted her at a sidewalk café in Paris. Or a casino in Monte Carlo. There was one man who took an oath on a stack of Bibles he'd seen Gail in a whorehouse in Tangier.

The truth, as usual, was much simpler.

Gail sold her Franklin house, dyed her hair brown, slipped on a pair of glasses, a frowsy housedress, and retook the name she'd been christened.

Then she bought a rambling old wreck in East Nashville, fixed it up, painted it yellow.

She didn't do much until her money ran out. Sold furniture at Sears. Opened a small antiques shop, did pretty well at that. Took up day care after she sold the store.

Gail Powell disappeared into the ordinary.

But *this* morning, she's whistling around that yellow house, cooking, bouncing babies. Finally Reola stops in the middle of a diaper change, says, "Let me guess. You've taken up with the paperboy."

"Nope. But you're warm. Try again."

"It's one of those contests. We're going for an all-expense-paid week in the Bahamas. Drink pink things with umbrellas in 'em till we can't anymore."

"Warmer."

Reola pats the freshly diapered toddler on the butt, lowers her to the floor, and lets her go. Then she stands back and stares at Gail.

When Reola Chandler stares at you, you know it. She is a regal six-footer. Very dark. Chest like the prow of a ship. Long red-and-yellow dress, silver earrings, her head is wrapped in cloth-of-gold. You'd mistake her for an African queen, easy. Watch her move, you'll put her at forty. But, like her best friend, she's crowding three score and ten.

Reola says now, "Go ahead and tell me what you did, before the cops pull up. While there's still time to call a lawyer."

Gail laughs and does, tells Reola—in between giving the tots their cookies and lemonade—about last eve-

ning's sit-down with Shelby Tate. How they're going
to have themselves a write-fest. This very evening.

Reola shakes her head, cannot believe her ears,
shouts, "What? You what? You *sang* for her?"

"Not exactly. Kind of half-sang, half-spoke. She
didn't *know,* Reola. Besides, even if she did . . .
You've always thought my hiding out was a bad idea
from the get-go."

Reola crashes down hard in a rocker. "The *get-go?*
The get-go was over thirty years ago. *Now* you're telling me, last night you said, Forget all that. Say, I'm
back, y'all. Hi, there. How you? Then sit down and
write something with the first delivery girl you set eyes
on. That's what you did?"

"She wasn't just a delivery girl."

"Well, good Lord have mercy, I hope not. Because
just *any* delivery girl would be on the phone this minute selling her story to the *National Enquirer.*"

"Oh, Reola, nobody gives a hoot about me anymore. Nobody even remembers."

"Oh, no. Unh-huh. Tell you what, wouldn't surprise
me if we didn't have reporters lined up on the porch
ten-deep before nightfall. TV cameras. Satellite
remotes."

"You are being so crazy."

"Crazy. Yes, ma'am, that's the next thing. We'll
have the loony-toons coming out of the woodwork.
Them folks that's always pestering the famous. Pre-
tending they're God knows who. And kinfolks you
ain't heard of in thirty years, they'll come for their
slice of the pie."

Reola gives a wave to the imaginary throng. "Hey,
there. Here we are. Come on, you extortionists. Grab-
bers. Grubbers. Robbers. Kidnappers." Then turns
back to Gail. "We're gonna have to get us a security
guard. Double-bolt the doors."

"I *am* Gail. Why can't I be myself if I want?"

"Oh, my God, baby. It's not that I don't want you to go back to being Gail, that'll make you happy. But couldn't you have *thought* about it a little? Given me a little warning?"

"I've had over thirty years of thinking. Besides—and this is the important part, so listen up. Shelby Tate was *sent.*"

"Oh, yeah? By who?"

"You'd know, you saw the golden ring shining in her eye."

"Absolutely. I bet I would. Makes all the difference, a gold ring. Yes, indeedy, it does."

Make fun, Gail says. Then she tells Reola how depressed she was last evening.

"I'm getting too old, Reola. You know I can't hear worth a toot. I *hate* that. I'll tell you, last night I was giving some serious thought to walking over to the river, jumping off. Or maybe riding up to the top of the ASCAP tower, doing it there. Taking up skydiving without a parachute."

"Oh, baby," Reola says. "Why didn't you call me?"

"Well, I was going to, I had my finger on the autodial, but then I found myself calling up information. Asking for the number of Sweet Willie's. It was like I was on automatic pilot, something was guiding my hand. The next thing I knew, I was talking to Willie, ordering a meal. Then up drives this Shelby Tate.

"One look was all it took. I'm telling you, Reola, it's a miracle. And you know I haven't believed in miracles since 'Me, Too' went gold."

"Baby, baby."

Gail ignores her, goes right on. "And it's not that Shelby looks like Patsy. Well, just a little. Doesn't sound like her neither—though she's got a touch of that old sob in her voice. But, hear this and hear it good, Reola. As sure as I know anything, I know that inside that chubby songwriting brunette with the gold ring in her eye, Patsy Cline lives. Patsy is alive and well here in Nashville."

# 19

MAC POINTS OUT THE CAR WINDOW AS HE AND LEROY turn right onto Twenty-first Avenue, into Hillsboro Village. "Do you see that store over there?" he asks.

Leroy sees a strip of one-story shops. A gas station. A bakery. Sweet Willie's. The gift shop where he'd found Shelby yesterday morning.

But none of it really registers. Leroy's preoccupied with what he's going to say when he and that cop come face-to-face, which Mac has assured him will be soon. Before or after they go pick up his truck near Shelby's, he's not sure.

Nothing's as important right now as Officer Capshew. How to make him understand that he, Leroy himself, has vowed and determined to rewin Shelby's love? It just isn't going to work with some cop lurking.

"That's Riflefire!" says Mac.

Leroy follows Mac's finger. The word, followed by an exclamation point just like Mac said it, is painted on an orange-red awning.

"The greatest Western wear in all of Nashville," says Mac. *"Very* fancy threads. Fringed leather jackets, every color of the rainbow, over a thousand dollars, some of them. Lots of turquoise. A silver-trimmed saddle that will knock your eyes out. Country artists in the clover, they spend buckets here."

Riflefire! is behind them now. They pass an ice cream store, a gas station, a pizza parlor.

Mac says, "You'll be strutting around town in clothes like that in not too long. Mac McKenzie, Esquire, too. We *deserve* some luxury, don't you think?" Mac smooths his right hand down his faded red Western shirt gaping over his gut.

Then he cuts a hard right. They pull into the parking lot of a low blond brick-and-glass building. Green shrubbery around it. Big blue plastic letters announce FIRST NATIONAL BANK.

"You got business in here?" Leroy asks. Mac hasn't mentioned it.

"Indeed I do. Reach in the back, please, would you? Hand me that grip."

Leroy hefts Mac's worn tan-and-yellow cardboard suitcase over the seat. Mac unsnaps the case, roots around in it until he comes up holding a little snub-nosed Smith & Wesson. It is hammerless, well, actually the hammer is concealed, and has a "lemon squeeze" safety that makes it virtually impossible for the gun to go off accidentally.

Leroy doesn't know what kind of gun it is. He just knows that he's looking at one, and he doesn't want to be looking at one. Guns scare the doo-waddy out of him.

"What the hell're you doing?" he asks Mac.

"Didn't I tell you back up on the hill where we saw that police car that I could make your officer come to us? And you said, yes, that would be good."

"Yeah, but you didn't say nothing about guns."

"And didn't I tell you that's the beauty part of riding shotgun with Mac McKenzie? You don't have to worry your pretty head about a single solitary thing?"

"I ain't riding shotgun or any other kind of gun." Leroy's voice is rising. "And I *told* you I don't want to have nothing to do with no bank robberies. Told you that when you picked me up. Right off."

Mac slaps his forehead. "You know, son, you are absolutely right. You did. And it *would* be stupid, wouldn't it, to go back in that same bank and try to rob it again? Plainly misguided to think that the security guard who eyed me before wouldn't recognize me again."

Mac slides a look at the side door of the bank, and just then, a large black man in a blue security guard uniform strolls out and lights up a cigarette. "Very wrong thinking. I agree with you one hundred percent."

Mac lays the Smith & Wesson down on the seat. "Okay, I give. Hey! I was just playing with you, Leroy."

Leroy doesn't think he believes that.

"But I do need to take care of a little business inside. Do you mind waiting just a minute?" Mac reaches for the door handle.

Leroy gives him a fishy look.

"This is my bank, honest." Mac holds up both hands. Innocent, see? Then pulls a scruffy brown wallet from his back pocket. Waves a navy blue bank card in Leroy's face. "I won't be but a minute."

# 20

JEROME BIBLE STANDS THE SEVEN-TO-THREE SHIFT AT the First National on Wednesdays, that being his day off from the fire department.

Right now he's taking a cigarette break, leaning up against the side of the bank building listening to WSIX on his Walkman. Concentrating, trying to see what it is Althea hears in this honky country music.

Money, honey, she says.

He doesn't hear anything but twanging and clanging, a bunch of no-talent white folks whining through their noses. Jerome has personally witnessed Billy Ray Cyrus twisting himself across a stage, the arms cut out of his funky shirt. What is that?

*Lots* of money, honey, Althea says.

Well, bless her heart. It would be awfully nice if she could make some, too, for a change, though Jerome doesn't know how this country thing is going to make a difference.

In addition to being the hope of his life—she and

her two kids, whom Jerome is crazy about—Althea is one of the best singers Jerome has ever heard. And that includes your Whitney, your Sade, your Aretha.

The thing about Althea, his short round brown Althea, she writes her own stuff. *Then* belts it. And Althea can flat tear up a room. She does a number like her "Momma Knows," it'll knock you down, walk all over your face.

The problem is, folks over at the lounge at the Holiday Inn where Althea has been singing for small change for years, they don't do much listening with their drinking. And folks out at the Cooker on Briley Parkway, where Althea's waiting breakfast tables to help keep the kids in Catholic school, they don't know she makes any sounds except, "Yes, sir. No, sir. Thank you, sir. I'll get that right now, sir."

Music City U.S.A. is a cold hard town for a musical black woman who wants to do something with her life.

But then, as Althea says, Where ain't?

So now she has this new thing working. She's taken up writing country songs with these two white women.

Althea's dragged Jerome to hear them, Shelby and Lynn. They call themselves the Wild Women, have made Althea a Wild Woman, too, like she wasn't already. It was an early-evening songwriters' gig at the Bluebird Cafe he went to. The *crème de la crème,* according to Althea, of the clubs where the country writers try out their own stuff. Keep it simple. Just a keyboard, a guitar.

Crème de ma ass, Jerome had said, dragging his feet into the place, but once they were there, he'd heard some music he liked. *Especially* Shelby and Lynn's. Some of their songs had a bluesy kind of thing, didn't seem like country at all to him, but he could see how Althea could relate to it.

**119**

That ain't the stuff they play on the radio, though, he'd said.

Yeah, said Althea, mostly that was true. You never heard the *really* good country music on the radio, the material that pushed the edge of the envelope. You had to go to the Bluebird, Douglas Corner, Ace of Clubs, the Sutler, other places like that to hear the *real* music.

Then what's the point, asked Jerome. That's like any other commercial music scene you're telling me you been knocking your pretty head up against the past twenty years.

Yeah, but *some* of it gets on the radio.

No way.

Then she said, You tune in WSIX, see if you don't hear Lynn's "Mysterious Love." You can hear it in person you come to our writers' night at the Sutler. Wild Women gonna turn some people loose.

And, son of a gun, if she wasn't right.

Leaning up against the side of the First National Bank on his break, "Mysterious Love" is what Jerome is listening to when Mac McKenzie walks up to him.

Jerome remembers Mac from Monday. He's the main character in the funny story Jerome was going to tell Jeff Wayne yesterday when his friend caught that call, had to leave.

Monday, Jerome comes in a little early for his three-to-eleven shift, he's standing around gassing with Hubert, who's just finished locking the doors, bank's closing. Hubert goes off to see about something, this little character comes up, bangs on the glass. Jerome strolls over, opens the door a crack, tells him politely he can't come in, but there's an automatic teller right outside. See that, sir?

The guy says, No, that won't do. He has to get into his safety deposit box.

Well, he doesn't look like a guy who'd have a box in the first place, but that's none of Jerome's business, and he's been wrong before. What is his business is that the bank is closed, the man'll have to come back tomorrow.

At that, the character goes berserk. Starts screaming about how he might not be here tomorrow, he has this inoperable tumor in his gut, cancer eating his insides up, he could die any minute.

Jerome thinks, well, he's got *something* in there, all right. Looks like a seven-month baby. But that still doesn't cut any ice. Closed is closed.

At that, the character starts pulling pills out of his pockets, spilling drugs all over the sidewalk. Jumping up and down, screaming. Waving medical bills from Vanderbilt Hospital up in front of Jerome's face. Says he needs to change his last will and testament, and he means now!

Jerome says he's real sorry, but the rules are the rules.

At that the character has another little foaming hissy fit, but finally takes himself off, yelling: *I'll be back and deal with you, my friend.*

Now here he is.

Jerome drops his cigarette, grinds it out, and says, *Well, look who's here.*

Mac pulls his *other* Smith & Wesson, twin to the one he left in the car with Leroy.

Fires.

# 21

LEROY'S STILL RUNNING HIS LINES, PRACTICING WHAT
he's going to say to that Officer Capshew. Nodding in
time to the song that's playing on the radio.

> *Love is a mystery that gives you no clues*
> *Wears a mask, dyes its hair, jumps out at you*

Good idea, thinks Leroy. He'll jump out at that cop,
that's what he'll do. Set him straight. Then get on with
the music bus business.

Now here comes Mac. The little man climbs back
behind the wheel. "Are you ready to roll?" Pats his
wallet.

"Ready when you are," says Leroy.

"Then hold on." Mac throws the car in reverse and
backs into an oncoming lane of traffic. Horns wail. A
blue station wagon rear-ends a white BMW. Mac pulls
away clean.

*Love is a mystery,* the blonde is singing. Or at least

she sounds like a blonde to Leroy. And he agrees with her. There's no way you can know a damned thing about love. Love *is* mysterious.

Lookit. There he thought for nine years that Shelby was crazy about him. She sure as hell hadn't said anything different. Then she up and left him.

Cold.

Maybe he'll tell the cop that.

Say, Hey, man, you don't want to be messing with the likes of her. Woman'll break your heart. I'm doing you a favor, here. So buzz off, okay?

Then Leroy looks up. They're back in front of that store Mac pointed out before. Riflefire! Mac's parking right in front.

"What are we doing now?" Leroy's getting impatient. "Shopping? I thought I was going to straighten out that cop. Then we were on our way to see about some music buses."

Mac grins. His dentures are bright white in the sunlight. Leroy doesn't like to think about those snappers jumping out of Mac's mouth. They could grab his leg. Land in his lap.

Mac reaches into the suitcase on the seat between them, starts pulling stuff from it. Black gloves, tan raincoat, a big floppy black hat. A single black stocking.

He puts it all on, the stocking over his head, mashing his nose, grabbing up pieces of his face, twisting them around.

"Climb over into the driver's seat," Mac says, working hard to make the words inside the stocking. "And keep 'er running. I won't be but a minute."

Then Mac leans back in and grabs the cold revolver he'd left on the seat earlier with Leroy, shoves it under his gut.

\* \* \*

For three long minutes Leroy sits there frozen, shallow-breathing through his mouth. Listening for gunshots.

Wondering, should he get the hell out of here, dump Mac? Or wait?

Leroy decides. Fuck this.

He's sliding the gearshift into Drive, when the little man flies through the door.

"Hit it!" says Mac.

# 22

THE DEMO SESSION FINALLY FINISHED, SHELBY'S FLY-
ing. Her feet hardly touch the ground as she and
Selma make their way back up to their cars in front
of Bud's.

Selma had her do *her* version of each of the three
songs they'd come to demo, along with Arlen's. Now
Selma lays a hand on her shoulder. "Shelby, that was
great work. But I don't want you to get your hopes
up. This is Nashville. Where money talks and bullshit
walks just as sure as if it were L.A., New York. This
is a *business,* Shelby. Big business."

Shelby slows. "I know." But she doesn't want to
hear it. Not one word. Wants to keep on flying.
Never stop.

"And the music business is no meritocracy. Most of
the time it doesn't *matter* how good you are. I hate
to say that to you. I hate to even think it. But you
know and I know that it's the truth. So, no matter
how cool that session was, no matter that we have a

DAT"—she waves the little plastic master cartridge
in her hand—"with your versions, you know what it
don't mean."

"Dick," says Shelby. "Don't mean dick unless some
man with *very* deep pockets thinks he can make 'em
even deeper with my sound."

"There's my girl."

"Yep," says Shelby, sucking it up. Putting one foot
in front of the other. She's still got time. She's not
skinny and she's no raving beauty and she's not as
young as they like girl singers these days, eighteen,
twenty, twenty-two, but look at K.T.

K.T. was forty-five when Diane Petty *finally,* dear
God, helped her get her career burning.

Shelby's not forty-five. Not yet.

*And* she's got Chris Cassel coming to hear her songs
tomorrow night. Hear *her,* too.

Miracles can happen.

A person who doesn't believe in miracles ought not
to come to Nashville in the first place.

And right now, what she's going to do, she checks
her watch, yes, she's got time before her rehearsal
with Lynn and Althea, is run back over to that gift
shop, buy that crystal star.

For yes, ma'am, Shelby's on a roll. No matter what
kind of rain Selma's pouring on her parade, she still
feels good. Yesterday *abounded* with bad luck, except
for the very end when she went over to East Nashville,
ran up on her old lady songwriter. That's when her
luck turned. Now things are going her way. Clear
through tomorrow night.

And that little crystal star might be just the specific
piece of magic she needs to make it all work.

"Thanks, Selma." Shelby gives her a kiss on the
cheek. And a hug. *Everybody* in Nashville hugs. A lot.

"I'll see you tomorrow night. You gonna be there early?"

"With bells on."

Shelby wheels toward her Toyota.

And there, sitting in his Metro Police car, big as life, is Jeff Wayne.

"Son," she says to him, leaning in his window, "are you strange or what?"

"What do you mean?"

"Explain yourself. What are you doing?"

"I'm sitting in my car. This is part of my patrol."

"Is that right? Everywhere I go, is that part of your patrol, too? 'Cause I tell you what, Officer Capshew, I appreciate all you've done for me, but I'm beginning to wonder about you. You're making me a little nervous."

"Oh, Ms. Tate, I sure don't mean to be doing that."

"Well, what exactly do you mean to be doing?"

Jeff Wayne glances around nervously, like maybe he'll find the words on Bud's front porch or down the sidewalk or maybe up at the TV tower. He clears his throat.

Then a woman's voice crackles on his radio, saying there's an armed robbery in progress at Riflefire! Custom Clothiers, 1801 Twenty-first South, the intersection of Twenty-first South and Acklen.

"See you later," says Jeff Wayne, gearing up and roaring off, his blue lights awhirl.

# 23

Leroy, wild-eyed, wheels the turquoise Camry this way and that away from Riflefire! Up through a maze of streets rising behind the red brick Belmont College.

Mac, ever cool, says, "Slow down, Leroy. You don't want us to get stopped for speeding. Good. Now, turn here. Pull over."

Leroy holds up in front of a ratty orange brick duplex. A butt-sprung couch sits on the lopsided front porch. Two broken bikes lie in the dirt. A hundred more brick units like it are scattered around the rolling hills.

But Leroy is way beyond taking in the public-housing architecture. Leroy is rigid with fear.

"Mac, what the hell is going on?"

Mac is paying him no attention. The little man has pulled a handkerchief from his pocket and is wiping down the interior of the Camry. Whistling like some kind of damned elf while he works.

"You grab that side over there," he says to Leroy. "Here, use this."

Mac produces a brand-new purple-and-green bandana from his Riflefire! shopping bag. Shoves it at Leroy. Says, "Rub off everything. You never can be sure what you touched."

"What is *wrong* with you?" Leroy screams.

He's getting the hell out of this getaway car. He jumps out and stands in the middle of the street. Which way to run?

Suddenly, from around a corner whiz four shiny mountain bikes. Four African-American teenagers pumping like madmen. Wearing big shirts, baggy cut-off jeans.

Leroy knows about ghetto crime. Baby drug dealers, toting Uzis. He jumps behind the Camry. The kids zoom by, yelling something.

Mac doesn't even look up. Keeps spitting on his handkerchief. Wiping, wiping, wiping all the interior surfaces. Now the door handles on the outside.

"Come on!" Leroy pleads. "Let's get out of here."

Mac flashes his bright store-bought grin, says, "Chill, Leroy."

Then Mac pulls a wrench and a heavy-duty screwdriver from his suitcase. Tosses the shopping bag at Leroy. Saunters over to a brand-new black Jeep four-by-four that looks out of place in front of the crummy brick cottage.

"Hold on a minute," Mac says.

He knocks in the right rear window. Opens the door, and a car alarm wails. Mac leans in, pops the hood, lifts it, and shuts up the alarm with one whack of the wrench. He has the Jeep up and running in ten seconds flat.

As Leroy sees it, he has two choices.

He can stay here and deal with the gigantic black

man running out on his falling-down porch. Jerking his pants over his naked butt. Hollering, "Stop, you motherfuckers!"

Or he can jump in the Jeep with Mac.

Leroy jumps. Then hunkers. Any second there'll be the whizzing of bullets past his ears. Then sirens.

But there aren't!

Instead Mac quietly ambles them out of the project in that Jeep. Back through a nice old middle-class neighborhood. A Sunday drive. Big trees. Two-story houses where nice people live. People who haven't just robbed a clothing store at gunpoint. Now, stolen a Jeep.

Leroy stares at the man, speechless.

But Mac has lots to say. "Mark my words, Leroy, this vehicle's hot as can be. Already was, I mean. No way that brother's going to report it nabbed. *And,* nine chances out of ten, those folks in Riflefire! are going to say it was a bro' who robbed them, too. That black stocking over my head, the wig, their native prejudices working, it'd be difficult to dissuade 'em. Then they'll find that Camry in the 'hood." Mac takes both hands off the wheel, shrugs. Case closed.

Leroy shuts his eyes and prays. *Dear God, get me out of this mess, I promise I'll go back home to Star and never bother You again.*

Mac's still talking. "Well, here we are, and there he is, Leroy. Just like I promised you." He brakes. Pulls the Jeep over.

Leroy opens his eyes. Cannot *believe* what he sees.

They've come full circle and have stopped directly in front of Riflefire! again.

Is Mac going to ask him to slide over, run in, and rob it for the second time?

Probably not. Considering the place is surrounded

by white Metro Police cars. Blue gumballs rolling and flashing.

"Do you see what I see?" Mac's pointing at Officer Capshew talking to a fellow in jeans, bright blue ostrich-and-inlaid-lizard cowboy boots, six pounds of turquoise. Riflefire!'s manager, has to be.

Leroy ducks. Curls head-to-stomach like a roly-poly bug in the passenger seat.

"Sit up, Leroy!" Mac won't quit. "There's your man. Big old policeman. Didn't I tell you we could make him come to us? And here he is, just like we special-ordered him." Mac looks tickled to death with himself. "Now, straighten up, old son. Get on over there and give him a piece of your mind."

Leroy stares up at Mac. "Man, you are effin' crazy."

Mac giggles. Can't remember the last time he'd had so much fun. Now he can't *wait* to get to the next part, over at that big yellow house in East Nashville. *That's* gonna be something.

# 24

SHELBY'S BEATING OUT THE RHYTHM OF "I WANTA Drive" on her steering wheel. *"Put the pedal to the metal. Let the rubber hit the road."*

She gliiides into the Natchez Trace's parking lot. Taps the brake at the last moment with the tip of her toe.

Yes, momma.

All right, girl.

Who's the hottest songwriter/singer in Nashville at this *very* nanosecond?

Shelby Kay Tate, and don't YOU forget it.

Shelby swings open her door, sashays out of her moldering wreck of a Japanese kiddie car as if it were a carriage of gold.

Bebops down the sidewalk.

*Gotta grab the shower I skipped this morning. Change my clothes. Run over to Lynn's, do this rehearsal thing. Wiiiiiiild Women gonna rock and roll. Then me and Miz King, we're gonna write us a song. Oh, yeah, baby, oh yeah.*

Then someone calls, "Hey, Shelby, wait up."
Shelby does a one-eighty.
Chuck.

He comes toward her, arms open, enfolds her in one of those Nashville hugs.

"How you doing, sugar?" he asks.

"Good. Great." Shelby pulls back, looks him square in the eye. "Real great." And once again, she can see herself, half-naked, diving into his embrace. She blushes, buries her face in her hands. "Oh, Lord, Chuck."

"Hey, darlin'." He laughs. Crinkles his eyes. Pulls her chin up. "It wudn't like you wrecked that train by yourself, was it?"

"No, but . . ." What can she say? "I feel so dumb."

"Ain't nothing the least bit dumb about good honest lust, sugar baby."

"Do you think maybe we could talk about this somewhere else?" Shelby flips a palm toward the very parking lot where, the day before, their dirty laundry hung.

"Why sure." He lowers his voice, filling it with insinuation. "What'd you have in mind?"

She slaps at him. "Don't you dare start."

"Awh, hon. Can't you take a joke from your Uncle Chuck?"

"Joyce didn't think it was a joke."

"No, she didn't. She sure didn't." And that's when Chuck begins to weep.

One foot in her door, Chuck notices the TV, says, "What the hell happened here?"

Shelby does a quick Leroy-update.

Chuck sets his iced tea down on her coffee table,

pushes back into the navy sofa. "Sure as the sun'll rise, them boys'll do you that way. Didn't I tell you so?"

"Yes, you did. And I'm just bored to tears, thinking about Leroy. So, can we move on? Let's hear *your* story."

"Well, hell, Shel, I don't know what to think. I'm bewildered, Joyce left me. How come she did that? She never did before."

"Before what?"

"Hon, I don't know how to tell you this, but yesterday was not exactly the first time I've ever been indiscreet."

"No shit? And here I thought we were practically engaged."

"Now, don't be like that."

"Like what? I don't know what I'm supposed to say here. Hell, I don't even know how I feel. Except weird. I know I feel weird. I didn't even get to *be* the other woman. Got all of the shame, none of the fun."

Chuck rolls out his sexy bass again. "And I can guarantee you it would've been fun."

"Stop. Okay?"

"You're right. I'm real sorry. I just keep putting my foot in it, everywhere I turn."

"I'm sorry, too. About the whole thing. Where'd Joyce go?"

"I reckon she went over to her sister Lucy's. Yesterday afternoon, she was packing up, she wouldn't say. She just kept slinging stuff in suitcases, shopping bags. Ruby was following her from room to room, wagging her tail. Thought she was going to get to go. Joyce was out the door, she said, 'Try not to let the dog starve to death.' Like I would."

"Did you try her at Lucy's?"

"Yeah. Lucy said she wasn't there, hung up."

"So she *was* there."

"Probably. It's hard to tell with Lucy. For a woman who makes her living off people getting married— Lucy's a wedding and party consultant—she has the worst opinion of men."

"Maybe that's *why* she does."

"Hey, is there something else you want to say here? Go ahead, woman. Take your best shot."

Shelby has to think about that for a minute. What *is* she feeling? "I don't know. It's confusing. There's a part of me that really feels for Joyce. I've been on her side of this story, you know."

"With Leroy." Chuck sits, rocking lightly back and forth. "So why'd you put up with him?"

"Good question. You looking for some insight, you and Joyce?"

"I guess."

"Let me ask you this. Did Joyce ever catch you in the act before?"

"No, not really. She didn't. No."

"More like she knew, but it wasn't staring her in the face, she didn't have to own up to it if she didn't want to?"

"Something like that."

"So maybe she loves you, jerk. Doesn't want to lose you, no matter what. But once you've rubbed her nose in it, her pride won't let her stay."

"Like when you found Leroy and that blonde in the pickup?"

"I guess. God knows I knew way before that. But, you're right, I saw 'em, it was over. No doubt about it." Shelby pauses. "Chuck, let me ask you something."

"I know. 'Why do I screw around if I don't want to lose her?' "

"Something like that."

"I didn't for years, not for a real long time. And then, well, it was like, hell . . ."

"What?"

"It sounds stupid, but, all right, it's the God's honest truth. Women kept throwing themselves at me. After a while, well, I was weak. I've been a hell of a lot better lately, though."

"Oh, yeah? What about me? What was that?"

"Well, Shelby, hon. Now, don't get mad, but *I* wasn't the one who got half-naked."

"That's it. Scoot. Git. Go on. Move. Hit the road."


Halfway out to his truck, Chuck remembers why he came over in the first place. He turns around, retraces his steps.

"Shelby?" he hollers, back at her door. "Let me in. Come on, now. I've got something real important to give you."

"Don't need no Girl Scout cookies," she hollers back.

"I'm not teasing. This is serious."

"So am I. Go on, now. I'm already late. Should have been over at Lynn's ten minutes ago."

"I'm gonna stand here and scream until you open this goddamned door. Somebody might call the cops again, thinking it's Leroy."

"Okay, okay." Hands on hips. "What?" Shelby steps aside, and Chuck throws his briefcase on her table. Opens it and starts sifting through seed catalogs, old song sheets, a T-shirt that says WE GROW OUR OWN.

"And I didn't even know about Leroy's showing up, trying to take advantage of you when I packed this up. But, that just goes to show you. Once a cop, always a cop. The instincts never die."

Please. Shelby looks toward the heavens.

"And now, well, there's no telling what he's gonna have in his mind, he gets out on bail."

"I beg your pardon."

Chuck turns. "Bail, Shelby. Leroy's most likely probably already sprung. Don't you know that?"

"What are you talking about? They locked him up."

"Didn't they explain all this to you at the police station? That the man probably would make bail before you can say Jack Robinson? Tell you to call them immediately, if he shows again?"

Shelby isn't sure. There was this woman officer who'd talked with her a long time, but she hadn't really been listening. Maybe she'd already had too much on her mind to concentrate. Shelby turns now, confused. The woman gave her a card. Where's her purse?

"But just to be on the safe side," Chuck says. Pulling a big Browning .380 automatic out of his satchel. Shoving it toward her across the table. "It's kinda heavy, but Leroy comes back, you don't want no cap gun."

Shelby steps back. "Are you nuts?"

"No. Now listen to me. You carry this with you at all times. Look here. See this? This is where the clip goes in . . ."

# 25

LEROY ISN'T RISING FROM HIS CROUCH IN THE FRONT seat of the stolen Jeep until Mac comes to a full stop. And assures him the coast is clear.

Then slowly he unfolds, takes a peek.

"Jesus H. Christ!" Leroy cries, ducking again.

Here they are, in broad daylight, back on Shelby's street. Pulled up behind his old green pickup, exactly where he left it yesterday, just down the block from the Natchez Trace Apartments. Officer Capshew could be over here any second, the way the man hangs around Shelby. . . .

"Don't be such a wuss," says Mac. "You said you wanted to pick up your truck. Not that we can't grab you a new one . . ."

"No! No more grabbing!"

"Leroy. Son. Are you going to turn out to be a disappointment to your father confessor, Mac McKenzie? And here we just got started good."

"I *told* you, I didn't want to be stealing things."

"And I'm willing to discuss that. But you must sit up, Leroy. It's impossible to carry on a con-ver-*sa*-tion with a man who's cowering."

Leroy slides up, partway. Rests his head against the back of the seat in a most tentative fashion.

"That's better. Now, Leroy, tell me what you have against petty theft."

*"Petty?* Two cars and a clothing store in one morning? Us fresh out of jail?"

Mac doesn't answer for a moment. They sit there, on the quiet street lined with two-story apartment buildings and townhouses. Everyone who's going to work or school has left. Won't be back for hours.

The two men watch a wren pull an earthworm from the grassy strip between the sidewalk and the street. The pinkish-gray worm stretches and stretches, then lets go of its hold on the dirt and slaps hard against the wren's beak.

Finally Mac says, "Your thinking is unsophisticated, Leroy. Based on a tired philosophy your parents taught you and your grandmothers taught them. And so on."

"Unsophisticated to think it's *wrong* to go around robbing? Not to mention dangerous. This kind of stuff could get a person killed. And I'm not studying going back to jail," says Leroy. "No way."

"Which is precisely why you're partnered up with the likes of Mac McKenzie. He can keep you out of harm's way. Free as that bird." Mac points toward the wren, who has made a quick lunch of the worm and is now shopping for dessert. "But *wrong?* Son, *wrong* is not a concept."

"What do you mean?"

"Let me ask you this. Do you think it's wrong that bird just ate that worm?"

Leroy shakes his head.

"Why not?"

" 'Cause it needs the worm to live."

"That's right," says Mac. "A bird will eat a worm, a cat will eat a bird, and a Chinaman will eat a cat, and so forth. It's always been that way. Always will be."

Leroy didn't follow the part about the Chinaman, but he got Mac's drift. "What *you're* talking about is survival. Creatures keeping body and soul together. But that's not at all the same as taking a man's car, holding up a store, robbing a bank."

"Why?"

"Because those things aren't necessities."

"How do you know that? Have you thought about what it takes in this modern world of America in which we live today to keep a man going? Preserve his self-respect?"

Mac is just warming up. "A man who has no car, do you think he's going to call himself a man? Additionally, how's he going to get around? How about a television? How the hell are you going to know what's happening in the world without one? There could be, oh, some sort of new rare disease which could kill you, one of those mutant African strains, and you wouldn't know about it, if you didn't see it on the tube.

"Children have to have their skateboards, Rollerblades, those fancy bikes, otherwise, they might as well give it up, because none of their little friends will speak to them. They'll wither and die from the lonelies—or the first thing you know, they've up and become serial murderers."

Leroy shakes his head. Mac is so intelligent, his mind so lightning fast, sometimes Leroy finds it impossible to keep up.

"And, besides which, how do you think those who are wealthy became that way if not by relieving others of their earthly goods? The Rockefellers, the Morgans, the Kennedys, they walked on the backs of the little men listening to their grandmothers saying Do unto others—all the while someone's Doing it to him."

"Are you saying Rockefellers *robbed* people?"

"Well . . ." Mac drawls the word out long, leaning back and patting his belly as if it were strung with a gold watch chain beneath a striped waistcoat and a dove gray vest. "I'm not claiming they pulled their stagecoaches over and said, Stick 'em up, but they might as well have.

"And look here. How about the bankers, those S&L crooks, stealing billions from little old ladies, the government didn't do a thing but pat them on the back? And Wall Street? Pshaw! I could go on and on, but what I'm telling you is the gospel truth. Nobody ever got anywhere by sticking their nose to the grindstone. That's for chumps.

"The *problem* is thinking any of the doing-what-is-necessary is wrong. It's all like that bird and that worm. It's the way of the world. It's what it is."

"Oh yeah?" says Leroy. "Then how come back in jail you were talking about stars in your crown? A man who believes in earning a place in heaven's got to believe in right. Doesn't he?" Leroy leans back, resting his case.

"Oh, yes," croons Mac. "Yes, yes." He is having such a good time. He is absolutely exhilarated. Times like this, his brain spinning, a chump like Leroy in the palm of his hand, he feels like he'll live forever. Which is hardly the case. "Okay. Yes, Leroy, I believe in right. Yes, Lord, I do." He smacks the dash of the Jeep. "You bet I do. Right is everything. And everything is right."

Leroy mulls that over a few minutes. Then begins

to get Mac's drift. "Are you're telling me you believe in right. But not in wrong. Is that what you're saying?"

"It's not that I don't believe in wrong, son. It's precisely as I said from the beginning. Wrong is simply not a concept." Mac drums his fingers on the steering wheel, then shifts the Jeep from Park to Drive, and that is the end of that.

Mac says, "Now, listen to me, Leroy. Go get in your truck and follow me over to the Hampton Inn. We'll check in, establish international headquarters for McKenzie & Mabry Custom Bus Enterprises.

"The location is entirely appropriate for our undertaking, the hotel having been built upon the site of the old hotel where Elvis used to stay when he came to Nashville. That *has* to be providence.

"Anyway, we'll check in, and then I've a few little errands to run. You can freshen up, we'll be off to inspect the music bus business as it exists in Nashville *pre*-McKenzie & Mabry. After today, it'll never be the same. What do you say, Leroy?"

Leroy jumps out of the Jeep and dives into his pickup. Gives Mac a thumbs-up. They're rolling.

# 26

Lynn called two seconds after Chuck left.

Shelby said, "You and Althea hold your horses. I'm on my way."

But Althea wasn't at Lynn's, waiting to rehearse. Althea, said Lynn, was at Vanderbilt Hospital waiting to see if Jerome, who'd been shot, was going to live or die.

Now Shelby hurries down the pale green hospital hall, following the signs to the ICU waiting room. Trying not to look into open doors. Bedpans. Needles. Tubes.

Jerome's too strong to die, Shelby tells herself, passing a little old lady in a wheelchair. *He'p me, he'p me, he'p me,* the woman chirps over and over like a whippoorwill.

Jerome's too young. Too big. Too good.

She turns the final corner and bumps into the waiting room. Rows of padded green plastic chairs. Magazines. Discarded food wrappers. Soda cans. Coffee cups. A TV tuned to Sally Jessy, the sound turned so low you can't make out what the whining is about. Althea, surrounded by a bunch of ladies.

"Althea, honey, I'm so sorry." Shelby falls into her arms. The short round brown woman smelling as always of baby powder and coffeecake. "How's he doing?"

"Holding on." Althea nods. "Doing good."

Althea's full bottom lip is tucked tight. You aren't going to see her crying. Not now. Not while her strength can help Jerome. Come the worst, there'll be plenty of time for tears.

"What happened?" Shelby asks.

Althea shakes her head. "Don't know for sure. He was doing his security guard thing at the bank, some fool walked up to him on his cigarette break, shot him."

"Christ," says Shelby.

A black woman in a yellow pants suit on Althea's left pops Shelby a look. Taking the Lord's name in vain doesn't play in this crowd. The woman says, "Lord Jesus'll take care of Jerome. Yes, He will." Nodding to the rhythm of her words.

On the other side of the yellow pants suit, a tall handsome woman in a long dress of blue and gold says, "Yes ma'am. Him *and* Vanderbilt Hospital."

Althea says, "Shelby, this is Mayretta and Reola. Friends of Momma's. She's gone on home to be with my kids."

"Lynn is on her way over there to see if she can help," says Shelby.

"That's awfully sweet. And sweet of you to come."

"Althea. Althea." Shelby shakes her head. "And they don't have any idea who it was?"

"No. Jerome's friend, here, is with the police, but they haven't been able to tell us anything yet."

Shelby looks up to see Jerome's friend, the cop. And here comes Officer Jeff Wayne Capshew down the hall, carrying a tray of coffee cups.

# 27

Patsy Angel grins at Shelby and Jeff Wayne. She's right in the waiting room with them and Althea. Not that anyone can see her.

Shelby says, "What are *you* doing here?"

Jeff Wayne demands, "How do *you* know Jerome?"

"Althea's one of the Wild Women. Me, Althea, my friend Lynn, we perform together."

"And Jerome's my best friend," says Jeff Wayne. "Isn't it a small world?"

Althea says, "I take it you two have met."

Now *there,* thinks the angel, taking a deep whiff of Althea, is a woman with some serious mojo of her own. She trails Shelby and the cop over to the Coke machine.

Shelby says, "I know this isn't the time to bring this up again, but, really, why are you following me?"

"Jerome *is* my best friend, Shelby."

"I know. I know you said that. But look." She ticks off the examples on her fingers. "Yesterday, you an-

swered the call to my apartment about Joyce. Then
you came back, saved me from Leroy. I finish my
demo session today, go outside, there you were. Now
here. What gives, Jeff Wayne?"

The angel smiles at Jeff Wayne, her designated run-
ner, knowing he isn't going to tell Shelby that she
missed one. She didn't see him trailing her all over
Nashville last night, over to Gail's house, then back
home again. Waited outside her window, made sure
she was tucked in tight.

And how can he explain himself when he doesn't
know *what* the heaven he's doing?

Doesn't know that Patsy Angel has picked him to
help her look after Shelby through what she had a
feeling was going to be a very bad patch.

Most of the time, of course, Patsy Angel does just
fine by Shelby without any assistance. She can certainly handle the musical aspect of Shelby's life. After
all, this is Nashville. And she was Patsy Cline.

The way that works? Well, Shelby came squalling
out of her momma at the very exact instant that Patsy's little plane went splat, nosedown in the dirt over
near Camden, Tennessee. March 5, 1963.

Shelby Kay Tate was the only girl child born at that
precise moment in the entire South. And it wasn't like
God, who was a country music fan Himself, was going
to waste Patsy's spirit on some Yankee. Or a girl baby
in some land where they didn't know "Sweet Dreams"
from "On Top of Old Smoky."

Once Shelby was chosen, Patsy Angel gave her perfect pitch and passion and ambition, but after that,
she stood back.

Her thinking was, if Shelby didn't have some tough
times, some rocks in her path, she couldn't exactly
write country music now, could she?

Oh, sure, Patsy Angel had come to her rescue when

Shelby was a little girl and a horse had thrown her and was about to kick her brains out.

And she'd sent Lynn to that songwriting seminar in Jackson.

She'd sat that blonde down at the bar next to Leroy that night after Dwayne exploded the walnut cake. When she thought it was time for Shelby to leave him, get on with her career.

And, okay, she'd pulled a few strings for Shelby when she got to Nashville.

But, heck, what was the point of having connections if you couldn't use them?

After that, Patsy Angel thought she'd just keep an eye out. Shelby had the goods. Her blessing. She'd be all right.

But then she heard the buzz that Rahab, one of the Seven Princes of Hell, was moving into her territory. Big Time. And Rahab, the Violent One—who'd been working for the Pharaoh when he tried to stop the Jews from crossing the Red Sea—had found himself a perfect emissary in Mac McKenzie, Esquire, one evil little son of a bitch.

Now with Rahab, Patsy Angel had her work cut out for her. But she was equal to the task. After all, what was her motto if not: Play hard, work harder, never say die?

Besides, there were perks to this assignment she'd never dreamed of.

Like seeing Gail. Her sweet old Peach. *Always* on her mind.

And setting her and Shelby up together, now, wasn't that a neat trick?

Now, over by the Coke machine, Shelby is asking Jeff Wayne, "Do you want a *date?* Is that what this is all about?"

Patsy Angel grins.

"No," says Jeff Wayne, "I don't."

"Well, why the hell not?"

Patsy roars. Sic 'im, girl.

"I *have* a girlfriend, Shelby."

"Yeah, well, I tell you what. If you were *my* boy-friend, and I caught you hanging around some other woman like you've been hanging around me, I wouldn't care *what* you said. Wouldn't matter a bit that you thought you had this *calling* to protect this other woman. Isn't that what you said to me yesterday? Said you had this *feeling* I needed you? I'd say, Jeff Wayne Capshew, use your noggin, son. Figure. It. Out. Fish or cut bait. Don't give me this mysto-schmysto crap about *callings*. And as far as *I'm* concerned, me, Shelby Kay Tate, you're making me real uncomfortable. How do I know you're not one of those pervert cops?"

Patsy takes a deep deep angel-lungful of the electricity, the heat, the energy zapping through the air. Boogies her angel-butt.

Oh yaaaaaaaas.

Isn't nothing in the Angels' Handbook that says an assignment, even one as dangerous as this, can't be a kick.

# 28

THE MINUTE MAC LEAVES THEIR HOTEL ROOM AT THE Hampton Inn, Leroy takes a shower and climbs into his new duds from Riflefire! Stone-washed jeans, dark blue boots, purple shirt with silver trim and genuine turquoise button covers. He'll be ready, when Mac gets back, to go calling on the music bus folks.

In the meantime, Leroy thinks he'll watch a little TV. Have himself a couple of drinks.

He reaches for Mac's bottle of Early Times.

But, setting his glass on the edge of the bathroom sink, wet-combing his blond curls back, Leroy can't help checking himself out. A man who looks this sharp can't waste it sitting around a hotel room with "A Different World." Now can he?

But Mac has said he's not to dare leave the hotel.

Okay. Fine. So what about the lobby?

When they'd checked in, a covey of chickies was fluttering at the desk. Here from Bristow, Oklahoma, to See Nashville.

Let 'em See Leroy, too. Couldn't hurt.

In the lobby Leroy takes a chair down a couple of steps by the TV. Looking up and out at the check-in desk. A good see-and-be-seen spot.

And sure enough, he's barely settled in, being careful not to crease his new shirt, when a cute Okie chickie with big brunette hair, healthy chest, tiny little jeans, comes up and says, "I've seen you before. Are you somebody famous?"

"Nawh." Leroy gives her his grin.

"Oh, yes, you are!" the chickie squeals. "I know you are. Who are you?" She starts jumping up and down.

"I'm just an old country boy," Leroy says from the corner of his mouth.

About then, this large woman in a pink polyester pants suit, her silver hair a World War II destroyer atop her head, comes over and joins the chickie.

"Look!" the chickie shrieks. Pointing at Leroy. "Look, Aunt Wilda!"

"Who do you think that is, sugar?" her aunt asks, like Leroy isn't even there.

"I don't know! But I know it's somebody!"

"Well, he looks a lot like Jerry Lee Lewis, Tiffany. But he's not." She aims her squinty black gaze at Leroy. "You're not, are you?"

Leroy gives them his Killer growl. *Grrrrrrrrrrrrr.*

They both jump.

"Come on now, Tiffany," says Aunt Wilda, jerking her niece by the elbow. "The bus is waiting to take us to Opryland."

Leroy watches them scurry out, then knocks back the rest of the drink he's brought down from the room. Thinking, Wouldn't it be neat for Shelby to see me like this?

Now, Mac also said, right before he left, "Leroy, I know I don't need to reiterate, but here it is. Do not make any effort—personal or telephonic—to contact Shelby while I'm out. You do, the police are going to be all over you like a cheap suit. Do you read me, Leroy?"

Loud and clear, Leroy'd said.

But, hey, that was before he'd cleaned up so good. Now, he was sure if Shelby could see him like this, it would make a real difference.

And once he's had that thought, Leroy can't be still. He's itching to get a move on. Mac could be back any second.

Leroy motates out to his pickup. Points it toward Shelby's.

On Broadway, passing sandwich shops, a Kinko's, Leroy catches a red light. Over to his right is the sprawling red brick Vanderbilt medical complex. A car is pulling out of the hospital parking lot.

A familiar car.

An old blue Toyota.

Jesus H. Christ, it's Shelby!

Shelby realizes there's nothing to be done, he's not going to stop honking, except get out and talk to Leroy.

She pulls over into a gas station. Seems a safe choice. There's plenty of open space. People around. One thing she doesn't want is Leroy following her back to her apartment again.

She picks up her purse, hefty with Chuck's automatic. Throws it over her shoulder. Not that she'll need it, she says to herself, but, hey . . .

"Hey, Shelby," says Leroy.

She watches him turning this way and that. What *is*

he doing? Showing off his clothes? "You proud of yourself, Leroy?" she asks. "Getting out on bail?"

A look of disappointment crosses his face. What does he think? She's going to congratulate him?

"No," he says. "I'm not proud. I'm ashamed, you want to know the truth. Sorry as I can be I raised a hand to you. I hope you'll find some way to forgive me."

"Piece of cake. You're forgiven, Leroy. Now go back home to Star."

"No!" He shakes his head. "I can't do that."

"Why not? You in trouble back there, too?"

"Of course not! What are you talking about?"

"Read my lips, Leroy. There is no percentage in your being here in Nashville. None. Zero. Zip. So. Leave. Me. Alone. I don't have *time* for this, Leroy."

" 'Cause you're so busy with your boyfriend, huh?"

"*Please*. We chewed this to death yesterday before you knocked me to the floor. I told you. Chuck's a writing partner. A buddy."

"I'm not talking about Chuck."

Leroy is getting loud. Shelby's wondering, Is he going off again? Well, she's not standing for that.

Shelby opens her bag. Rummages around the automatic for her change purse. Pulls out a quarter. Starts for the pay phone, right over there. Says to Leroy, "You're going to be like that, I'm not talking to you a minute longer. You're not supposed to even come near me. Not talk to me either. Don't you know that? I'm calling the police. They'll remind you good."

Leroy slams his fist hard into the side of his truck. "What I know is that I want you to come back home so bad I can taste it."

"Well, I'm real sorry about that, Leroy." She lifts the receiver.

"Listen to me!" he shouts.

A mechanic steps out of the service bay and takes a good hard look, first at Leroy, then at Shelby. "Are you okay, lady?"

"I don't know," she says, then turns back to Leroy. "Am I, Leroy? You drunk? Going crazy again?"

Leroy falls to one knee on the grease-stained concrete. Holds his hands up. "Crazy for you, Shelby."

"I'd go ahead and make the call, lady," the mechanic says.

"You shut up!" Leroy screams. Then grabs onto one of Shelby's ankles. Lowers his voice to a whisper. "Please, baby. Please, Shelby. Listen to me. Since you left, I've been so lonesome I thought I was going to croak. I missed everything about you. Things I hadn't thought about before. Your nightgown on the back of the bathroom door. The way you smell."

Shelby still has her finger on the nine of nine-one-one. But she's listening. Maybe if she hears him out, then she can talk some sense into him. And, in a way, despite yesterday, she feels sorry for Leroy. Poor old dumb thing. He never should have married a woman like her in the first place.

Leroy is saying, "It was a bottle of Chantilly that did the trick. Call me crazy, but about a week ago, I was in a drugstore, and my eye fell on this big old bottle of the stuff. I screwed the pink top off, took a big whiff, and it was like you were standing right there beside me in the Eckerd's."

"Oh, Leroy," Shelby sighs. She knows what he means. That longing. It's like a hole in your heart. Not that she has it for him. But she wants *somebody, someday. . . .*

Leroy is saying, "I bought that very bottle, took it home, sprinkled it all over the bed. I guess I thought it'd make me feel better, but it worked the opposite.

Made me want to go out and lay down in the middle
of the interstate, let a big rig turn me into roadkill.

"It was the very next morning I woke up and decided I was coming over here to get you, Shel."

Shelby drops the receiver back on the hook. "Leroy,
hon," she says. "Try to get your mind around this.
I'm not ever coming back. Not now. Not ever. Amen.
Don't you get it?"

Then she tucks her loaded purse under her arm,
climbs back in her Toyota, and drives off.

# 29

THE MIRRORED EXERCISE STUDIO IS FILLING WITH women in brightly colored Spandex workout togs, the latest exercise shoes. They're stretching, up and down, side-to-side, while checking out the competition.

Joyce McGivern says to her sister Lucy, "I feel like an absolute fool. All these girls are at least ten years younger than us. Maybe twenty."

"No way."

"Even so, I don't like doing this in public. I work out with Cindy on the TV."

Joyce is wearing black shorts and a T-shirt belonging to Lucy. ELVIS RECYCLES it reads. Her golden ponytails sport black ribbons.

Lucy is tiny, just like Joyce, and her Spandex shorts match her hair, a shade her colorist calls Five Alarm.

"What's your problem?" she asks. "We're skinnier than most of these gals. Anyway, I'm hoping this class will perk you up. I can't stand watching you mope."

"Say the word, Lucille. I'll move right over to Momma's."

"No, you won't. She'll be weeping and wailing and praying for the ruins of your marriage, have Brother Parker over, he'll be praying and weeping and wailing, too."

"I can move to a motel."

"You're too cheap."

Joyce stares at the door. "You think this teacher's gonna come, or are we going to stand around all day picking at one another?"

Right on cue, a tall lean blonde in a shiny turquoise body suit and chartreuse tights bounces in. "Hey, y'all." She grins. "Praise the Lord!"

Her big white teeth could stun a deer, thinks Joyce.

Around her the class echoes, "Praise the Lord!"

The blonde punches on her tape machine, and the big room booms with hand-clapping, amen-ing, and testifying of a full-out gospel song. Southern white gospel. Contemporary Christian.

Danielle's bouncing, smiling, introducing herself to the beat. "For anybody who's new today, I'm Danielle. And this is Moving with the Spirit, a fifty-minute Christian tuneup of your body and your soul."

"Amen," calls a large woman in the front row wearing a black-and-white polka-dotted leotard.

Danielle, never letting go of that big old smile, begins to move her feet to the right, to the left, clapping her hands wide and slow.

*Jesus loves you,* the Dove Family croons on the boombox. Soft seventies harmonies. *Loves you in the morning. Loves you at noon.*

Joyce can just imagine the Doves' outfits. Lots of fringe. Spangles. Western jackets on the men. Fat men. Fatter ladies. Fat hair, too. Her own golden ponytails bounce.

"Knees!" Danielle shouts as the Doves sing out, picking up the tempo.

*Loves you in the afternoon.*

Danielle leads them through her Christian routine. First comes a slow-moving warm-up: head-rolling and limb-stretching. Next is the serious business of lifting those feet, those knees, swinging those arms, balling those jacks, pivoting on the balls of the feet, sliding, hopping, skipping, jumping, twisting, turning, mamboing, cha-chaing—except Danielle doesn't use any of that ballroom terminology.

No sirree. She calls: "Step, step, step-step-step closer to Jesus!" while the Doves shout, *"Walking with the Lord. Talking with the Lord. Lord, Lord! It's Your sweet face I'm longing for."*

"Single knees. Double knees. Single back-step. Double back-step. Pivot right, step, step, pivot right, step, step, pivot right, step, step, making it foursquare for Jesus!"

*And I say. Oh, I say. Yes, I say. Lord Jesus is my friend. My friend in deed. My friend in need.*

"I bet there was never a choir lady ever in her whole life jumped around like this," Joyce says to Lucy as they almost collide with one another in the middle of a diagonal slide-together-step-hop.

"Not wearing Spandex. But I bet they do some sweating under those robes."

"You think Jesus likes sweat?"

"Jesus owns stock in Gatorade." Lucy grins.

The woman in the polka dots gives Lucy a look, but Lucy laughs.

"Why wouldn't He? You think Jesus don't know a happening product when He sees one?"

Five more songs and they've clocked twenty minutes of aerobics, the magic number that some cigar-smoking fat guy in Bethesda, Maryland, had, in the middle of a long session of the Fitness Subcommittee of the American Health Council Annual Meeting, doodled onto a notepad along with a drawing of a naked woman with bouncing boobs. Twenty minutes of aerobic activity it is—adopted, announced, and promulgated—the ideal and the optimum. Now part of every heart-attack-fearing American's common wisdom.

Which means that the women in the noon class of Moving with the Spirit at the Franklin Road Workspace, Nashville, Tennessee, having precisely twenty minutes under their belts, can now fast-walk around the room in a big circle, cooling down, before they do their floor routine of stomach crunches, leg lifts, and pelvic tilts. The Doves give them a helping hand with "Me on the Mountaintop."

"I feel better already," Joyce says to Lucy, striding right beside her. "I really do. I think the Lord has lifted me."

"Don't tease, Joyce. I'll take you out in the backyard when we get home and turn the hose on you."

"No, truly." Joyce waggles her ponytails. "In fact, I feel so good, I think I'm going to drive into town and find that fat bitch and wring her neck."

"I swear. What kind of talk is that?"

"It's what I honestly feel. I feel *strong*." Joyce beats herself on her chest with her little fists, right atop Elvis.

"Well, you *sound* stupid. I think you completely missed the point of Moving with the Spirit."

"What exactly *is* the point, Miss Lucille?"

"Releasing your tensions. I had hoped the music would flush out some of that anxiety you walk around with all the time."

"Lucille Beemis, I am one of the most peaceful people I know."

Lucy rolls her eyes and keeps on moving. They're slowing down now, other women passing them, the rhythm of the room growing a little erratic as Danielle changes the tape for something slower.

"Peaceful as a Chihuahua on diet pills," Lucy says.

"I don't know why you're so hateful. You didn't used to be this hateful before Malcolm left you."

"I left him."

"Whatever. You were nicer when you were married."

"I was miserable."

"You still are."

"I'm a different kind of miserable."

"Well, you were a heck of a lot nicer."

"That's because I was getting laid regular."

"Lucy, I swear. You'll say *anything.*"

"You just wait, missy. You think this is hell? Just wait till you been on your lonesome a while, the anger starts fading. You get horny, *then* you'll be singing a different tune."

At that, Danielle, gliding by the two sisters, slows down and holds even.

"I won't get horny," says Joyce.

"Yes, you will. And I'm here to tell you, Joyce, you might as well go to Eckerd's right now and buy yourself one of them vibrators. 'Cause if you think, get shut of Chuck, you'll go out and find yourself a new flavor of manflesh, you're wrong. You'll be lucky if you ever even *see* another whanger except on little boys at the water park."

"*What* are you talking about? I'm still a good-looking woman."

"You're fifty, Joyce. Dead meat in the marketplace. Flies is all you're gonna draw."

"Are you crazy?"

"Even the seventy-year-olds, they want younger

flesh than yours. You're history, sis. *Ancient* history. My advice to you would be, get over yourself. Crawl back to Chuck on your hands and knees before somebody else nabs him."

Danielle leans closer.

Joyce says, *"She's* already nabbed him. Made a good stab at it anyway. But just you wait till I get my hands on her. That bitch, Shelby Kay Tate."

"Shelby *who?*" cries Danielle.

# 30

"I'M TELLING YOU," REOLA CHANDLER IS SAYING over her shoulder, lifting the tail of her long blue-and-gold skirt as she traipses down Gail's front steps, "I don't like the look of it. Not one bit." She stops at the bottom and looks back up at Gail.

"You're overreacting." Gail stands behind the front-door screen. "Ask me, *you're* the diva. Always were."

"Go ahead. Make fun. But there's not one thing funny about Jerome lying up there in the hospital, tubes coming out of him every whichaway."

"I'm not saying there is. It's just that somebody's shooting your friend Fontella's son-in-law has nothing to do with me."

Reola narrows her eyes. "Don't you think there's something awfully coincidental, I go to the hospital to keep Althea company, in comes this Shelby Kay Tate? The *very one* who was here, listening to *you* sing, Miss Throw Caution to the Winds, the night before?"

"Didn't Althea tell you they are writing partners, she and Shelby? Perform together, writers' nights?"

"Unh-huh. All the more reason to be wary of her, I'd say. You let her come back over here, let her into the house, you're asking for it."

"Reola. I think maybe you need to go have them check your hypertension medication, sugar. You're not making sense."

Oh, yes, she is, says Rahab, the fallen Angel who is sitting down the street beside Mac McKenzie in the shiny black Jeep four-by-four. Rahab's consulting the master game plan resting in his lap. The woman's making great sense. Going to have to watch out for that Reola. Keep her in your sights. Do you hear me, Mac?

Mac doesn't know that the same exact thoughts running through his mind are Rahab's words, but he nods all the same.

Yes, Mac nods. Keep an eye on that big black one, if I want to have myself some fun with Miss Gail.

And fun's what Mac has in mind. The ho ho ho of stealing Gail Powell's guitar, the very one that belonged to Patsy Cline. It is Patsy's, isn't it, the one he heard Gail playing the night before? Even if it isn't, what difference will Leroy know? Leroy doesn't know dick. Leroy'll believe anything Mac tells him, if he thinks it'll get him one inch closer to Shelby.

And Mac is hoping he'll have enough time to turn even that around. Get Leroy going in a different direction. Potentially a much more interesting one. Promises to be a *much* bigger yuk than this adoration business.

Oh, you dirty dog, you. Mac McKenzie, the Svengali of Nashville, pulling the strings. Winding 'em up, letting 'em go.

Though not too far, of course.

Ah, yes, the perversity of the mischief-maker. The fun of the trickster. The glee of fucking with folks. Give those suckers a crumb, a taste of hope, raise those expectations, then *Whomp!* Pull out that rug.

And if a little blood is spilled along the way, well, hey, isn't that the ultimate control? Life and death rolling in Mac's hands like a couple of dice, isn't that just the most getting-down, rip-snorting, buck-dancing hoot of all?

"Humph," Reola says to herself, making her way on down the sidewalk from Gail's. "Not making sense, my ass. *I'm* making good sense. Woman dudn't have enough sense to listen, that's all.

"Ain't no such thing as coincidences, anyway. Look at it: Gail, that Shelby, Althea, Jerome. Coincidences ain't nothing but harmonic convergences of energy. Folks with their eyes open, they see 'em all the time. I myself long time ago ceased to be amazed. Just say, Unh-huh. Thank you, Jesus. Then I pay attention. Do what I gotta do, make the most of the convergences. What I say to do with this one is Lock the Door. Don't let that Shelby Kay Tate in, not anymore. Woman's trailing bad juju with her. That's what I think."

Reola is at the corner where she'll turn left. She lives only two blocks down that way in a pink house with a lacy cast-iron balcony running across the front of the second story. It's the only one of its kind in Nashville. The man who built it grew up in New Orleans, the same as Reola.

Now, suddenly, out of nowhere, a short little white man with a great huge gut strolls right up in Reola's face.

Says, "Excuse me, ma'am."

He's fitted out in a tangerine-colored cowboy shirt

with pearl snaps gaping over his melon of a belly. Gray Western pants. Black lizard boots. A black ten-gallon hat. He looks like a fool.

But then Reola has lived among Southern white men her whole life, so nothing they can wear or do or say is much of a surprise to her.

Though the "ma'am" is a little different. It puts her on guard.

"Yes?" she says, looking down at him from her height.

"I was just wondering, I hate to bother you, but, gosh, I feel so stupid. I just ran out of gas." He points back down the block. "That's my Jeep back there. And I've been walking up the street looking for somebody who'll let me use their phone to call Triple A."

"Unh-huh." Reola pauses.

The man seems nice enough, but you just can't be too careful these days. Robbers, rapers, killers come in all kinds of colors and flavors. Not to mention this flap with Shelby Tate. For all she knows, this man might be a reporter from *People* magazine, Shelby called him up. Next thing you know, there'll be a profile, "At Home with Gail Powell," every newsstand in the whole damned country. After that, it'll be Katie, bar the door.

Reola says, "I'd be happy to help you, but I can't."

"Well, how about the lady in that house back there? The one I saw you coming out of?" He points back at Gail's.

"No, I don't think she can help you, either."

It's a fine line she's walking as a black woman, here in Dixie at the very buckle of the Bible Belt, talking with a white man. Even now.

Especially saying *No* to him and leaving off the *sir*. The entire history of the African-American experience comes to bear at such intersections: slavery, the War

Between the States, as it was called in these parts, Reconstruction, Jim Crow, Little Rock, Selma, Albany, Birmingham, Watts, lunch counters, Affirmative Action, school busing, Malcolm X, Martin Luther King, Spike Lee, Aretha, welfare mothers, crack cocaine, Rodney King. Not to mention this little cracker's own accumulated baggage.

"Doesn't she have a phone?"

The little man's mud-colored eyes narrow. He runs a hand across his yellow mustache. Reola notices the long nail on his little finger.

The more she sees, the less she likes. This fink is up to no good.

"It ain't that," she says lightly, the fear stepping up and causing her to give him the tiniest drop of Stepin Fetchit. "I'd let you use it if it was my house, but it's not."

"You don't live there?"

Reola can see through his airs, knows he is the worst kind of white man. Mean trash. Has to blame his pitiful hard-scrabble life on someone. Guess who that is?

She says, "No, I sure don't live in that yellow house." With that, Reola steps back. She can run if she has to. A miler when she was young, she's still pretty good.

He steps forward. "But you know who does." Then he laughs a high dry laugh showing very white teeth that definitely aren't his own. "I mean it's not like you just ran out of there having ripped off the silver."

"What are you talking about?" Reola throws her shoulders back, draws herself up to her full six feet. "I ain't ripped off nothing in my entire life."

"Hey, hey, take it easy. I was just funning." Showing her those fake teeth again.

Reola remembers the bad old days, the white cops

who smiled like that right before they hefted the base-ball bats, aimed the water hoses.

"Kidding," he says. "But, seriously, the lady who does live there, you think she'll let me use the phone?"

"I bet she would if she was home. But she was going right out when I left."

Reola looks down the deserted street. Not even a car in sight. Everybody still at work. Wouldn't do any good to holler. Miz Murphy, who lives in the big white house they're standing in front of, her little concrete chickens pecking in the yard, is deaf as a post.

Of course, Reola could just turn, leave him there, trot on, but she knows that won't be the end of it.

He'll follow her home.

If he lets her get that far.

"Excuse me," he says, pointing back at Gail's. "Who lives there anyway?"

"A friend of mine."

"Does she have a name?"

Well, now. Here it is. Time to fish or cut bait. Jump one way or the other. Is she Miss Scarlett's whining Prissy, doesn't know shit from shinola, or is she Reola Chandler?

"Sir," she says, "I don't mean to be rude, but I just don't see exactly how that's any business of yours. Anyway"—she points behind him—"if you walk two blocks that way and take a right on Eastland, you'll come to a gas station another block over."

That isn't true, but he won't know that until he gets there, will he?

"Does she call herself Ann?" the man purrs, deep in his throat. It's the kind of voice men use when they're thinking about kissing you.

Reola steps back.

"Does she wear red hightop shoes?"

Trucking. Reola is moving on down the line. Doesn't give a hoot whether he follows her or not.

He skips up and down behind her. An exuberant little son of a gun. *Delighting* in his badness.

"Does she smoke a cigar? Own a guitar?" he flutes.

Jogging, Reola'll see if she can make it to the fire station.

Then he begins to sing . . .

> *You say this chill is all my fault*
> *I'm only to blame*
> *But if you'd hug me, kiss me more*
> *I could burst into flame*

One of Gail's. Reola wheels, and her anger jumps in front of her fear. "What do you want, little man?" she thunders.

"Oh. Hey. Wait." He's laughing now, walking backward, his hands raised like she said, Stick 'em up.

Then she's the one advancing. Barreling down on him. "What's your game, mister?"

"Does that mean I'm a good guesser?" he teases.

"It means if you don't get out of this neighborhood, I'm going to knock you upside the head."

"Oh, I don't think so." Sliding his right hand back inside his jacket. "I think you're going to tell me everythin—"

But before he can finish, Reola does exactly what she said she was going to do.

Draws back and doubles up her fist. Puts her one-hundred-and-eighty-eight pounds, hardly any of it fat, behind that fist. Delivers a right hook that drops Mac flat on the pavement.

His Smith & Wesson pops out of his belt and flies up against one of Miz Murphy's chicks.

It rebounds, and Reola jumps, snatches the pistol

up. She whirls and takes a stance. Legs wide, knees bent, she shouts, "Freeze," just like the cops on TV.

But the little sucker is up and running.

And Reola doesn't have what it takes to shoot another human being, even this one, in the back.

So there she stands, the pistol lowered and dangling at her side, watching him jump into his Jeep and roar off. She can't read his license plate from this distance.

But even if she could, what is she going to do about it?

Having disappeared into thin air right in the middle of Nashville, Tennessee, thirty-odd years ago with Gail, Reola has long been out of the habit of calling the cops.

# 31

M_AC'S HEAD IS STILL RINGING FROM R_EOLA'S RIGHT
hook when he picks up the house phone in the lobby
of the Hampton Inn.

"Leroy," he says. "Come on down here."

Then he grabs himself a cup of the hotel's free coffee, plops on the nubby blue sofa in front of the big
screen tuned to CNN.

A few minutes later, there's Leroy stepping off the
elevator. "Get on over here, son," Mac says, waving.
"Sit down for a minute. Hey, you look awfully sharp,
in your new threads."

"Yeah, I know I do." Leroy grins, giving him his
hand. "A friend of mine picked them up for me."

"Did he now?" Mac winks. Then takes a sniff, says,
"You have a few, Leroy?"

"Just a couple. You know, take the edge off."

"What you got to be worried about, old son?"

Leroy shakes his head. "Nothing. Not a thing. Just,
you know, relaxing."

Mac leans closer. "You wouldn't be worried about that Jeep, would you?"

"Oh, no. Sure wouldn't."

"Good. 'Cause I got rid of it."

"You did?"

"Yep. Traded it in."

"No kidding?"

"Yep. Got us something a little more comfy. So, what you been doing while I was out taking care of business?"

"Nothing much. Cleaned up. Had a couple of drinks, like I said. Watched a little TV."

"Didn't go anywhere? Didn't drive your truck?"

Leroy doesn't even blink. "Nope. Came down to the lobby for a few minutes. That was it." Leroy reaches for Mac's cup. "Can I get you a refill?" Jumps up and heads for the big thermos that's a trademark of the Hampton Inn. Looks back over his shoulder at Mac, his short legs spread like a fat lady's, only his toes touching the brown carpet. "I been right here."

"Well, now, son," Mac drawls, "I'm sorry to hear you say that. Makes me real sad." Mac reaches his arms wide as he can on the sofa back.

Leroy sits back down with the coffee. "Why's that?"

"I sure do hate this." Mac shakes his head mournfully.

"Hate what?"

"Having to cut you loose."

Leroy's eyes grow wide. "What are you talking about?"

"Son, what do you think your mileage was on that truck of yours when I left here?"

"I'm sure I don't know." Holding his chin high, but knows he's toast. He parked in the same spot, completely forgot about the odometer.

Mac says, "Well, I know. One hundred and forty-two thousand, six hundred and fourteen point three miles. And how many miles do you think were on it when I got back? Six hundred and fifteen point five." Mac slams his fist down on the coffee table. "Damnit to hell! You got yourself one point two unaccounted-for miles. A man can get into a shitload of trouble in one point two miles, Leroy. A real shitload."

Mac stands, pulling down his pants legs. He wheels, flies up the two steps to the main entryway, and hangs a right toward the double front doors. The little man is trucking.

"Wait!" cries Leroy.

"Stay where you are, son!" Mac points a finger. An accusing finger. He's got old-timey preacher indignation in that digit. "You *lied*. And that was *wrong*, Leroy."

Leroy's voice goes high and wild. "But you, YOU, said yourself that wrong wasn't a concept. Didn't you, huh? Huh?" Leroy runs and grasps at Mac, but Mac jerks free.

Then Mac reaches inside his jacket.

Behind the desk, the two clerks freeze.

College kids in maroon blazers working part-time to help put themselves through college, their worst nightmare is that some little argument will escalate into fisticuffs, then into gunplay, and end with dead bodies clogging up the lobby.

It happened in Topeka.

It happened in Glendale.

There is nothing to say it can't happen in Nashville.

Except that Leroy is falling to his knees again on the scarlet indoor-outdoor carpet. "Please, I'm begging you, Mac. *Please*, don't leave me."

The desk clerk named Lucinda Weaver starts to giggle nervously.

Which causes Grover Giles, who is standing next to

her, and who plans to live long enough to be the first black governor of the state of Tennessee, to kick her a lot harder than he intends to.

"I'm sorry, Mac. I really am." Leroy is groveling.

"Where did you go, son? Now, wait before you answer. Hold up. Think about it."

"I'm gonna tell you God's honest truth, no matter if it kills me." Deep breath. "I went looking for Shelby."

"Good boy! And did you find her?"

"No, sir, I did not."

"Praise the Lord!" Mac raises his little arms like that old preacher delivering the benediction.

Then in a blue-sky voice, the storm clouds of his anger blown past, Mac says, "Get up off your knees, son. Let's us go look at some music buses."

Leroy scrambles to his feet. "Yes, sir. Yes, indeedy," he says all the way out the double doors.

Back inside, Lucinda Weaver hauls back and slaps Grover Giles hard enough to leave her handprint on his cheek.

She says, "You *ever* kick me again, you're gonna be the first African-American governor of the state of Tennessee with no dick, and I ain't playing. Son."

# 32

SHELBY KEEPS AN EYE ON HER REARVIEW MIRROR
driving over to East Nashville. Watching out for
Leroy, his green pickup truck.

Leroy's knocked Jeff Wayne clear out of her head.
So she doesn't see his Trans-Am, hot on her tail.

Jeff Wayne just missed Shelby's run-in with Leroy
coming out of the hospital parking lot, went the
other way to the police barracks to turn in his
cruiser and sign out. But once in his own car, he's
flipped on his scanner, is picking up the signal from
the tiny transmitter he planted under Shelby's right
front fender.

Flicks on his monitor, watches the blinking red dot
move through the grid that is Metro Nashville. Zeroes
in, tighter and tighter. Closes in on her, live and in
color, on Gallatin, just before she turns right onto
Greenwood.

*   *   *

Shelby's listening to Mary Chapin Carpenter's latest on WSIX. Thinking about Leroy. God, please let this be the last of him.

And Jeff Wayne, too.

What the heck does that man want?

Maybe she'll talk with Ann King about men. It'll be a great warm-up for working on "I Still Miss My Man." Too bad they can't write tonight, but Shelby has to run back over to Lynn's now, decide who they'll call to replace Althea. Or, should they just do the night, the two of them?

Shelby would have saved herself the trip, called Ann, if she'd had a number.

But there's no Ann King listed in Nashville info. No A. King either. Nothing even close.

# 33

MAC HAS EXCHANGED THE BLACK JEEP FOUR-BY-FOUR for a pearly white Lincoln Towncar. He's driving it now to Goodlettsville, a northern suburb of Nashville and center of the music bus industry in the known universe.

Stroking Leroy. Leading him along. Feeding the man's fantasies.

And Leroy is into it big time. Especially after the reprieve Mac has given him. Bad boy, taking off in his truck and lying about it.

As if Mac really gave a rip.

Listen to Leroy now. Running his mouth. Offering his past like a dog, belly-up.

He's telling Mac about a revival preacher he saw at church back in Mississippi when he was a little kid.

Leroy's talking: "I swear the man was seven feet tall. Thin, he was like a skeleton, his navy blue suit flapping on him. His hair was so short, more like a three-day beard really, you could see his skull. Bony old thing, lots of pits and craters. He got up there in the pulpit, and he started talking about what Judgment Day was gonna be like for the sinners, all of us not washed in the blood of the Lamb. The wrongdoers, naysayers, backsliders, and the youngsters like me who hadn't shouldered their responsibility to the Lord. Doomsday, he's talking about, legions of the damned rising out of their graves, gonna come and lay their bony hands on the lost, snatch them up. Just looking at him, his black eyes burning in his skull, you could see what he was talking about. You could believe that the damned, they'd look just like him.

"Then this tall skinny preacher got to preaching so hard and so fast about all these terrible lost creatures—the grave stench, rotten flesh hanging off their bones, howling sounds they made—he got to going so fast, spit was flying every whichaway. And then he got to moving in time with his words. Jerking, lurching, humping. Man, I'm telling you, it was something to behold. The next thing I knew, he'd jerked himself right out from behind the pulpit, he's sidewinding down the aisle.

"Folks are drawing back. They don't want any of what he's got getting on them.

"He's coming closer and closer. The clattering of his hard-soled shoes on the wooden floor is awesome. I'm getting real scared.

" 'Cause that sound's the bones of the damned banging on the inside of their coffins, raging to get out, go back, do it all over again the right way.

"And me, I'm slap up on the aisle. My daddy's next to me, Momma over on the other side of him.

"I'm wishing it was different. Wishing I was in the middle. Or even better, over on the other side of Momma so I could hide, press myself into her skirts, the preacher man wouldn't even see me.

"But I'm not. I'm right out there on the edge, exposed, and Daddy's next to me in his hard black suit. There's not a soft spot on him.

"And when that preacher draws up even to me, his feet thumping, his eyes burning, his mouth working and slobbering like a mad dog, my daddy says, *This here boy's bad!*"

"And pushed you right out in front of him," says Mac. Then swivels his head to watch the amazement rise on Leroy's face like the morning sun.

Leroy. Jesus. It's like shooting fish in a barrel.

"He did! He pushed me! The preacher man reached out, and I went *kerplunk* in the aisle. Dead to the world."

"Yep," says Mac, driving along, passing a Mayflower moving van, "and you think that's what I'm going do to you, too, son, don'cha? Think I'm going to hang you out to dry because you lied to me about seeing Shelby?"

This time Mac doesn't even bother to turn his head. He can feel Leroy's twitch, knows he's struck bone. "I know that you saw her yesterday when you said you didn't. And I know you smacked her the day before. The two of you wrestling on the floor, you popped her one, didn't you, Leroy? Couldn't resist it, could you?"

It's gorgeous out here in the 'burbs, real country coming up. Trees leafed out all over. New green so proud you can almost hear it sing. Can smell it, for sure. Sun. Rain. Rich loamy earth. For a second Mac thinks about pulling over, leaving Leroy behind, walking out in that field, rolling in the grass. Trying to get some of that LIFE on him.

But for what?

It's way too late. No point in his thinking about renewal. Not with that goddamn disease eating at his gut. Not much of anything left for old Mac except the fun of fiddling with Leroy.

Mac turns back to his toy. "Leroy, son, do you know you give yourself away every time you lie? You have a tell. Here, look at me."

Leroy doesn't want to. He can barely meet Mac's gaze.

"Now, this is what you do." Mac scrinches his neck to the left side like he has a crick in it. "Each and every time you're about to tell a lie, you do that. Some people blink. Some people look away. Some hold their breath. The possibilities are endless."

Mac can feel Leroy's amazement. And he, in turn, is amazed at how little attention people pay to one another, when most people truly can be read like a book. It's like there are diamonds lying on the ground, they're just shuffling through them. Or, is it possible that lately his own vision has become more acute?

Mac lets the stunned Leroy stew, his own mind meandering as they pull off the highway, wander the two-lanes toward the town of Union Hill, idle past cow pastures, a little crossroads and a barbecue stand, and then they see a sign, MONROE'S CUSTOM MOBILE, and Mac stops.

"Come on, Leroy," he says kindly.

Leroy jumps out like a pup who's puddled in the house, had his nose rubbed in it, is *dying* to prove how good he can be.

Pick Monroe, a long raw-boned man with huge ears, comes out to greet them. A man of few words, Monroe points in the direction of a green Quonset hut of corrugated steel, which holds half-a-dozen customized buses. Then he goes back to the business of tearing an engine apart.

The buses are real beauts. Long bullets of maroon, candy apple, gold flake, baby blue. The colors so rich, the surfaces so smooth, it's hard not to step up, take a lick.

Their interiors hold the same delight as anything in miniature, perfectly tooled. A music box. A toy train. A dollhouse. There's something thrilling about the very idea of taking a four-bedroom house, scaling it down, putting it on wheels so it can do ninety miles an hour, whoosh through the night from Nashville to New Orleans, make a pot of coffee, do eggs easy-over, too.

As they traipse in and out of the buses, Mac making cooing noises, saying, How you like this one, son? Leroy's eyes are wide as if Mac has just handed him the moon.

Finally Mac thanks Pick Monroe kindly, takes his card, and says, yes sirree, they'll be giving him a call. Mac points the Lincoln back toward town.

Mac's asking Leroy, "Did you like the red one? The blue? Wasn't that hibachi something, just hoist it up on the back when you're stopped, have yourself a bar-becue? What'd you think about those folding beds? Those triple-level cabinets? Do you think you can build something like that, Leroy?"

Mac knowing all the while that if he hasn't had Leroy in the palm of his hand before this, he does now. He's instilled the perfect mix of guilt and longing in the man.

Leroy is his. One hundred percent.

Mac grins, heads the Lincoln Towncar toward East Nashville. And more devilment. Steps on it.

# 34

SHELBY PARKS HER TOYOTA RIGHT IN FRONT OF 301 Greenwood Avenue. Jumps out and is halfway up the steps when suddenly a large black woman looms over her.

She's seen this woman before.

At the hospital. In the waiting room. There was Althea, the woman in the yellow pants suit, then this one. What *is* her name?

"And where do you think you're going, missy?" the woman thunders from above her on the porch.

"I'm here to see Ann King."

"No, you're not."

"And why not?"

"Because I said so."

"Ma'am, is there a problem here?" Jeff Wayne has pulled up behind Shelby, steps out of his Trans-Am. Not sure that he ought to be interfering. Not knowing what Shelby wants here, but the fact that she wants it, whatever it is, is enough for him.

But not for Shelby. "What are *you* doing here?" She turns on Jeff Wayne.

Reola choruses. "And *who* are you?"

"Jeff Wayne Capshew, ma'am." Tipping his Nashville Sounds baseball cap to Reola. "Metro Police. Off-duty."

"And what do *you* want?" Reola demands.

"Forget him," says Shelby. "*I'm* here to see Ann King. We have an appointment."

"You skedaddle," says Reola. "Now."

"Says who?" That's Shelby.

"Mrs. Reola Chandler, that's who." Reola speaks over Shelby's head to Jeff Wayne. "I help Miz King run a day care in this house. No visitors allowed."

"Why's that, ma'am?" Jeff Wayne asks.

"I guess you gonna tell me that we don't have the constitutional right to keep people off these private premises?"

Shelby remembers Ann mentioning a partner. Reola, yes, that's the name Althea said. But what's *this* noise all about? She says, "I met Ann last night when I delivered her dinner from Sweet Willie's. She asked me to come back, work on a song."

"Over my dead body."

Shelby says, "Ma'am, I saw you at the hospital a little while ago . . ."

Jeff Wayne nods. He noticed her, too. But then, he's a cop.

"Did I say something there that offended you?" Shelby asks.

"Nope."

"Ma'am, don't you think maybe we ought to ask your friend if she wants to see Shelby, here?" Jeff Wayne asks.

"No, I do not. I know what she wants. Wants to be left in peace."

Shelby has had just about enough. She took the time to drive over here, when time is what she's got precious little of, wants to make sure Ann can write with her tomorrow morning, her absolute last shot, what *is* this woman's problem?

She says, "Ma'am, I don't mean to be rude, but I don't know how you can presume to speak for Miz King."

"Git!" Reola says, as if Shelby were a cur who's come up in her yard. "Git now!"

"Officer Capshew." Shelby turns to him with the sweetest little quaver in her voice. "One of the reasons I wanted to come over here this evening is that Ann King told me last night that she was growing afraid of this woman."

"Watch out, little girl," says Reola. "I'll bite your head off."

"She said that she didn't know exactly what was wrong with this Reola, but she was acting very strange, and she was worried about her."

"Suck your blood out."

"Now, Mrs. Chandler, you don't want to be talking like that," says Jeff Wayne.

"Munch you up in little pieces when you're dry."

"I'm afraid maybe something has happened to Miz King, and that's why Reola doesn't want us to go inside the house."

"Chew you up and spit you on the grave of that little sucker you sent over here."

"*What* little sucker?" Shelby asks.

"Like we wouldn't notice," says Reola. "Him following right in your footsteps. But I gave him a good one. When you see him, ask him where he got that bruise upside his head."

"What little sucker are you talking about, Mrs. Chandler?" asks Jeff Wayne, the cop.

# 35

MAC LOOKS OVER AT LEROY, SAYS, "NOW, WHAT we're about to do is edge up on that large yellow house. Do you see it up there? Then I'm going to run in and snatch Patsy Cline's guitar . . ."

Leroy doesn't say, "Oh, no, you're not. They'll catch us and throw us back in the pokey." Nor does he say, "Mac, excuse me, but Patsy Cline's dead." Though Mac is fairly sure that even Leroy knows that.

Instead, Leroy asks, "How much is it worth?"

"About fifty thousand dollars, if we find the right buyer. Of course, we'll have to be rather careful. Make a nice little down payment for Operation Music Bus, don't you think?"

Leroy's eyes glisten like a kid's on Christmas morning. The heavy Lincoln creeps up toward the yellow house.

Then Leroy blinks. Looks at Mac. Looks back. For there, on the stage of the steps of the big yellow house stands Shelby.

And the Cop.

Gazing into one another's eyes.

Two women, one short and white, one tall and black, bit players, stand off to the side.

Shelby and the Cop glow, stars in the spotlight.

Mac grins. Couldn't have been more perfect if he'd stage-managed it himself.

"Goddamnit!" says Leroy beside him in the Lincoln. "Goddamnit to hell! She puts me off. Says, Get along, Leroy. Says, I'm too busy with my career. Says, No, no, there ain't nobody else. Then everytime I look around, there's that *po*-liceman."

"Man with a hair on his ass wouldn't put up with it," purrs Mac.

"No, he wouldn't, would he?"

"So what are you gonna do, Leroy?"

"Put a stop to it. I can't have her, nobody will." Leroy turns and raises his right hand and takes an oath. "Nobody. I'll kill her first."

*Yesssssss,* Rahab hisses into the dying light.

# 36

THURSDAY, THE DAY, TEN A.M., SHELBY AND GAIL—
whom Shelby still knows as Ann—have *finally* settled down to write. Ten hours till Showtime at the
Sutler.

Reola has planted herself on Gail's front porch.
That little sucker comes back, he'll have to deal with
her first.

Thursday and Friday are Jeff Wayne's days off. He's
sitting in the other rocking chair, beside Reola. He
spent last night on Shelby's sofa. She told him she
didn't need his protection, he was nuts, but finally, she
just gave up, threw him a pillow and a blanket and
went off to bed. He hasn't spoken with Danielle since
yesterday morning. If she's been home, she hasn't answered the phone.

Shelby and Gail face each other from two easy
chairs. Shelby's in a big yellow shirt over black tights,
black cowboy boots. Gail's jumpsuit is baby blue. The
two floor-to-ceiling windows that open onto the porch

have been thrown up. The room is soft with the balmy air of a Southern spring morning.

Gail holds Shelby's song in her hands, bouncing the pages gently up and down. Shelby's baby. "Who's this song about?"

"I was pitching it like my momma was writing the song about her rotten husband, Dwayne."

"But it's not working?"

"Nope. I think I got started on that gun business because of the hook . . ."

"And it led you down a road you didn't want to go."

"Right. It's too tough, don't you think?"

"Yep. I also think the whole thing'd work better if you were writing it closer. To you, I mean. Forget your momma. Do Shelby."

"Yeah, I know. Write from your heart. Write what you know. But if I'm determined to work with this hook, then who's the man *I'm* missing?"

"Leroy? Your ex?"

"There is *nothing* about Leroy I miss. I just want him to go on back to Star, leave me alone."

"And why won't he do that?"

"Because he misses *me*. He's got it in his head he can convince me to come on back home. He's got this cockamamie notion we're still married, even though we're divorced."

"Unh-huh," Gail says, picking up her pencil. "Go on. Tell me about Leroy. Tell me about your life together. Did he fool around?"

"Does a bear shit in the woods?" Shelby laughs.

"What else? How about your songwriting? Did he go for that?"

The next thing Shelby knew, it came tumbling out. Gail and Jeff Wayne and Reola out on the porch, heard all about Leroy's resentment of her writing. How he made fun of it, put her down. His drinking and fooling around. How he never helped around the house, if you could call that double-wide mobile home a house. His thing for fried chicken—and her boobs. How the love between them had died, and how he refused to accept that. Says now he can't live without her, is going crazy, and it's all her fault.

"So *he's* really the one doing the missing?" says Gail.

"Yep. I see what you mean. We've got to figure out some way to make it go both ways."

"How about this, for starters?

> *That girl you say you're missing*
> *Ain't your missus anymore*

Shelby throws her hands over her head. "Did I tell you? I *knew* this was going to be good." Then she picks up paper and pencil and scribbles for a few minutes.

> *She ain't frying no more chicken*
> *She ain't scrubbing no more floors*

"Yes! I like it. She ain't—" Gail starts. "What else ain't she doing? No, wait, next let's say what she has been doing."

"Let me think," says Shelby. "She's, let's see, the rhyme we're headed toward is *floors. Floors, bores, mores, snores, doors. Doors.*"

"Knocked me through the door? No, that's the violent thing again. I think we're looking for some humor here, don't you? Lighten the whole thing up? I mean, the title, the hook, they're *funny.*"

"Yeah, I think you're right, but let's lean on the

humor in the chorus. In this first verse, at least, aren't we setting it up that she's just sick and tired of him?"

"Sick and tired of what?"

"His drinking. Running around. Not being who she wants to be."

"Did she, did you, *tell* him that? Up front, or did you hide it?"

"Well, I sure as hell wasn't as outspoken as I've gotten to be, once I left. Found my tongue."

*"Door?* What'd she do behind that door? Doors?"

"Cry? Cry, cry, cry behind the door?"

*"She's cried behind the door."*

"Behind locked doors."

*"She's cried behind locked doors."*

"Maybe, okay. So what's the line above?"

> *That girl you say you're missing*
> *Ain't your missus anymore*
> *She ain't frying no more chicken*
> *She ain't scrubbing no more floors*
> *Duh duh duh duh duh duh duh*
> *She's cried behind locked doors*

Shelby says, "She's done something else. Something sad. Something he made her do. A *reaction* to him, right?"

"Right. Is she afraid of him?"

"Not really. No."

"Okay, but what if we fudge it just a little, just to lean on the idea of her unhappiness?"

"Spit it out."

*"She's trembled in your shadow."*

Shelby laughs. "I just can't imagine being in Leroy's shadow. It's not even *big* enough."

"Shut up," says Gail. "It's a song, not the absolute truth. And I like it."

"I *love* it," says Shelby, jumping up and giving Gail a big Nashville hug. I absolutely purdee *love* it! I *knew* this collaboration was going to work!"

"Don't get too excited yet, girl," says Gail. "We ain't got much time, and we've got a *long* way to go."

# 37

"GOOD MORNING, LEROY!" MAC FINALLY AWAKENS about noon.

He sits halfway up, focuses on Leroy sitting in the one upholstered chair in Room 505 of the Hampton Inn. "Son, I seem to have a persistent pain in my abdomen. Do you think you could search around in my grip and find me my pills?"

After Mac has swallowed a handful—one white, three green, a couple of large orange-and-yellow ones—he asks, "So, what would you like to do today?"

"Kill Shelby." Leroy knocks back a shot of Early Times. *Early* Early Times.

"Now, Leroy. Come, come. Didn't a good night's rest change your mind?"

Then Mac sneaks himself a little look. Hot-diggity, the man's still fuming. Probably didn't sleep a wink all night. *Now* they're getting down to it.

"Gonna kill her dead, Mac. I am."

"Leroy, be serious. Have you ever killed anyone?"

"No. But I figure there's a first time for everything."

"Now, as I remember, the reason you came over here to Nashville was because you love Shelby."

"That's right. I do."

"But you want to kill her?"

"Right."

"Does that really make sense?"

"It does to me."

"Maybe it's the morning hour and this pain in my abdomen that are slowing down my thought processes. Explain it to me, son."

"Can't stand the notion of her *wanting* it with him." Leroy pours himself another two fingers of Early Times, then stares down the outside of his pants leg at the toe of his black cowboy boot. "The very next time I lay eyes on her, she's dead. I swear."

"All right then," says Mac, hauling his tiny legs off the side of his bed. He's wearing a sleeveless undershirt and Jockey shorts scrunched way down under his stomach. "I think it's an absolutely grand idea."

"Damned straight."

"But"—Mac scratches under one armpit—"everything in its own good time. Not that we're gonna dawdle over this matter I know is of such importance to you, but we need to insure your safety, too."

Leroy nodded. That was Mac, always thinking.

"Here's what we're going to do. We'll raise even more money than we'd originally planned so that we can make sure that, post–Operation Shelby, you have a successful getaway. Not to mention a considerable nest egg—while you lie low."

"And you, too, Mac? You'll lie low after Operation Shelby with me?" Leroy was starting to feel all puffed up inside. These operations, two of them now, making him feel *very* important. He is a man of purpose. Of import. A man with achievable goals.

"Oh, yes. Me, too. I'll lie very low, most assuredly."

*Lying low* has resonance for Leroy. The words make him think of foxholes. Combat. Bullets whizzing overhead. Or, maybe, big-time crooks who'd secreted themselves in a hideaway. A castle—in the deep dark woods. In Leroy's mind, lying low is a very romantic concept.

"So, in addition, Leroy, to lifting the Patsy Cline guitar, we need to call on your cousin."

"Chris?"

"Unless you've got another one's rolling in clover."

"You think Chris might be good for another loan?"

Mac just grins.

# 38

JOYCE MCGIVERN, HER SISTER LUCY, AND DANIELLE, Jeff Wayne's girlfriend, are having lunch at the Sunset Grill. The trendy health-conscious restaurant, a favorite of the Belle Meade crowd plus the hipper country music element, is going full tilt.

Conversation zings off the gray metal rafters. Armani suits rub up against leather Western jackets. Thai chicken offers flavor-of-the-moment with 340 calories, 7.5 fat grams, 139 milligrams of cholesterol, and 243 milligrams of salt. Which isn't to say you can't have a burger, a club sandwich, or meat loaf.

The three women—the sisters in neat pastel dresses, Danielle in skintight jeans and a silver bodysuit—have all ordered lean-style and are settled into the business at hand.

Dishing Shelby.

"I just don't understand her problem," Joyce says between bites of poached salmon. "First my Chuck, then your Jeff Wayne. One man at a time's not enough for her?"

SARAH SHANKMAN

"I guess not," says Danielle. "Some women are like that." Touching at her big blond hair. Sneaking a look at the older ponytailed man at the next table who's been staring at her since she sat down.

"So, what are you ladies going to do about her?" That's Lucy. Miss Down-to-Business Lucy of Parties and Weddings Unlimited, who's feted and fed about half the folks in this restaurant. Especially the well-heeled Muffies and Biffs, whose names adorn the rest rooms.

"You have any suggestions?" asks Joyce.

"Well, you could shoot her," says Lucy.

"Nope," says Danielle. "Too quick. Not nearly painful enough."

"How about grilling her? Roasting her?" suggests Lucy.

"Steaming her? Smoking her?" says Danielle.

"Barbecuing," Joyce said firmly. "Old piggy thing. Stick an apple in her mouth and turn her ever-so-slowly on the spit."

"Douse her from time to time with gasoline? Is that what you have in mind?" asks Lucy.

"Sounds good to me," says Danielle.

"But seriously, ladies," says Lucy. "How about it? You going over to her apartment, read her the riot act?"

"I don't know." Joyce shrugs. "That seems so, I don't know, so *ordinary*. I'm *mad*, Lucy. Pissed."

"Me, too," says Danielle. "*Real* mad. I mean, who does this Shelby think she is? I tell you, every time I think about her ..." Tears spring to Danielle's big blue eyes.

Now Joyce starts in, too. The two of them, sisters-in-betrayal, weeping into their seafood specials.

"Ma'am?"

The ponytailed man standing before them is a stylish piece of work in his three-piece gray linen-and-cotton suit with the white polo shirt and silver-buckled alligator belt.

"Ma'am?" he says again, offering Danielle a fine white handkerchief. "Is there any way I could help?"

"Well, actually, there's this woman . . . ," starts Lucy.

"Hush," orders Joyce.

"It just breaks my heart to see you so upset," he says to Danielle.

Ignoring Joyce as if she weren't crying, too. And she's the one with the most reason! But, on the other hand, she isn't twenty-two and built like a brick shithouse.

"Listen," the man is saying, "here's my card. I'm a talent manager, based on the Coast, in town 'cause one of my up-and-comers is doing a gig at the Bluebird tonight. I'd love it if you could be my guest."

"Well, I don't know . . ." Danielle bats her baby-blues.

"Tell you what. I'm staying at the Loews, you can give me a call if you want to go, or, if you want to decide at the last minute, you can come on ahead. Just mention my name at the door. Here." From under his arm he pulls a copy of the *Nashville Scene,* folded to the week's music listings. He circles the Bluebird's notice and hands the paper to Danielle. Nods at Joyce and Lucy and takes his leave.

"Well!" say the sisters in unison.

"Oh, I don't think so . . ." Danielle shrugs. But she's pink with pleasure.

"Did he write you a love note?" asks Lucy. "Give me that paper." She reaches over and grabs the *Scene* from Danielle. Examines it closely. Says, "No, he just marked the Bluebird." Then her eye runs down the listings. "Oh, my God. Oh, my *God!*" she screams.

"What?" her companions cry.

"You won't believe it!"

"What!?"

"Guess who's performing this very evening at a writers' night at the Sutler? Live and in color right up on that very stage? Where the likes of us could go and heckle the bejesus out of her? Make a scene? Boo? Be the three bitches from hell?"

"You don't mean?"

"Oh, yes, I do!"

# 39

JOAN CASSEL IS STANDING OUT ON THE FRONT STEPS OF her red brick Georgian mansion in Belle Meade. She is a very pretty dark-haired woman with ivory skin and violet eyes. The periwinkle of her silk overblouse and slacks make her look like a younger, smaller Liz Taylor.

But Joan is frowning into the sun at her yard's expanse of St. Augustine grass.

"You're gonna get wrinkles between your eyes, you do that," calls her next-door neighbor, Lizbeth Meems, who's pulling past in her powder-blue Mercedes convertible.

"Don't I know it," says Joan. "But this surprise party tomorrow for Chris's gonna be the death of me anyway. I've got a million things to do . . ." She waves the list in her hand.

"Aren't you using Lucy Beemis?"

"Yes, but you know, there's still always something. I'm out here trying to decide if I need the yardman to come again. What do you think?"

"Looks perfect to me. But, honey, if you're the least bit worried about it, I say, call him. What the hey? It's only Chris's money."

"You're probably right. Okay, thanks, let me let you go. I need to get running." With that, Joan dashes back into the pale gray cool of her marble foyer.

She lifts her purse from the burled walnut side table. Checks to make sure she has her keys, her wallet. Grabs the garment bag holding her orchid taffeta party gown. She's lost a couple of pounds since it was fitted. Needs to run by Harry B's, have it scooched in just a tad in the bodice.

Making her way back past the living room, the dining room, through the kitchen, she checks her list one last time.

Harry B's, then Levy's to pick up a new tux shirt for Chris. Chris thinks they're going to a benefit for the Literacy Volunteers tomorrow night, which they are, but only for a little while. Then she'll have a headache, and they'll come back here. Surprise!

After Levy's, she'll stop at the Corner Market. Lucy said they had this new St. André cheese she ought to try, see if she wants it for the party. Oh, and somewhere in here she needs to make a stop at the Sunset Grill. The owners, who are friends, want to do Chris's favorite voodoo pasta for the party, they need to talk.

So many errands to run. But then, she'll do anything for Chris. Fifteen years they've been together, and it seems like fifteen minutes.

She'd been Joan Mathers, a nobody from Ellabell, Georgia, sitting out at the receptionist's desk at RCA, when Chris came walking in the door. Strutting like he was *somebody*.

But when he saw her, he froze. Couldn't remember his own name when she asked, Whom shall I say is calling, sir?

Joan laughs at the memory. Chris, Chris, God, she adores him. She worships the very ground he walks on. She throws open the door from her utility room to her garage, steps through it.

Leroy grabs her.

Joan can't see a thing from inside the black garbage bag. She can't scream because her mouth is taped. Her wrists are tied behind her back. She can kick, though.

"You keep doing that," warns the one who's doing all the talking, she thinks there are just two of them, "we'll kill your Chris. Dead as a doornail, I promise."

She stops. Immediately.

"Good girl," he says. *Smart* girl. Sit down here, now."

One of them pushes Joan back against the edge of a straight-back chair, then starts tying her ankles together with soft rope.

"Don't need to worry your pretty little head about a thing," rasps the talker. "All you need to do is relax. And pray, of course, that Mr. Chris loves you as much as you think he does."

He says to the other one, "Open the back door. This side."

They lift her, chair and all, and carry her a few feet. Tilt the chair forward, and she rolls out of it, smacking her head. She bounces off something, falls about a foot, and she's wedged.

Of course. She's in the back seat of her car. She knows its smell. Her silver BMW, still parked here in the garage.

Somebody pushes at her feet, tucking them in. She waits for the door to slam.

Then the other guy speaks. "What do you think, Mac? Should we leave her some water or something?"

"Goddamnit!" says Mac. "Do you hear what you

said? You've gone and used my name. We've got to kill her now. No way around it."

"Oh, no. Kill her? Are you sure?"

"It's her or us."

Inside the car, Joan struggles. She shakes her head, trying to tell them, No, I didn't hear a word.

Mac says, "Tell you what. You believe in fate, right? Believe it was fate brought us together, set us along this road?"

"Yes, sir, I do."

"Okay. Then let's let fate call this one. Here's the deal, Leroy. See this quarter? I'll flip. Heads, she lives. Tails, she dies."

The silver coin whirls high, higher.

# 40

IT'S TWO O'CLOCK, AND SHELBY'S RUNNING LATE FOR her hair appointment.

"Can't you drive any faster?" she asks Jeff Wayne. He'd insisted they take his car, leave hers at home.

"I'm doing seventy."

"What are you afraid of, you're going to get a speeding ticket?"

"It could happen."

"Then what's the point of being a cop?"

He turns and peers at her over his sunglasses. "You know, somehow I thought you'd calm down a little, once you'd finished your song."

"What difference does that make? I'm thrilled it's done, and I love it to pieces, but I haven't *practiced* it. Ain't nowhere near *at home* in it. Plus I've got so little time and so much stuff to do. The salon. That'll take an hour and a half. Still got to run by the cleaners. This is the exit, here. Then you're gonna go left like you're headed for the Green Hills Mall. Riqué's is off to the right, down behind a cleaners. I'll show you."

"Is that the cleaners where your shirt is?"

"No, no. That's back by my apartment. And you know what? I just remembered, and this is *your* fault, Jeff Wayne, I got so discombobulated when I came out of my demo session yesterday and saw you there, I clean forgot to go pick up my star."

"Your what?"

"Get over to the left here. There's the cleaners, see? My star. A crystal star from a shop in Hillsboro Village. On a gold chain, it's a necklace. And I just know it's going to be my good luck piece."

"How do you know *I'm* not your good luck piece?"

"Hell, you hang around me enough to be, don't you?"

"You are one tough woman, anybody ever tell you that?"

"Folks been calling me all kinds of things I was never called before I came to Nashville." She's out of the car now. Headed toward the door of Riqué's. "So are you coming in, or are you doing your bodyguard thing from out here?"

"Shelby?"

"What?"

"Come here for a minute."

"I'm in a hurry, Jeff Wayne."

"Just for a minute. I want to give you something."

Shelby throws her head back and gazes at the clear blue skies. Up toward the heavens. "Can this wait?"

"I don't think so."

She leans in the window. "Okay. What is it?"

Jeff Wayne reaches up and out and grasps her gently by the back of the neck, pulls her toward him, and gives her the sweetest kiss.

Not a particularly sexy one. But certainly loving. Just the slightest flutter of his tongue against her lips.

Shelby steps back, stunned. "What has come over you, Jeff Wayne?"

"Your guess is as good as mine."

# 41

Danielle is standing, hands on hips, staring into her closet. What is she going to wear tonight?

Something killer, that's for sure.

Something that shows lots of boob.

Skintight.

And shiny.

Danielle pulls out a black-sequined catsuit, stares at it a long moment, throws it across the bed.

Joyce said Shelby is on the hefty side. So, no doubt about it, this is the time to strut her stuff. Show the heifer what's what.

Besides. Jeff Wayne might be there, too. It's possible. Or is that probable? Danielle doesn't know how far this thing has gone.

All she knows is, he talked about the woman in his sleep. Used the lame excuse that she was one of his cases, some poor defenseless woman, her husband tried to beat her up.

According to Joyce, somebody *ought* to beat her.

And, here it is, Jeff Wayne's day off. Where is he? Where was he last night?

He left a message saying he had an emergency.

She'll give him an emergency, all right.

Danielle begins pawing through the closet, searching for that gold lamé dress cut down to the patootie. She wore it to a Christmas party last year. The music director of her church said it really made him feel the Christmas spirit.

Here it is. Danielle pulls it out and inspects it. Maybe.

Which shoes? Her gold-and-lucite catch-me-do-me-sandals? She looks up, inspecting the rows of labeled shoe boxes, when suddenly she feels as if they're about to tumble on her. She'll be buried alive in an avalanche of slingbacks and slippers and pumps.

Or is it Shelby Kay Tate walking all over her?

Jeff Wayne giving her the boot?

Peering up into her closet, she feels dizzy. She can *see* Jeff Wayne kissing that cow. Feathering her lip with his tongue. Then running the stubble of his jaw along Shelby's cheek. Whispering something in her ear.

(Rahab being a wizard of mind control and special effects.)

"No!" Danielle screams into the depths of her stuffed closet. Into the thicket of skirts and blouses and jumpsuits and dresses and slacks. "Nooooooo, you won't, you bitch!"

She flings herself out of the closet, out of the bedroom, and down the hall to the big locked double walk-in where Jeff Wayne keeps his guns.

She jerks so hard on the door, she hurts her wrist. She's forgotten that Jeff Wayne keeps it locked.

Danielle rummages around in her memory for the key. Comes up with it.

# 42

CHRIS CASSEL MOVED TO NASHVILLE TWENTY YEARS ago, hoping to make it as a singer/songwriter. However, Mrs. Cassel raised no stupid children, and after two years of banging on Music Row's doors, he gave up that dream.

But Chris turned out to have a natural bent for A&R: finding the repertoire of songs for artists under contract. Now the brass-and-wood nameplate sitting on Chris's desk at Liberty Records proclaims him to be Exec. VP, A&R.

"If I had any more letters behind my name you'd think I was a can of alphabet soup." Chris says that a lot.

He laughs a lot, too. For an executive in the record game, he is one hell of a nice guy. He actually *relishes* finding great songs by new writers and giving them the Big Chance.

The tall, dark, and handsome Chris is nice to everyone. He's nice to the staff of A&R people under him. He's nice to their assistants, some of whom wouldn't know a hit song if it bit them in the ass. He's even nice to Pammie, the new receptionist, who keeps losing the phone calls that are his life's blood—but then he has a soft spot in his heart for receptionists, considering Joan was once one.

So when Pammie interrupts Chris to say that there is a man with her out in the lobby who needs to talk to him right away about his cousin Leroy, Chris says to Dianne Petty—who's on the line inviting him to have a drink before the show at the Sutler tonight—"Darlin', could I put you on hold for just a minute?"

Then he leans back in his black leather chair and asks Pammie, "Is he a policeman?"

"Oh, no, Mr. Cassel. I don't think so. He doesn't look like one."

"Well, looks can be deceiving, darlin'. But why don't you just watch my line, and when I've finished this call, send him on in."

Then Chris whirls his chair around so his back is to the door. He's staring at his credenza and a picture of his darling Joan.

"Dianne," he says, "I'm sorry I don't have time for the drink, but like I told you, I'm hot for your Miss Tate's songs, so I'll most definitely be there tonight. The only thing that might keep me away would be your failing to promise me the first dance at that CMA party next week."

"You wanta cut the crap?" growls a voice from somewhere behind Chris.

He whirls. A very short man with grizzled red hair and a humongous paunch is planted squarely on his three-thousand-dollar Navaho rug.

"Let me call you back, Dianne."

Chris stands.

A very impressive six-foot-four inches of muscle and sinew, Chris has always found it useful to rise to his feet when he's doing any kind of business with people he doesn't like.

And already he hates this little pissant.

But Chris is nothing if not polite. "Can I help you, sir?" he asks.

"I hope so."

"Are you the man who's here about my cousin Leroy?"

"I am."

"And what might be your name?"

"I'm the Bearer of Bad Tidings."

"And I'm the Big Bad Wolf. You want to cut the shit and tell me why you came barging into my office without so much as a by your leave?"

Mac smiles his thin-lipped smile. This is going to be more fun than he'd even thought. "I'm afraid the sad news is that your cousin Leroy finds himself in a bit of a tight again, and he needs your assistance."

"Then why doesn't my cousin Leroy come and talk to me himself, Mr. . . . ?"

"Mr. Bigg," says Mac McKenzie, drawing himself up to his full five-foot-three-and-a-half. Then he gives Chris his squintiest grin. "You like that? A big galoot of a guy like you, accustomed to pushing your weight around? Lording it over the sweet tiny perfect parcels of humanity such as that which you see before you this very instant?"

Chris starts toward the door, which he intends on opening and propelling the smartassed little intruder through. He hasn't quite decided yet if he'll use his hands or his feet.

"Before you do anything rash," says Mac just before Chris draws even with him, "you might want to listen to this tape recorded by your lovely Joan."

Chris freezes in midstep. "Don't be joking about my wife."

"And why would I joke?"

# 43

CHUCK MCGIVERN HAS HAD A ROTTEN NIGHT.

At first Ruby was restless, following him from room to room with her soft brown eyes. Worried about her momma. Finally, he said, "Come on, then." The dog jumped up, delighted to be *on the sheets*. Laid her head on Joyce's pillow, was snoring in half a minute.

Chuck didn't sleep a wink.

He was too busy feeling guilty. Thinking about that picture of Jesus hanging on his momma's living room wall. How Momma always said Jesus knew. He knew if you did wrong or right. Loved you anyway, but it sure would be easier on you, son, Momma said, you stick to the straight and narrow.

Too bad Chuck just wasn't a straight and narrow kind of guy.

There've just been too many temptations in his path. Lovely temptations. Seductive temptations. Like that blonde there. Pulling up in the driveway of the doctor's house where he is right now, hefting rocks with his crew.

Chuck has held onto his landscaping service—specializing in high-end jobs in fancy neighborhoods like Belle Meade, Green Hills, Brentwood—that's paid the bills until a few years ago when he began to hit the inside track of the songwriting business. These days he rarely gets dirty himself.

Unless it's a day like today. He has a need to expel some evil.

And wouldn't you know? Just when he's working up a good sweat, the devil goes and sends another one of his minions.

Look at her.

A pretty woman in sunglasses, pulling into the doc's driveway in a powder-blue Mercedes convertible. Bright pink scarf laced through her blond hair. Waving at him.

"Yoo-hoo. Excuse me, but are you Chuck McGivern?" Her voice is high, flutey. Younger than she is. But most Belle Meade belles, they have voices like that.

"Yes, ma'am, I am. Is there some way I can help you?"

Chuck runs a hand through his wet hair, plastering it back over his bald spot, though he knows from experience that hair, or the lack of it, doesn't seem to make much difference to horny women.

"I certainly hope so." She lowers her sunglasses. Can send Morse code with those eyelashes. "My friend Matilda called and said she saw you over here. Said you hadn't been in the neighborhood for a *long* time. Said you do *wonderful* work."

"Well, ma'am, I appreciate that. 'Preciate the word of mouth."

"Oh, Matilda, she couldn't say enough nice things about you."

"Well, Miz Matilda, she's a right fine lady herself."

The blonde laughs, not too loud, not too long, a laugh she's been practicing since she was thirteen. Then she twists pink-tipped fingers through the ends of her blond curls. "I was wondering if you could come over to my house and do some work for me. I'm Lizbeth Meems. I live right over on Lynnwood." She turns and points down the street.

Chuck says, "Why, I imagine we could help you out. How big a job did you have in mind?"

"Oh, very big." Lizbeth laughs again. "Real big. Might keep you busy quite a while. Especially if you're as good as Matilda says you are."

Ten minutes later Chuck is climbing out of his truck in front of a forties yellow brick manse. Red tile roof. Mediterranean shutters and grillwork.

"Stay, Ruby," he says to the dog through the open truck window, then takes a good look at the house.

It would go twenty, twenty-five rooms, easy. Three million, maybe four with the land. And a nicely manicured plot of land it is. Looks like Joe Fujikawa's work. Chuck can't see a single solitary thing he'd change.

"Miz Meems, you got yourself a right nice place here," he says.

She's standing beside her Mercedes now in the tiniest white tennis skirt he's ever seen showing off long tanned legs.

"*Lizbeth*, please, and thank you very much. I've always been real fond of it myself. That's why Judge Meems left it to me."

"I'm sorry for your loss," Chuck says.

Lizbeth Meems laughs. "Oh, the judge's not dead. We've just gone our separate ways."

"I see. Now, tell me"—Chuck surveys the yard—"what exactly was it you had in mind?"

"Come, I'll show you."

She walks him around the grounds. Says all the azaleas, there must be three hundred of them, have to be pulled up and replaced with something that doesn't look so plug-ugly when it's done blooming. She wants an all-white cutting garden. A gazebo with latticework and screening. A whole wall of trees to hide her new tennis court.

"You mean full-grown trees?"

"Oh, yes. Up to the top of the fence. Twenty feet." She stretches, swanlike, one arm out long.

"That's gonna cost you a pretty penny."

She smiles sweetly. "The judge was very generous. Now, why don't you come into the house? We'll have a glass of iced tea and talk about the details."

Chuck has had this glass of iced tea before. He knows he'll barely empty his glass before Miz Meems will invite him upstairs to help her see about something.

It won't be rearranging any pictures of Jesus, either.

Sure enough, he's downed three sips when Lizbeth, who's sitting on a kitchen stool right across from him, raises her right foot, giving him a straight shot up her tiny tennis skirt. Slowly unlaces her tennis shoe, pulls off her sock, wiggles her pretty pink toes.

Says, "Matilda mentioned you were awfully good at helping out. And I've got something upstairs that really needs to be turned around."

# 44

Over at Lucy's house, Joyce is cleaning out her sister's kitchen cabinets, a freshly scrubbed sugar canister in her hands, when she has a sudden flash.

Chuck, this very instant, is up to no good.

There's not a doubt in Joyce's mind. She's had hunches plenty of times, but this is strong.

Son. Of. A. Bitch. Does he think he can just do anything, get away with it?

Him and that Shelby Tate?

Joyce stares at the kitchen cabinet before her. Straight at a wooden block full of keenly honed knives.

She chooses carefully. The boning blade isn't the longest, but Joyce isn't adverse to getting close.

Then, too, it will fit nicely in the giant bag she carries, the one Chuck teases her about. "Got everything in there but the kitchen sink."

She'll just see who has the last laugh, she pulls this shiv from her portmanteau.

# 45

THREE MINUTES LATER CHUCK AND LIZBETH ARE sprawled across her bed. Lizbeth's other shoe, sock, her polo shirt, little bitty tennis skirt, and lacy underthings are scattered from here to kingdom come. Things are just getting interesting when Ruby, whom Chuck has left in his truck in Lizbeth's driveway, starts in howling.

So is Lizbeth. "Oh, God," she moans, "you feel so good."

Ruby's persistent, an admirable trait in a hunting dog. *"Ooooooooruh. Ooooooooruh,"* she calls.

It sounds to Chuck like she's treed something. A squirrel? A possum? This is a really woodsy neighborhood. Has she jumped out of the truck?

This speculation causes Chuck to lose his concentration.

"Lizbeth," he says, "sugar, I'm sorry, I'm not doing any good here. Let me get up, run outside, see what my dog's up to. I'll be right back."

"What?" Lizbeth sputters. "Have you gone crazy?"

"I don't think so. But us older guys, we can't be doing but one thing at a time. And right now, that's listening to my dog cut up." Chuck's out of bed, pulling on his shorts. "Your next-door neighbor have a cat or something?"

"Joan?" Lizbeth sits up. "I don't think so. Chris's allergic."

Chuck takes both her hands, rubs his mouth across them, then tucks them between her legs. "Hold that thought, and I'll be back in a flash."

The next-door neighbor's house is an acre of admirably groomed St. Augustine grass away. And sure enough, after he crosses it, Chuck finds Ruby, pointing a baby raccoon atop the neighbor's garage.

Furiously barking at the little coon, then at Chuck. Can't he see?

"Ruby, girl, what are you doing out of the truck?"

The setter ignores his silly question. Goes right on bawling. Giving him her best machine-gun chop. *A raccoon! A raccoon!*

"Hush, Ruby!" Chuck orders.

The gyp stops bawling, though reluctantly. This is *her* coon.

"You ought to be ashamed of yourself. Little bitty thing like this, lost its momma. Scared enough without all your carrying on."

He stares up at the young coon. It stares back at him, scared stiff. It's not going anywhere.

"Tell you what, baby," he says to the coon. "I'm gonna ring this Miz Joan's bell, see if she's home, I can borrow her ladder. We'll get you down from there. Lock Ruby up. Turn you loose. What do you think about that?"

The coon is silent, as is the response to his ring at Joan's door.

"Okay, okay. Plan B. I'll go back over to Lizbeth's, see if she has a ladder."

He thinks about that for a minute.

"You know, something tells me Miz Lizbeth ain't gonna be in the mood to direct me out to her garden shed or wherever it is she keeps her rescue equipment."

Chuck sits down on Joan's steps. Ruby sits beside him, reluctantly. Chuck runs his hands over her deep red coat, can feel the *Coon! Coon!* coursing through her sinews.

"What do you think, girl? Think the old man's gone nuts, like Miz Lizbeth said, he cares more about a little baby raccoon than rich-lady pussy?"

Ruby rolls her eyes.

"Truth is, given the choice between tromping around in the woods with you or rolling around in the hay with an ex-debutante, it's never been any contest. You just can't take the country out of the boy, Ruby, my love."

Ruby mutters something deep in her chest about his not being *very* serious about country, he'd walk away from a tasty bite of coon like that.

"Well, hell," Chuck says, standing, dusting his knees off, "don't look like this Joan Whoever She Is is home. But let's go make sure 'fore we give up and tangle with Miz Lizbeth again, maybe Joan's garage door ain't locked after all."

# 46

CHRIS CASSEL IS THE CHILD OF THRIFTY COUNTRY people who hoped for the best but expected the worst and taught their son to spread his savings around.

Which is why he and Mac and Leroy have already visited three banks. The First National is the fourth. Withdrawal of Chris's savings being the object.

Chris pulls the pearly Lincoln into the First National parking lot and stops. Mac and Leroy occupy the backseat. Mac warned Chris at the outset, right in front of Liberty Records, "You signal to anyone, involve us in a wreck, pull out in front of a policeman, do the tiniest thing that could be construed as cute, you can kiss sweet Miss Joan bye-bye."

Leroy registers the low blond brick-and-glass building edged with green shrubbery, the blue plastic letters spelling out FIRST NATIONAL. "Here we are again. Small world, ain't it, Mac?"

"It certainly is. Yes, indeed, it gives one hope that

maybe there's some sort of overall plan after all,
doesn't it?"

Leroy pauses. Does Mac mean Operation Shelby—
or is he talking philosophy again, like wrong not being
a concept? Leroy says, "Unh-huh, it sure does."

Chris, still behind the wheel, resists the temptation
to tell his cousin precisely what flavor of idiot he is.

Neither did he scream *Help! Help!* at any of the
other banks, from which he has withdrawn a total of
thirty thousand dollars. Ten thousand a pop is the
limit Mac thinks they can safely withdraw, in cash,
without arousing major suspicion.

*Minor* suspicion, says Mac, well, what the hell? No
pain, no gain. And isn't the blast of adrenaline what
this whole adventure is all about? It makes a man feel
*A L I V E.*

"Okay," Mac says now, opening the rear door on
his side, "are you ready to roll, Mr. Hotshot?"

Chris nods, climbing out.

The less he says, he figures, the better, and the
quicker this nightmare will be over. He hopes. Mac
said the clock is ticking on Joan.

He wouldn't elaborate on the details, so Chris's
imagination has run wild.

Joan is locked up somewhere, suffocating. Drown-
ing in a slow-filling tub. Or is it fire? Drugs?

Dear Jesus, the possibilities are endless. *Please,* he
prays, *look after her. Please, Dear Lord, keep my sweet
wife alive.*

The Lord handles that end, he figures he can kill
these sons of bitches later, on his own.

Now Leroy's climbing out of the backseat. "Mac?
Do you think it would be better if maybe I went in
this time? Given that, you know, you were just here
and all?"

"You mean yesterday? I only made a withdrawal, Leroy."

"How about the day before?"

"Whatever it is, I don't want to know about it," says Chris, clasping his hands over his ears.

Just then a tall long-legged blond man who's exiting the bank stops and waves at them. It's Ken Hite, country superstar.

"Uh-oh," says Leroy. "Oh, boy."

"Not to worry," says Mac. "Everything is under control. And you'll be the soul of discretion, won't you, Chris?"

Oh yes, Chris nods. He'll be good as gold.

Now Hite is upon them. "Hey, hoss!" he says, enveloping Chris in a big manly hug. "I thought that was you. How you doing?"

"Just fine." Chris smiles. "Doing just great."

"Mr. Hite, I'm a huge fan of yours," says Mac, stepping forward with his hand out. "McDonald Bigg's the name."

Hite looks like he doesn't know whether or not the little man's for real. Chris's famous for his practical jokes. Is this one? "Happy to meet you, Mr. Bigg," he says finally.

Leroy, not to be outdone, offers his hand, too. "And I'm Leroy Mabry. Gosh almighty, ain't this something? Could I get your autograph?"

"Why, you bet. I'd be honored."

Leroy begins to hunt around in his pockets for something for Hite to sign. Today he's all in black—cowboy shirt, jeans, boots.

"That's a very cool shirt you're wearing," says Hite, inspecting the silver tips on his collar. "Riflefire!?"

"Sure enough." Leroy grins.

"Listen," says Hite, "you don't have any paper there, why don't y'all come over to Sweet Willie's with me, let me buy you a cup of coffee? We'll find a napkin or something."

"Thanks a lot, bubba," says Chris. "But we're gonna have to pass. Got a little business to tend to here at the bank."

But Mac doesn't want to miss *any* opportunity for fun. "Awh, come on, Chris," he says. "It's not everyday, is it, a man is asked to sit down with a megastar country recording artist. Is it, Leroy?"

"No, it sure ain't."

And then Leroy wonders if maybe he ought to remind Mac that Sweet Willie's is where Shelby works.

Maybe it wouldn't be too cool if they ran into her there, right out in the open, seeing as how he's taken a vow to blow her away the very next time he lays eyes on her?

Then Leroy tells himself, Nawh, go with the flow.

# 47

SHELBY, HER WILD MOP OF RED-BROWN CURLS FRESHLY tended, has decided to ignore the kiss Jeff Wayne gave her out in Riqué's parking lot. Not that it wasn't nice, but she just doesn't have time to think about it right now. It's three o'clock, four hours till she has to be at the Sutler.

"I really could have done without Riqué *insisting* that I drop these products off for Willie," she says to Jeff Wayne, as they pull into Sweet Willie's employee lot. "But he gives all Willie's employees a discount, he and Willie are old friends, it's not like I could say no." Out of the car she says, "You gonna just wait for me here?"

"Well, I was kind of hoping maybe we could stop for a little bite." Jeff Wayne looks at his watch. "You gonna eat before your performance?"

"I wasn't planning on it." She watches his face drop. "Oh, hell. Come on then. Or the next thing I know you'll be lecturing me about how it's bad manners to starve your bodyguard."

Outside in Sweet Willie's side lot, four car doors slam: Chris, Mac, and Leroy exit the pearly white Lincoln Towncar. Ken Hite's out of his black Jeep Cherokee, the exact same model as the one Mac and Leroy had two cars back, or was that three?

"Y'all know this place?" Hite is saying to Mac and Leroy as they head toward the door. "Best meat-and-three in all of Nashville. And the coffee ain't bad either."

"I heard the waitresses are sluts," says Leroy, sliding a look over at Mac.

Mac giggles. Chris looks at him, then at his cousin Leroy, the two sons-of-bitches in whose hands lie the life of his sweet Joan. *If* she was even still alive, that is. Ticktock, ticktock, how many hours, minutes, oh Jesus, did she have left? A howl of despair rises in Chris's throat, and it's all he can do to keep from throwing his head back and letting it spiral into the warm blue afternoon.

"Well, I wouldn't know about that," Hite says, his hand on Sweet Willie's door. "I'm a family man myself. But I can sure speak for the coffee."

Shelby and Jeff Wayne are settled into a booth waiting for Wanda, one of her least favorite waitresses, to get back to them with a cup of coffee.

"She is *so* slow," Shelby mutters to herself. "I don't know why Willie puts up with her."

Jeff Wayne looks up from the menu. "Really? She was the one waiting on us, me and Jerome, day before yesterday when I got the call that took me over to your apartment. And now look. Here we are, Jerome's in the hospital . . ."

Suddenly Jeff Wayne stands, grabs Shelby's arm. "Come on."

"Don't you want to eat?"

"Sure, but we need—" Jeff Wayne stops as if he's listening to something. "We need to eat somewhere else."

"What are you talking about? I don't have *time* to go running around town to another restaurant."

"Back here," Jeff Wayne's pulling her. "Back in the kitchen, okay?"

*Yes,* says Patsy Angel, shoving them along. *Move. Move now!*

"Well, why did they do that?" Wanda is wondering out loud when a familiar voice calls, "Hi, there, Wanda, how you doing?"

It's Ken Hite. The star. And with him Chris Cassel, Liberty A&R. Two of the handsomest men in Nashville, but can a girl even get a smile from either one of them that isn't brotherly? Well, she can't, that's for sure.

"And this is Mac," Hite is saying as the four of them slip into a booth, "and this here is his friend . . ."

Wanda doesn't hear Leroy's name for the roaring in her ears. Doesn't see him all that well either. Everything's a blur except for his face.

She looks through a prism that Rahab, *mightily* pissed at Patsy Angel's fiddling with his stratagems, slips before her eyes. The long grooves running down either side of Leroy's nose, she sees as character lines. His blond curls are a diadem. His spooky blue eyes are deep pools. Wanda sees pure sex in Leroy's black cowboy shirt, tight black jeans, black boots.

Leroy grins up at her, and shivers run all through her.

"Maybe I'll take this little lady's autograph, too,"

Leroy says. "Don't y'all think she looks like she's gonna be famous?"

"She sure doesn't look like what you said out in the parking lot," Hite teases.

"And what's that?" Wanda's breathless.

"Oh, nothing," says Leroy. He scowls at Hite. Just because the man's famous doesn't mean he can go around embarrassing people.

"Don't you remember, Leroy, you were talking about a woman who works here?" says Mac.

Leroy stares at his partner, astonished. Mac siding with the singer, the two of them ganging up on him? What the heck is going on here?

"Y'all know somebody who works here?" Wanda asks.

"Shelby Tate." The words pop out of Mac's mouth. Just like his flying dentures.

"You know her?" Wanda is disappointed. She doesn't like Shelby, who thinks she's hot stuff. Shelby, who just pushed past her back into the kitchen with that blond cop in tow. Said something about going to see Teedell.

"Oh, yes," says Mac. "In fact, Leroy knows Shelby *very* well. I think he'd like to say hello to her. You know where she might be?"

Wanda looks at this strange little man with the strange way of talking, the gut, the big fat yellow mustache. She looks at Leroy, her heart going pitty-pat. She looks at Hite. Then she focuses on Chris, who looks just awful, come to think of it.

There is *something* going on here.

Wanda glances back toward the kitchen. "Well . . . ," she says.

# 48

Teedell, Sweet Willie's chef, is making up a batch of dumplings when Shelby and Jeff Wayne fall into his kitchen. He looks up from the flour, shortening, salt, egg, and milk he's mixing with his hands, and says, "Hey, Shelby. How you feeling?"

"Fine, Teedell. Just fine." She introduces Jeff Wayne.

"What brings y'all back here today?"

Jeff Wayne looks at Shelby, waiting for *her* to explain. "Well," she stutters, wondering why the hell they *are* there, "I thought maybe we'd just hang out with you a bit. Do a little tasting off your stove. You know, your vegetables." She nods toward the huge pots of green beans, black-eyed peas, squash, greens laced with fatback—all simmering.

"Oh, yeah?" Teedell's looking at her like she's gone crazy.

"Jeff Wayne's a ... TV producer," she says. "You know that new food channel on the cable? Well, Jeff

Wayne's here scouting for a show on real Southern cooking. I told him, you can't do any better than eating off Teedell's stove."

"Well, now," says Teedell, straightening up and smiling at Jeff Wayne as if he's known all along that if he waited long enough, someone would come back in his kitchen and ask for a cooking demonstration that might lead God knows where. He could be the first black male Southern Julia Child. This is a TV man, after all, in Nashville, the town of boundless opportunity.

He hands them each a plate. "Well, now, why don't y'all just help yourselves. Meanwhile, Mr. Capshew, let me show you how I make my dumplings. You see I'm gonna roll this ball of dough out." He picks up a rolling pin. "Until it's about a half inch all around. Then you take your knife." He holds it up. "Cut it in strips like this about an inch to an inch-and-a-quarter wide. Then you cut those strips into your dumplings, about two inches long. The size is really up to you."

Back in Sweet Willie's dining room, Mac asks, "Is she out in the kitchen, Wanda?"

"What?"

"Is Shelby out in the kitchen?"

Wanda slides her amber eyes off Mac's mud-colored ones. This man reminds her of the pervert who used to wander around her neighborhood in Birmingham, saying, "Stick candy, little girl?" until they locked him up in the loony bin.

Wanda looks at Ken Hite, who just looks back at her, nothing on his look. Chris Cassel, on the other hand, is blinking so fast you'd think he'd been smoking some high-grade weed. He's already spilled a cup of coffee. There really is something bad wrong with Chris.

Then Wanda looks at the cute blond guy in black, Leroy, the one whose grin makes her want to rip off her slinky dress, the one she bought on sale at Retro Pieces.

"Is Shelby out in the kitchen, Wanda?" Mac asks again.

"Not that I noticed," Wanda finally says.

"I think you're a lying little bitch," Mac says, then stands.

"Whoa!" says Ken Hite. "Hold on just a minute here."

*Run.* Chris mouths the word to Wanda.

*Damnit!* Rahab hisses. He hadn't counted on Chris's taking the risk.

Wanda turns and flies. She doesn't stop until she's out the front door, across the sidewalk, and standing in the Esso station four doors down, where her friend, Broder, who owns the station says, "Well, Wanda, I think that's awful nice of you to bring that pot of hot coffee right over here to me, but, hon, you really didn't need to."

Back in the dining room of Sweet Willie's, Mac starts back toward the kitchen. "Leroy, Chris," he says, "you two come on in here with me."

Teedell is saying, "Now, the stock you already had going. It's got your chicken parts, I like leg quarters 'cause they're richer, and your whole stalk celery and your onion and salt and pepper and a little water, and you already cooked that till your chicken is done, and you've pulled it out and cooled it and deboned it. You're gonna drop your dumplings in that stock about twenty—" Teedell stops, staring at the trio walking through his double doors.

Mac snaps, "Who the hell are you talking to, boy?"

Teedell, who has never in his entire life responded

to rudeness, goes right on. "—twenty-five minutes covered, your heat on low. Then add your chicken meat, cut in little pieces, back to warm, adjust your seasonings, and that's it."

"Let's get out of here," Mac says, looking around the kitchen for the absent Shelby and noting that Teedell is holding a twelve-inch chef's knife in a hand that could have been a heavyweight contender's, easy.

Back in Sweet Willie's dining room, the booth where the four of them have been sitting is empty. Ken Hite has disappeared.

Mac turns to Chris. "You signaled something to Hite, didn't you? Now tell the truth."

"No! I swear I didn't."

Mac stares off into the distance. Then he says to Leroy, "Tell him."

Leroy leans over to his cousin. "Mac hates lying. Hates it worse than anything."

Chris doesn't even turn his face in Leroy's direction.

"You said something to him or gave him a signal," Mac goes on. "What you're thinking is you'll play along as if everything were copasetic. Your friend Hite's gone to the police, the SWAT team will swoop down and obliterate us, bye-bye bad guys."

"I didn't say a word, I swear." Chris is holding up his right hand as if his left were on a Bible.

"And why did Wanda turn tail like a bunny?"

"I don't know. I swear I don't."

"Well, now." Mac pats Chris on the arm. "Don't let yourself get upset. We'll find that little Wanda and bring her back so you can have her, Chris. Didn't you think she was cute? I saw you making eyes at her."

*Chris* could have her? Leroy is astonished. What the hell is Mac talking about?

"And we're even going to clear the decks for you.

No divorce. No waiting period. Just *ka-boom!*" Mac reaches into his jacket.

Uh-oh, Leroy thinks. Uh-oh. Oh, Jesus. No, Mac, don't!

But it isn't a gun that Mac pulls from his pocket. It's something that looks to Leroy like some kind of fancy TV remote.

"You know what this is?" Mac croons to Chris.

"No, I sure don't." Chris's staring at the thing like it's a snake.

"Are you sure?" Mac asks again. Getting a real big kick out of this. Oh yes, this is rich.

Chris shakes his head. It's something awful, has to do with his baby. The light of his life.

Mac says slowly, "It's the detonator for the bomb we left with Joan."

"You son of a bitch!" Chris lunges.

Leroy scratches his head. He doesn't remember seeing a bomb, but then he doesn't always pay such good attention, his mind being on Shelby.

"Uh uh uh," Mac warns Chris. "Now, the way I've set this up is, you see this big switch, well, you jiggle it, bye-bye, Joan." He flirts his thumb across it.

Chris shuts his eyes and moans.

"Of course, that's only one way the bomb works. Now the other is pretty automatic." Mac makes a show of checking his watch. "There's the clock I left with it. So, whether I push this or not, eventually . . ." Mac raises his little hands in an exploding motion, makes a sound with his cheeks.

Chris begs, "Why? You have the money. Why do you want to hurt her?"

He sounds so pitiful that Leroy feels sorry for him. But, as Mac has taught him, whatever it is Mac is doing with this remote thingy, it must be right. It has to be right if it is going to result in a successful Operation Shelby. And their lying low. It probably just doesn't *feel* right to Chris right now because he is still hung up on the concept of wrong.

Mac is saying, "So even if Wanda or your friend Mr. Hite has gone to the authorities . . ."

"I didn't say a word to Wanda!" Veins pop in Chris's forehead. "And I don't know where Ken's gone!"

"I'm right here, guys," the tall rangy singer says, stepping out of the men's room.

"Well, lookahere." Mac gives Hite a great big grin.

Leroy can see his dentures hovering on the brink. Will they jump out? Bite Ken Hite? But, no, Mac slips his whole self out of the booth, taking the country star's hand in both of his. "It *certainly* was good meeting you. Now I hope you don't mind if we run along. We've got some *pressing* business to tend to."

# 49

FIVE P.M. SHELBY IS PICKING UP BURGER KING WRAP-
pers from her dinette table. She says, "Okay, Jeff
Wayne. Here's the game plan. I'm going back to take
a quick bath. Then I'm running through my new song
about forty-two times, or until I think I can sing it
without embarrassing myself. I'll need half an hour or
so to get dressed, put on my warpaint. Twenty minutes
to get to the Sutler. That oughta do it, unless you've
got some other crazy idea up your sleeve."

They'd stopped for fast food after Jeff Wayne suddenly decided they couldn't eat Teedell's slow food
after all, had to get out of his kitchen. Another thing
he couldn't explain. Said he just had this feeling they
had to move.

Now Jeff Wayne waves Shelby away. "I'll finish
picking up this stuff. You go on ahead. Get cracking."

Then he dials the hospital.

Jerome is stable, holding his own.

Dials Metro.

Nothing yet on who might have shot Jerome.

Nor on the man who'd assaulted Reola, he'd called in her description.

And nothing on Leroy, for whom there's a pickup order, his having forfeited his bond, approaching Shelby.

There's no answer when he dials home.

Mac says to Chris, "If I were you, I'd just try to relax." He and Leroy are about to take their leave of him.

They haven't driven all that far. They're still in Davidson County off Pettus Road, only a mile or so from the DeBerry Institute—the state hospital for the criminally insane—which Mac once called home. Houses are few and far between around here, especially in the woods along this creek bottom.

Chris's trussed and gagged and propped up against a tree.

Back up on the road waits the dark blue four-year-old Oldsmobile Mac and Leroy have taken in trade, so to speak, for the pearly white Towncar.

"Now here's the principle you want to be sure not to forget," says Mac to Chris as he and Leroy begin walking away. "That detonator mechanism is *very* sensitive. So the slightest motion you make with your hands will flip the switch which activates the bomb in the trunk of her car."

"And blow up your house, too," Leroy says helpfully.

Mac turns and gives him a cold look.

"What?" says Leroy.

"Mr. Cassel here didn't know the location of his wife's car, did he, Leroy, until you informed him?"

"Oh, God, I'm real sorry, Mac."

"Well, that's okay. It just means we have to go ahead and kill him."

Leroy jerks back. They're gonna kill his *cousin?*

"Why don't *you* do it?" Mac reaches inside his jacket.

Chris lurches frantically. Moans from behind the tape across his lips.

"Now, I'm warning you this one last time," Mac says to Chris. "If you keep that up, flip that switch, your Joan's going to be splattered from here to kingdom come." He glances down at his watch. "If she's not already, that is. That alarm clock's ticking." He cuts his quick little grin, showing his snowy dentures. Then he says to Leroy, "What do you think, son? Do you want to use my piece? Or did you have something else in mind?"

What Leroy has is a real problem. Shelby is one thing, but Chris is his blood relation. On the other hand, if Mac wants him to . . .

He says, "Okay, give me the gun."

Chris tries to simultaneously wriggle and be still. To save his butt without blowing up his beloved's.

Mac grins. Leroy's his boy, all right. Right in his pocket. He says, "Nawh, forget it. Let's get going. Say good-bye to your cousin, Leroy."


Ken Hite is driving out Harding Pike on his way to a songwriting session, flipping through stations on the radio. But he can't stop thinking about the scene back at Sweet Willie's with Chris Cassel.

Something about it was fishy.

Those two guys just weren't the kind of folks Chris would hang with.

Sure, songwriters can be pretty scruffy-looking, but those two weren't songwriters. Didn't say they were musicians, either. Didn't say who they were, for that matter.

And Chris looked awfully white around the mouth.

The more he thinks about it, the more Hite thinks he ought to check with Chris, make sure he's all right. He reaches for the car phone.

Nope, says Pammie, the receptionist at Liberty, Chris isn't in. And, no sir, she isn't supposed to say this—but if he is *really* Ken Hite, can he sing a little to convince her? Well, my goodness, she guesses it won't hurt to tell *him* that Mr. Cassel never did come back from lunch.

Now, what Pammie really wants to know is, is Ken leaving his wife like all those newspapers . . .

Ken is looking down at his car phone, punching in the number of the Metro Police, when he crashes into a Chrysler turning left at the Country Store. That takes care of the front of his Jeep, and the pickup behind him accordions the rear.

It will be twenty-four hours before Hite—who has a concussion and a broken clavicle, not bad, considering—will regain consciousness in Vanderbilt Hospital, much less remember who he was dialing. Or why.


"Happy birthday to me, Happy birthday to me, Happy birthday, dear Shynelle, Happy birthday to me."

Shynelle Simon, six and a half years old and not the least bit shy, is lisping her favorite song through the gap where she is missing her two front teeth. She is walking along the edge of Devil Creek. That isn't the creek's real name, but her momma is always saying to her, "Shynelle, the devil's gonna get you, you go near his creek." Right now Shynelle is trying to figure out how she's going to hide the presents she got at school for her pretend birthday.

Shynelle is just crazy about her birthday, and it doesn't come nearly often enough for her. So whenever a chance presents itself, she gives herself another one.

Miz Roberts, her first-grade teacher, going on maternity leave was such a chance, and Shynelle has taken advantage of it, telling Mr. Bloomer, their substitute, that yesterday was her turn to stand under the plastic birthday tree over in the corner, eat chocolate-covered cupcakes, and gather up all the loot she could carry.

Most of it was stuff like broken crayons and cookies that other kids didn't want, but how about this Barbie with one arm? Shynelle, a redhead whose hair is straighter than Barbie's, pulls the doll out of her bright blue backpack and admires it.

Being a child with a first-rate imagination, Shynelle has spun a dozen tales about the catastrophes this one-armed Barbie has met: the battle with the pirate with the flashing silver sword, the fall from the very top of the very highest magic mountain in the whole wide world. She is lost in a tale of Barbie fighting off a band of wild Apaches when suddenly she hears someone singing.

The song's about some woman named Lucille and it being a fine time for her to leave. He sounds kind of hoarse, like maybe he'd been singing for a long time.

Shynelle can't see him from where she stands, so she walks a little farther. It's slow going along this boggy creek. He comes to the end of that Lucille song, and then he stops for a few minutes.

That's fine with Shynelle because the song is not a good sound track for her story about Barbie and the Apaches massing up on top of a ridge.

Then he starts in on another song about a woman named Ruby taking her love to town.

That one doesn't fit Shynelle's scenario either.

So she hollers down the creek, "Hey, would you please be quiet?"

That seems less rude than Shut up! Her momma is always telling her not to be so rude.

So, seeing as she hasn't been, she isn't surprised that the man *is* quiet. But for just a minute.

Then he starts in yelling, "Help! Help! Please help me!"

When Shynelle finds him, it doesn't take but one look for her to see that he must be an awfully bad guy, somebody has needed to tie him up and tape his mouth. It must have taken a lot of work to get the tape off without using his hands.

Driving back toward the Hampton Inn, Leroy tells Mac they should go on over to Shelby's. Wait for her if she isn't there, get this thing over with.

Kill Shelby, then his new life can begin, his and Mac's.

"I can't do that right now," Mac says. "I need to go back to the hotel now, Leroy. I'm having a little sinking spell. Shelby'll have to wait a bit."

"Okay, you take a nap, and then we'll go over there, take care of her, get on with our lying low?"

"Sure," says Mac. His voice is ragged, weak.

But Leroy's not paying much attention. Leroy's dreaming. "Maybe we could go to a deserted cabin somewhere in the woods."

Mac's listing to the left behind the wheel of the Oldsmobile. The malignancy in his gut has stepped up, taken itself a great big bite.

Leroy's off in the Land of Make-Believe. "Take ourselves a bunch of supplies, some canned goods. Beans, Vienna sausages, bacon. We can get ourselves one of them little cookstoves like you see in the magazines. Or, if we have enough money, we won't have to find an empty cabin."

Mac's slumping. Still driving. But leaning way over to the left.

"We can buy one of them pop-up tents, you don't even have to pound the stakes. Go up in the Smokies, maybe. I saw a story once about the Smokies in a magazine. They're real pretty."

"We'll see," Mac manages through the pain.

"Hey, if you don't like that, we could do some other kind of lying low." Leroy thinks about it for a minute. "I know! Somewhere with a beach. How about Panama City?"

One more inch, Mac won't be able to see over the wheel at all.

"Or Miami," says Leroy. "No, wait, I've got it. An island! Yeah, an island. Yes sirree, that's *really* lying low. One of those Caribbean places. Jamaica! That's the ticket! Where you sit under a grass hut all day, they bring you fancy drinks with cherries stuck on those little umbrellas."

"Let's talk about it later." Mac can hardly speak. He's holding on to the dark blue Olds's wheel so hard his fingers look like little white radishes. Not that his color anywhere is good.

Leroy finally notices. "Hey, are you all right?"

"Fine, I'm fine. I just need to take a little lie-down, like I said. You can clean up, get ready for your Big Surprise."

Surprise! Leroy loves surprises. What could this one be? He begins imagining. Sees himself on a plane. A *cute* stewardess is leaning over him. Asking him what he'd like . . .

Over on Preston Road, Shynelle is telling her momma, "And he said his name was Chris."

Momma says, "Shynelle, eat your supper and stop your fabricating."

"Chris Cassel," the birthday girl says, poking at her food. "And he says his wife, Joan, is locked up at their house, and there's this bomb that's going to go off."

"Don't play with your sweet potato. Eat it."

"I *am*. And then he started crying. I felt real sorry for him."

Momma shakes her head. "What am I going to do with you, Shynelle?"

# 50

$\int$IX O'CLOCK. SHELBY IS SITTING IN FRONT OF HER dresser in her black lace bustier and a pair of matching panties. She's leaning into the mirror, her lips parted, as she applies a third coat of mascara. Blasting in her face is a tape she just made of herself singing "I Still Miss My Man."

She's listening hard, trying to figure out what she might do differently. On the tape, she's winding into the chorus.

> *Do I miss you*
> *Well I guess I do*
> *Like Joan of Arc might miss a barbecue*

The rhythm of the second line is tough. She has to juggle with it, try for a little syncopation.

And go real country on the "cue," in the third, the joke, line. Get it way up in her nose and let it hang

240

there for a long count. Then *swoop* down on that next line.

The music's so loud, she's concentrating so hard, she doesn't hear Jeff Wayne at her door.

"Shelby?" he calls. Knocks again. "Shelby? It's the phone."

> *I'm tired of your demands*
> *I've had more than I can stand*

"Shelby? Somebody calling to wish you good luck."

> *Yeah, I still miss my man*
> *But my aim is getting better*

"Shelby?" Jeff pushes open the door. He's been in the living room, practicing his quick draw.

Shelby doesn't see him. Still doesn't hear him.

He hesitates. The woman's in the very black lace bustier she was saying Leroy planted the fried chicken in. Unless she has two.

He taps her on the shoulder.

Shelby screams. Jumps up.

"It's only me," he hollers. "The phone? Somebody wants to talk to you."

Shelby's backing away. Bumps into her bed. She's thinking about Chuck, herself half-naked, in this very bedroom. She screams over herself singing on the tape, "There's not gonna be any reruns of that fiasco, thank you very much, Jeff Wayne."

"It's the phone, Shelby," he tries again.

"I learned my lesson, day before yesterday." She's still loud, though the tape has stopped. "Besides which, that kiss was nice, but, well, it wasn't like the earth moved or anything. I mean, I might could work my way up to it, your being an awfully good-looking man, not to mention real kind, and myself being hard up and all. But it wouldn't be right. Your having a girlfriend.

"Besides which, Jeff Wayne, I just don't have the time." She taps on her watch to make her point. "Got to be out of here in less than half an hour, and furthermore, well, it's just like you guys before the big game. I never do it before I perform, no matter *how* tempted I am. Got to save every drop for the big stage."

"Bet your momma's proud to hear it." Jeff Wayne hands her the phone.

# 51

"So what do you think?" Gail asks Reola. She's standing at the bottom of her stairs, twirling in a circle, showing off her pretty things.

Black cowboy boots with scarlet flame insets. Tucked into them a pair of neat black slacks. Above that, the gol-dangdest red sequined cowgirl jacket ever in the history of country. Dripping with fringe. Rainbows and cacti and a long highway among the details. PEACH spelled out in silver sequins across the back. A gift from Patsy.

Reola can't say a word.

"Well, I don't think the jacket looks all *that* bad," says Gail. "Considering that it's been thirty years, and I've gained at least that many pounds. I mean, it's a little snug, but don't you think it's okay over this shirt?"

Finally Reola speaks. "And where do you think you're going?"

"*We're* going out."

"Oh no, we're not."

"Yes, we are. So why don't you go on home, get yourself spruced up. Wear your black dress with the sparkly trim and your gold do-rag. I love that one."

"You've gone insane. You think you're going to hear that Shelby sing, don't you?"

"Sing our song. Yes, indeedy, I am."

"Thirty years underground, and you're just going to fetch yourself up in a music club, music folks all around, like nothing ever happened?"

"Reola, listen to you. What *did* happen? How many times did you tell me, back then, 'Gail, it's not like you did something wrong. Not like you *murdered* Patsy.' "

Reola opened her mouth. Then closed it.

"That's right. There's nothing to say, is there? I did that then. I'm doing this now."

"Are you telling me you're going to walk right in the Sutler, say howdy to the folks, take up where you left off?"

"Take up what? My career? Don't be ridiculous. I'm an old lady, and that's ancient history. I'm just going to put my party clothes on, go take a listen to my new friend. Now, are you coming or not?"

Reola glowers. It's *hard* to change oars in midstream. Especially when you've been paddling in one direction for so long.

# 52

LEROY HEFTS THE BOTTLE OF EARLY TIMES AND POURS himself another one. He's getting quite a buzz on, sitting around the Hampton Inn, waiting for Mac to finish his lie-down.

But the booze isn't making him feel one bit better. Every time Leroy closes his eyes, all he can see is that policeman and Shelby. Doing the nasty.

Leroy has drunk his way into a *real* foul mood.

Now he stands and paces the little space at the end of the beds. Chugs back the rest of his drink. All spruced up in his last new shirt from Riflefire!, bright yellow and with big red roses. He's ready to get this show on the road.

Finally Mac moans, groans, struggles to sit up.

Leroy thinks back. Shit, it was hardly forty-eight hours ago, the first time he saw this old man rise, playing possum in that jail cell. And now it's like Mac's run out of steam. Maybe that's it. Talking ninety-miles-a-minute, he's schemed and planned and boogied them down the road so far and fast, in *so* many different vehicles, the man's just pooped.

"You ready?" says Mac, sitting up in his drawers and undershirt, his gut peeping out as always.

It's not a pretty sight. Leroy looks the other way.

Mac lifts his hands over his head, stretching this way, then that. Yawns, his mouth a bottomless black cavern, belching villainous fumes.

Leroy steps to the window. Looks for a way to open it for a breath of fresh air. But it won't open.

"Ready to perambulate over to East Nashville?" Mac's standing. Making his way toward the bathroom.

"East Nashville?" Leroy's alarmed. "What the heck are we going over there for?"

"Got a date to take that Patsy Cline guitar, Leroy. Can't you remember these details?"

"Yeah, I remember, all right." He takes a very deep breath. "But I don't want to do it."

Mac stops in his tracks. "What do you mean?"

"I mean I don't want to go over to East Nashville. I don't want to steal any cockeyed guitar, I don't care if it belongs to Mary Magdalene. I want to kill Shelby. Get that over with. Go do our hiding out. That's it. That's all I want to do."

"What do you think we'll be using for funds, son, in this great adventure of yours?"

"What about the thirty thousand we got from Chris? Ain't that a start? Would have been *forty* thousand, you hadn't wanted to dick around with that Kenny Hite."

"Leroy!" Mac is amazed. He can't believe the pitiful fool is standing up on his two hind feet. "What the hell's come over you?"

"I told you. I want to get on with this thing."

"You feel it in your gut, Leroy?"

"I feel it all *over* me. It's like there's red ants or

scorpions or something racing all around in my veins.
I want to do this, Mac. Do it now! And, furthermore,"
says Leroy, in for a penny, in for a pound, "I want to
drive. I'm tired of your chauffering me all over town
like I was some kind of kid. This Shelby part, it's my
show. Beginning to end."

Mac narrows his eyes and snakes his neck around,
sussing out Leroy. The boy's developed some *passion*.

Mac likes passion. It's a good thing. Passion can
lead a man down all kinds of crooked avenues and
around all kinds of corners he might not have dared
before.

Now, if Mac can just keep body and soul together—
if you can call the potato chip that passes for Mac's
spirit a soul—long enough, they might dare Lucifer
knows what.

But in the meantime . . .

"Leroy!" Mac bellows, reaching down to his toes
for the blast of energy. "You're right. You're absolutely right. Let's quit dicking around with this thing.
You drive us over to the Sutler, let you destroy that
adulterous twat, we'll get on with our men's business.
Warriors!" Mac slaps himself on his scrawny chest.
"Crusaders marching to our next conquest!"

"The Sutler?"

"It's a music club, Leroy. And Shelby's going to be
there tonight. Right up on the stage. Lights shining on
her. No way you can miss her." Mac reaches over on
the dresser, picks up one of his Smith & Wessons,
twirls it like a gunslinger.

"Shelby'll be singing?"

"Yes, Leroy. Doing that very thing that brought her
to Nashville. Took her away from your loving arms."

"Why didn't you tell me this before?"

"Didn't want to ruin your Big Surpriiiiiiiiiise!"

# 53

"SHYNELLE, WHAT IS THIS MESS?"

"I don't know, Momma."

"Little girl, don't you lie to me. These aren't your crayons. And *where* did you get this broken Barbie?"

"A new girl at school gave it to me." Shynelle pulls the covers up over her head.

Momma narrows her eyes. "Did you have *another* birthday, Shynelle? Now, think about it before you say no. Think what I told you about lying."

"Yes, ma'am, I did." Under the covers, the little girl is talking to her toes.

"Child, you keep this up, all these birthdays, you're going to be an old lady before you're twelve. And what is *this?* Shynelle, don't pretend you're asleep. Where'd you get this business card? And all this money! Why, there's ... Shynelle, this is three hundred, my God, almost four hundred dollars!"

The covers flop, and the little girl sits up. "I *told* you about Mr. Chris Cassel, the singing man. He said for me to take that card and his money out of his wallet and buy myself a birthday present. And then I told him that it wasn't *really* my birthday, and he said that's okay because tomorrow really is *his*. Truly. And he said it would be the best birthday present in the whole world if I told you that he's tied up down there in the creek bottom, and his wife is in her car at her house, and there is this bomb that's going to blow her up, and you need to call the police. So I told you. But you wouldn't listen."

# 54

AT THE LAST MINUTE, SHELBY WAS JUMPING INTO HER
car, insisting to Jeff Wayne that she needed to drive
herself to the Sutler, wanted the time to get her head
together—when she remembered she'd never bought
her crystal star.

Her magic charm was still shining in the window of
that gift shop in Hillsboro Village.

She hoped.

Six-forty, the two of them, she and Jeff Wayne, are
standing in Gordon's Gift Shop. Shelby, not trusting
him to pick the right one on his own, led the way in
her Toyota.

"Well, it's awfully pretty," he says, holding the
necklace in his hand where it looks like a star shining
on a ham. "I'll take it," he says to Betty, the big
brunette behind the counter.

"What do you mean?" Shelby asks him. *"You
will?"*

"Come on, Shelby. Let me give this to you as a

little present. A good luck charm doesn't have the same magic if you buy it for yourself."

Shelby gives him a look. What is this *really* about? But, hell, what is *any* of this business with Officer Jeff Wayne Capshew about? His bird-dogging her like Leroy's going to jump out of the bushes at any minute, shoot her down in cold blood? The whole thing is crazy.

"Fine," she says. "You want to buy a poor starving songwriter a good luck charm, have at it, son. And thank you kindly."

But five minutes later, they're still standing there. The computer's down, and Betty can't get an approval on Jeff's credit card. Jeff doesn't have enough cash on him.

"Here, let *me* pay for it," Shelby says. "I've got to *go*, Jeff Wayne."

"No. Absolutely not. I insist."

"Then, hon, I hate to be rude, I'm gonna go on ahead, I'll see you over at the Sutler."

Jeff Wayne is torn. He really doesn't want Shelby to drive there by herself. But on the other hand, he knows that she *really* wants this good luck piece, and the gentleman in him just can't take her money, even as a short-term loan.

"Okay," he finally says. "But you promise me you'll be careful. Keep a lookout for Leroy. You see him, you dial nine-one-one. Do you hear me?" He hands her his cell phone.

"Okay, okay." And Shelby's out of there. Her purse with Chuck's pistol over her shoulder.

She hasn't been gone two minutes, Jeff Wayne's about to take a hike out of the shop up the street to the First National and a money machine, when the door to the shop slams back.

A large red-faced man with thinning dark hair

combed over his bald spot lumbers in. Jeff's seen him before. Booked him for drunk driving about six months earlier.

"Betty!" the man shouts. "This is it! Now, you come on home to me, right this instant, or I'm shooting you and then me." The man is waving a Charter Arms .44 Bulldog, an ugly gun that will definitely do the trick. "I can't live without you, Betty. Don't want to anymore. Won't."

"Frank, what are you doing?" Betty screams.

"Shut up!"

Jeff is maneuvering, trying to slide over to where his right arm is out of the man's line of vision, he can pull his service revolver. Thinking, he can't take the chance on ordering the man to Drop it! Frank could kill Betty in an instant. The look of him, wild-eyed, sweat rolling off of him, chances are real high he would. Jeff Wayne thinks his best bet is to just shoot the sucker in the foot.

"You!" Frank shouts, turning, waving the .44 at Jeff. "Hit the floor. Now!"

Jeff Wayne does, and Frank starts kicking at him, not hard, patting him down with his foot.

"Pull it out real slow, Mr. Copper," he says, clearly remembering Jeff Wayne, too. "Toss it over there. Any funny stuff, I'll kill Betty, here. I swear I will."

Jeff Wayne does as he's told. And settles in for the long haul as one of goddamn Frank's hostages. Shelby flying toward the Sutler—and God knows what.

"I cannot freaking believe this," Jeff Wayne mutters to the floor.

# 55

SHELBY RACES THROUGH THE FRONT DOOR OF THE
Sutler. Seven-fifteen, the place is already filling up,
smoky, thick with the smells of whiskey and beer. People are pouring in behind her. Clint Black's singing
on the jukebox.

A few familiar faces at the bar. Two musicians,
three guys who are songwriting friends of hers, a
skinny girl singer. Two assistants from Bandit, her
music publisher.

Shelby makes the polite noises.

But she's looking for Lynn. She scans the large
room to her left. A tangle of standard-issue Formica
tables, chrome and plastic chairs before the stage.
Dark cinnamon walls plastered thick with photos,
country artists grinning.

Lynn grabs her from behind. "Hey, girl!"

The woman's *something* in a long swishing black
skirt, silvery ruffled off-the-shoulder blouse. The platinum streak in her hair shines. Lynn's humming with

excitement. "I was praying you'd been hit by a truck. I was going to sing every song I ever wrote, then every one you ever wrote, then I was going to take requests. Counting on a call from Letterman when I got home."

"Yeah, well, you can forget that." Shelby tells herself, I'm here. Lynn's here. I made it. Everything's cool.

Now Lynn's pulled away by her husband, George. Something about the equipment setup, the sound check.

The cyclone of noise and anticipation is gathering momentum. Another face pops out at Shelby. "Hey, darlin'. How're you feeling?" It's Dianne Petty, Shelby's fairy godsister from SESAC, tall, skinny, and sexy in a black catsuit. "Great evening coming up." She waggles long fingers. "I can feel it in my bones."

And here's Selma, sleek as a panther in black leather pants, dittoing the sentiment.

Shelby doesn't see Chris Cassel. Where is he?

"Don't worry," says Dianne. "He'll be here."

Now a crowd of well-wishers surges up. Kisses and hugs on all sides. Shelby's feeling overcome. " 'Scuse me," she says. "I'm going back to the ladies' room to throw up."

She's headed in that direction when Chuck catches her by the arm. "Hey, girl. Let me buy you a drink. You look like somebody in dire need of a couple of shots of Southern Comfort."

He plops her on a stool, then launches into a tale of trying to get a baby raccoon off the top of some lady's garage. Ruby barking her head off. Garage was locked, he couldn't even get in. Had to drag Ruby into his truck.

Chuck leaves out the part about running back in to Lizbeth, saying, he's real sorry, but he's kind of lost the impetus. Maybe another time. But not meaning it.

Shelby's trying to pay attention. But she can only focus on the odd detail. The old musket up over the bar. The bright blond curls swirled up atop the head of the pretty girl with the body to die for who's stepping up to the bar. The sweetness of the Southern Comfort, Janis's favorite drink.

Before she knows it, Lynn's at her elbow.

It's showtime.

Shelby slugs back the last of the bourbon, slaps high fives with Chuck, hits the stage cranked.

This is it. There ain't no place better tonight.

And Shelby's saved it *all* up. She's got her game face on. She's jazzed. Ready to kick ass and take names. Show them what she's got.

(Hoping and praying it's good enough.)

She steps behind her keyboard, leans into the microphone. Rita Hayworth face above a Bette Midler body wrapped in a big taffeta shirt that flashes now green, now purple beneath the lights.

Shelby opens her mouth. Croons, "How y'all feelin'? Y'all feelin' good?"

Oh, yes!

It's a hot crowd. Pumped and primed. The room is packed with a happy Nashville gaggle of friends and fans and folks looking for a good time.

Ready to *listen up*.

"Well, *we're* feelin' good," says Shelby. She riffs up and down the keyboard. Delaying, *just* one more moment. Playing with their anticipation. Running her fingers down into that bass as if she were searching for something just a bit sticky. Giving the crowd her scarlet smile. *Sexy* scarlet smile. The one that *knows* some secrets.

Then Lynn chimes in with *her* opening rap. Shelby scans the audience. Registers lots of familiar faces.

# SARAH SHANKMAN

Arlen Tapert, the demo singer. Isn't *that* sweet, that he'd come? And there's Ann King! Shelby waves.

But no Chris Cassel. Where *is* the man? The man she's been busting her hump for. Man's going to give her her big chance. Her rainmaker, a no-show? Shelby's seriously considering being pissed.

But she doesn't have time, for Lynn's jumping with both feet into "Turn Your Faith On," a barn-burner. Zero to ninety in five seconds, it's a risky way to begin. But the Wild Women like risks. Lynn bangs the opening chords on her guitar. Shelby's backing her on this one, this *BIG* song that says, Girl, when your world's at its lowest, its darkest . . .

> There is a flower that blooms through the snow
> There is a fire that's hotter than cold
> There is a river inside you
> That's ready and willin' to flow

The song pours out of Lynn's fingers, her toes. It pokes at the crowd. Pull yourself up by those bootstraps, honey. You've got what it takes. You've got the faith.

> There's a light down inside you
> Put there to guide you
> Turn your faith on
> Turn your faith on

These are folks raised in church. Yes! they pound on tabletops. We believe! We have the faith! Lead us! Lead us on! They give up waves of applause.

And now . . . it's really really showtime.

It's Shelbytime.

Shelby stares out at the crowd, sucking energy from their faces.

Reminding herself of what she heard Dolly say once.

They're on your side. They *want* you to be wonderful. They're dying for you to succeed. Because, as Dolly put it, "People don't come to the shows to see you be you. They come to see you be *them* and what they want to be."

Shelby closes her eyes for a long moment, gathers herself, takes a deep breath.

She's fourteen again. Where all the *very* best material comes from. Ten to seventeen or so, those *oh so longing* years.

She's dancing around on her front porch, her best friend, Rita, right beside her, dancing, too. The two of them *desperate* for her momma's permission. Another mother, down the street, is driving five of them, giggling girls, up to Brandon. To the roller rink.

Shelby winds up. Let's go.

*Momma always said, darlin', be good.*

Shelby's jumping off that porch. Holding hands with Rita, they're racing for the neighbor's car. There'll be *boys* at the roller rink. Strangers with slicked-back hair. *Hoods.* Anything can happen.

*Do what we taught you, do what you should.*

And what did Momma teach Shelby? Taught her how to roller-skate, that's one thing. Here's Shelby, scooting out onto that floor, Rita beside her. They're taking the first loop slow. Checking out the possibilities.

*Said I'd try my best, I really would.*

Shelby shakes loose. Can't be holding hands with a girlfriend when a tall boy with dark hair and a flashing smile is giving her the look. She skates on by him. Pretends she doesn't see him, of course.

*To do the right thing, best that I could.*

The best she can do? That's got to be whirling, back

to front, flipping her short skate skirt. Giving him a little peek. Now giving him her big smile as he cruises up. Says, Hey. Offers her his hand.

> *Best that I could*
> *Be*
> *But . . .*

Shelby's shouting it now. *Leaning* on the *be*. Hanging on the *but*. Letting the crowd hang, too, making 'em *ache* for the next thought. Word. Note. Making 'em beg for it. Come on. Come on. Come on, girl, give it up. Give it to us. Give us what we want.

So Shelby does. She's *in* the song now. She's whirling around the stage like she twirled around that roller rink so long ago. Fourteen, so full of juice and hope, she's a ripe peach about to burst.

"She's *good,*" says Danielle, The pretty blonde Shelby noted earlier at the bar. Picking up drinks for herself and her friends, Lucy and Joyce. Turning to them now. "I hadn't thought she'd be good."

"Humph," says Joyce. Holding her big old purse with the knife in it in her lap. Just in case. She hasn't really defined what that case is. But she's ready for it. Searching the room for Chuck, but not seeing him. Still seething. And aching. Wanting her husband back. Now.

Chuck's standing alone in a corner. Listening. Listening hard.

Lucy says, "Girls, I don't know about you, but I'm kind of having second thoughts about giving this Shelby a tough time in a room of what sounds like her friends. They might turn on us."

"I don't see Jeff Wayne anywhere," says Danielle.

Shifting her bag to her other shoulder. Jeff Wayne's pistol's a lot heavier load than she'd thought.

Shelby and Lynn are almost through their first set when Althea comes bustling in the swinging front doors wearing a long dress striped like a rainbow.

"Y'all couldn't wait?" she yells up at the stage.

"Althea! Get yourself up here!" Shelby yells back. Then tells the audience about Jerome being the fireman who was shot at the First National yesterday.

"And he's doing so much better, y'all!" Althea is jubilating into the microphone, her round arms raised high, the red, green, blue, gold of her dress pouring back from them.

Beaming as if these very people have been praying for her Jerome. And who knows? Maybe they have.

"A little while ago, George Hildebrandt, Lynn here's husband, called us in the hospital on that pay phone over yonder." She points at the back wall. "Wanted to see how Jerome was doing. Jerome and I were listening to these two Wild Women hogging all the glory, sopping up y'all's applause, and Jerome said, Althea, girl, I want you to get yourself right down there, and sing those people my fav-o-rite song."

Shelby pounds out the opening bars of Althea's "Big-Legged Woman." Lynn joins in on the guitar. Those who have heard the song before stand up, waving their arms.

Althea grins. "Now, y'all gone hush so I can sing? And my sweet Jerome can hear me? George, you got my baby on that phone again?"

Then she lets 'er rip.

*Momma told me to quit writing songs*
*About lost love, found love, want to be in love*
*Momma said write about "real life"*

*So I decided to write a song to let the*
*World know what it's like to be a*
*Beautiful, brown, round, pleasingly plump*
*Bodaciously big, Kentucky-fried, broad-breasted*
*Double D brand, big-legged woman in a Barbie*
  *doll world*

"So what do you think about *that?*" Gail's asking Reola as Althea belts her way into the chorus. They're sitting at a table on the right, about halfway back from the stage.

Reola sniffs.

"Do not tell me that you're not having a good time. This is *fun*, Reola. Those girls are *good.*"

"It's tolerable. But just you wait till somebody recognizes you. Then all *hell's* gonna break loose."

"Ain't no chance of that unless I get up and sing," says Gail. "If I do that, you can just excuse yourself to the ladies room."

"You get up and do *what?*"

Out in front of the Sutler, Patsy Angel is keeping watch. Fluttering from one side of the parking lot to the other. Peeping in on folks. Listening to a couple in a Saab convertible having a beef.

He: "I *told* you I didn't want to come."

She: "You never want to go anywhere. You just want to stay home and watch that damned TV."

Patsy Angel flashes a little picture in the boyfriend's head. Girlfriend's stepping out with somebody else. With a lot more hair and more money in his jeans.

He: "I'm sorry, sugar. I don't know why I'm being so grumpy. Let's go on in. Have us a *good* time." Gives his girlfriend the sweetest kiss.

Patsy Angel grins. And that's good and that's fine, but that's also lagniappe. Not what she's here for.

Patsy's on the lookout for Leroy and Mac McKenzie, that nasty little son of a bitch.

She can smell them in the night air. Smell Rahab's
sulfurous breath pouring off them.

They're in the neighborhood.

Inside, the second set is beginning. Around and
around the three friends go.

Lynn does "I Gotta Jones for You." Wallowing in
a love that's bad as a drug habit she can't cut loose.

Althea beats up on one she calls "Beach Nights."

Shelby wants to drive. Wants to go. Puts the pedal
to the metal. Lets the rubber hit the road.

The Wild Women are cooking.

But still, Shelby scans the room once more, no
Chris Cassel.

And still no Jeff Wayne.

Where has *that* boy gone? Shelby asks herself.

With her good luck star?

"You know what?" says Danielle, scooting back
from the table. "I think I'm gonna go on over to the
Bluebird, see if that nice man from lunch today still
wants to buy me a drink."

"Unh-huh," says Joyce, paying Danielle no mind.
She's been scouting the room for Chuck. *Still* hasn't
seen him.

Lucy says, "That looks like Dianne Petty over there.
Damn, that woman looks good. How does she do
that? Joyce, do you mind, hon, if I step over there for
a minute, say howdy to her?"

"Just keep driving," says Mac. "We're almost there.
Slow down now. It's up here on the left."

Leroy's fairly well drunk. Slogging around in his
own personal slough of despond. Digging up every

261

bad thing Shelby ever did to him. Chewing on that day in that Mississippi courtroom. Acting like she was *thrilled* to be shut of him.

Then that courtroom downtown here. Telling all that garbage to the night court judge.

Like she didn't know him.

Didn't know he was Leroy.

Didn't know he'd just had one bourbon too many, was eaten up with *love* for her.

But no. *His* love wasn't good enough for her.

Not for Miss High and Mighty.

Unh-uh.

Shelby didn't care.

Shelby didn't care.

Shelby didn't give a shit about poor old Leroy.

Chuck's hanging out now at the far corner of the bar, on the way to the men's room.

He's sipping a Scotch. Reviewing all his sins. Thinking about how Momma was right. The straight and the narrow is the best way. If he hadn't hoed his row so wide and curvy he wouldn't be in this mess today.

Up on the stage, it's like Althea's reading his mind. Singing one about Jesus knowing what you do.

Just like Momma said. That picture of Him on the wall. Sees all. Knows all.

Chuck steps back to the men's room for a quick pee. Stares up at a little TV hanging from the ceiling. Usually it's tuned to the Nashville Network, but right now he's looking at the news.

The camera zeros in on a pretty woman in a blue dress. She's standing in front of a house that looks vaguely familiar to Chuck. It's the house he was at this very afternoon! The one next door to Lizbeth's. Had that little raccoon up on its garage.

The woman in the blue dress's saying, "This is Abigail Chang coming to you live with a News Flash from WKRN here on Lynnwood Boulevard in Belle Meade. And with me here I have Shynelle Simon, six and a half years old, of Preston Road—"

A little red-haired girl smiles right at Chuck.

"It was Shynelle who began the chain of events which happily resulted in Mrs. Joan Mathers Cassel, wife of Liberty Records executive Chris Cassel, being rescued from her car here at her home—"

Chris Cassel! That was Chris Cassel's house with the little coon!

Chuck stares at a shot of the garage. The door is up and open now, a little silver German car inside it with both doors and trunk wide.

"—where she'd been bound and gagged for the past nine hours, while her husband, Chris Cassel, who himself had been kidnapped at gunpoint by Mrs. Cassel's abductors, feared that she was to be blown up by a bomb, which was later found to be a hoax.

"There *was* no bomb, it was discovered, after Shynelle Simon led the police to Mr. Cassel, who had also been bound and gagged and abandoned in a wooded area near Shynelle's house. Taped to Mr. Cassel was a computer joystick that the kidnappers had told Mr. Cassel was the control which would decimate Mrs. Cassel. Now both Mr. and Mrs. Cassel are safe inside this, their luxurious Belle Meade home, where they are being interviewed by the police."

Holy shit, Chuck breathes. He was inches away from rescuing that woman. Chris Cassel's wife. Good grief! And *that's* why the A&R man ain't here. Lord, wait till he tells Shelby.

Abigail Chang puts her arm around Shynelle. "If it weren't for the brave little girl, Shynelle Simon, who *knows* what would have happened to these people?

Even though the bomb was a hoax, they were both in danger of their lives and owe a lot to you."

Shynelle smiles up at her and says, "I hope Mr. Cassel has a really happy birthday tomorrow."

Chuck's flying out of the men's room. Then hears Abigail Chang say, "And now we take you to Gordon's Gifts in Hillsboro Village, where the hostage situation we were following seems to be ending peaceably. Cut to you, Matt." Chuck puts on the brakes.

"This is Matt Kelman at Gordon's Gifts. And the man you see coming out first is Officer Jeff Wayne Capshew of the Metro Police."

Chuck can't believe his eyes. It's the cop from day before yesterday at Shelby's! Walking out slowly, his arm around the shoulder of a huge old son who's sobbing like a baby, wiping his tears on his sleeve. Behind them is a big brunette woman.

"Held at gunpoint an hour and a half by Mr. Gordon, here, who seemed to be distraught by his wife's, that's Mrs. Betty Gordon behind them, filing for divorce."

The camera zooms in on Officer Capshew. From one hand dangles something Chuck can't quite make out. Something glinting in the TV lights. Shining, like a star.

Chuck has *got* to go tell Shelby all this. Tell her, when she finishes this song, what happened to Chris Cassel. Let her know that he's not blowing her off. The man was in danger of his life! Him *and* Officer Jeff Wayne Capshew!

Chuck makes his way toward the stage, scrambling and crouching, trying to be quiet, creeping around tables and chairs. He bumps into Gail Powell. "Excuse me, ma'am," he whispers.

Then snags his foot on something and trips, falls facefirst.

The something is Joyce's foot.

Joyce saw him coming. Wanted him to stop. Was afraid that he wouldn't, afraid that he'd just fly on by. Afraid that she'd lost him forever.

Chuck rolls over in a mess of folks' feet, peanut shells, cigarette butts. Sits up. Sees Joyce staring at him.

And the past three days wash over him. A huge tidal wave of guilt and regret.

"Darlin'," he whispers.

The next thing he knows, Joyce has slipped off her chair and is sitting in his lap. Face-to-face, her legs wrapped around him. Like in the old days. Back when they were first married, thirty-five years ago, he used to carry Joyce around like this, like she was his little baby.

"Yes, Chuckie?" Joyce says.

Chuck pulls his one and only beloved to him and kisses her.

Now, the kiss that Chuck lays on Joyce is not an ordinary kiss.

It is the kind of kiss that makes mermaids rise from the sea to sing upon the rocks.

The sort of buss that stops angels midflight.

In fact, outside, Patsy Angel halts, sniffs, says, What the heck was that?

A smooch that calls to mind Clark Gable, Cary Grant, Valentino. None of the new faces will do.

It is the kind of smooch that causes Lucy to take one look down at her sister and brother-in-law and say to her friend Dianne Petty, You mind if I just stay over here with y'all?

Then Chuck says, "Can you ever forgive me?"

"You bet." Joyce grins.

They're moving. Though Chuck's a songwriter to the core, he knows that Shelby and Lynn and Althea will forgive him if he splits. This thing he's dealing with here, this is the real thing. The actual life experience that the songs sing of.

Chuck'll be halfway home, way outside the city limits, before he even remembers the business about Chris Cassel. Or Officer Jeff Wayne Capshew.

Speaking of which, the second Jeff Wayne can get loose from Frank Gordon, turn him over to the SWAT team, Jeff Wayne's on the horn, trying to explain to HQ that they need to get a car over to the Sutler, ASAP. He's real nervous about Leroy.

"Leroy Mabry?" asks the dispatcher.

"Leroy Mabry. We have a pickup order on him. Order of protection he blew, from his ex-wife. She's performing tonight at the Sutler."

"We have an APB out on one Leroy Mabry, Officer Capshew. Caution warning, armed and dangerous. He's one of the two suspects in the kidnapping of a Belle Meade couple earlier today. Can you hold one second, let me patch you over to Captain Amis?"

"Park right there, Leroy. That's good."

Leroy's jangling with excitement. He's a lightning bug in the dark interior of the Oldsmobile.

Mac's leaning his head back against the seat. Barely holding on. Sweat and stink pouring out of him. The man is running on fumes.

But Mac has no intention of letting a hospital lay its paws on him again. He's said *No way* to doctors prodding and poking, humming to themselves while he lies sweating in a high bed.

Mac's goal is to remain viciously ambulatory until the very last jot and tittle and tick of his mean little self has tocked.

Or has just plain old been et up from the inside out, which seems more likely.

Seems to be happening this very instant, in fact. The gnashing in his malignant gut has shifted into high gear.

"Get me out of this car," he grunts at Leroy. "Come on, boy. Give your old pardner a hand."

Leroy runs around the car. Grabs the door handle.

Patsy Angel knocks his hand away with a swipe of her wing. *Out of here, Leroy. Go home. Git. Leave my Shelby alone.*

Leroy shakes his head. Reaches for it again.

Patsy Angel rears back, and Rahab catches her by the tips of both wings. Holds on. Pinions her. Patsy's struggling and screaming oaths and imprecations that are pretty shocking, considering her exalted status.

Then Rahab kicks Leroy in the butt.

Up on the stage, Shelby's said *Forget you* to Chris Cassel. She's gotten over her disappointment. No longer gives a rip about Mr. A&R Man, breaker of promises.

Because she's having such a good time—pouring out her songs to the folks, them pumping their love back, the songs like a big old four-lane, their love and their lust and their longing to be free of the ordinary old everyday that holds 'em back, keeps 'em poor and hungry, stands in the way of 'em realizing their most basic dreams, all of that roaring back and forth on that highway of songs. And if that ain't the point, well, what is?

The Wild Women are cruising into the home stretch now. It's getting to be time to think about letting these folks who have been so nice to them go home and get some shut-eye.

"I've been working on a song here for a while to

do for y'all tonight," says Shelby. "Finished it just this morning with a wonderful songwriter I discovered a couple of days ago. I think maybe y'all need to discover her, too. Ann?" Shelby beckons toward Gail. "Would you do me the great favor of coming up here and helping me sing our song for the folks?"

Gail turns and gives Reola a wink. *Told you this might happen.* Stands.

"Don't do it," says Reola.

The double doors of the Sutler slam open, then bang shut, framing Leroy and Mac. Gunslingers.

Above and behind them Patsy Angel and Rahab jockey for position, invisible to the human eye, of course. Patsy Angel pulling. Rahab pushing.

Stage center, Gail's saying, "Shelby Tate, here, came into my life a couple of nights ago and woke me up. I'd been sleeping a long time. I'm talking about a *long* time. Now, I know I don't look like Cinderella—" She laughs and turns to Shelby. "You ready?" Lynn passes Gail her guitar.

"Would you look at that?" says Mac. "Do you believe it?" He and Leroy have stationed themselves at the bar.

Leroy nods. Speechless at the sight of Shelby up there. Star-bright in front of all these folks. He doesn't realize Mac's talking about Gail Powell.

Outside, about a mile away, police sirens rip the thick night air. A convoy of Metro Police are descending upon the Sutler.

"Ann and I wrote this song about my ex-husband," Shelby is saying.

Leroy freezes.

"I'd been working on another version of this song for a long while," says Shelby, "but it was going nowhere till I met Ann, and she showed me that the song had the wrong attitude. But maybe I ought to shut up, and we'll just sing it for y'all. What do you think, Ann?"

Gail strums Lynn's guitar. Hits the opening chords. And they ram at the song together.

> *That girl you say you're missing*
> *Ain't your missus anymore*
> *She ain't frying no more chicken*
> *She ain't scrubbing no more floors*
> *She's trembled in your shadow*
> *She's cried behind locked doors*
> *She's taken all she can*
> *And she ain't taking it no more*
>
> *Do I miss you*
> *Well I guess I do*
> *Like Joan of Arc might miss a barbecue*
> *I'm tired of your demands*
> *I've had more than I can stand*
> *Yeah, I still miss my man*
> *But my aim is getting better*

The crowd is howling. Clapping. Calling for more. Dianne Petty turns, wide-eyed, to Selma Phillips. "Do you hear what I'm hearing? Do you know who that old woman is?"

"I can't believe it," says Selma. "Do you think we've died and gone to heaven?"

"Take the second verse, girl," Shelby says to Gail. Gail rears back and slams into it.

> *You lied to me and cheated*
> *You made me feel ashamed*
> *You told me I was worthless*
> *Said I was to blame*

SARAH SHANKMAN

*For making you go crazy, the cause for all your*
  *pain*
*Not once was I a winner*
*In your heartless stupid game*

"Good *Lord* have mercy," Dianne says.

"It is," says Selma. "It's her."

Up on the stage, Shelby's looking over the old woman's head at Lynn, and Lynn's staring back at her. They know it, too. They're singing with the dead come back to life! With one of country music's all-time legends!

Leroy is reeling with the song's words. "Why is she saying those things?" he whines to Mac. "Why's she being so hateful?" Leroy's holding his chest as if her words have pierced his very heart. "That spiteful bitch."

"Kill her," Mac hisses, echoing Rahab, who's leaning in his ear. "Kill her now."

Boiling down Franklin Pike, their lights flashing red and blue, the police convoy cuts a horribly familiar swatch through this American cityscape. What fresh hell is this, citizens on the sidelines ask themselves. Who's shot? Maimed? Blown up? Beaten to a bloody pulp? How many children torn to bits? Whose children? Whose loved ones? Mine? Please, God, not mine. Not mine or anyone's I know.

Shelby and Gail join forces on the second chorus. The crowd howls this time at the Joan of Arc and her barbecue.

Patsy Angel and Rahab are locked wing to wing, cheek to jowl, foot to foot in a battle to the death.

Shelby takes the bridge.

*I'm aiming for the stars*
*I'm gonna shoot the moon*
*And somewhere there's a real man*

# I STILL MISS MY MAN . . .

*With a love for me that's true*
*Boy, is anything I'm saying getting through?*

"I *am* a real man!" Leroy insists from the bar. Slipping away from it now. Sliding toward the stage. And Shelby.

A few heads swivel. A few folks stare. But only a handful, as more and more of the crowd realize whom they're hearing.

*Gail Powell. It's Gail Powell.* The buzz is beginning.

Oh Lord, Reola moans to herself. Shuts her eyes. She's too *old* for this.

Shelby hasn't seen Leroy. Hasn't heard him, either. She's *into* the song. Into the singing. Into, Jesus, Gail Powell.

They head for the chorus one last time. And a tag.

*Yeah, I still miss my man*
*But my aim is getting better*

They soar on that last word. Lift off. The audience lifts off, too. Rushing the stage. Shouting their names.

"You know what?" Gail Powell says into the mike. "I like this so much, I think I'm gonna do a comeback album with this little lady. Yep. The two of us. Singing our own songs. What do y'all think? Think we can get anybody here in Nashville interested in doing that?"

Shelby can't do anything but grin. Hug Gail Powell and grin.

Dianne Petty and Selma Phillips are both punching in numbers on their cell phones. Interested? Are you kidding?

Outside, the Metro Police is rolling rolling rolling into the parking lot. Jumping out of cars before they're fully stopped. Officer Jeff Wayne Capshew is among the first.

"Bullshit!" Leroy screams into the rolling wave of applause. The sound crashing down on his ears. "It's all bullshit!" Then he's charging the stage. His arm is rising. His fingers squeezing one of Mac's Smith & Wesson .38s.

"Goddamn bullshit!" Leroy screams.

Shelby whirls toward his voice. The spotlights are in her eyes. She can't see him. *L E R O Y,* she mouths.

She dips beneath the spotlight and sees him.

He lunges toward her in slow motion.

Then, it's as if a locomotive is blowing, long and lonely at some country crossroads, a train picking up all the players, and they rumble toward their fate.

Patsy Angel and Rahab tumble over and over in the air, down the bar, across the floor. A hoop of feathers and fire. Patsy Angel pulls loose, one wing bent and dangling. Broken. Useless. Still, she plunges toward Leroy.

*Now!* Rahab screams.

*Shoot now!* orders Mac.

Leroy fires, but Patsy Angel bumps him at the crucial instant. The shot goes wild, slams into the ceiling.

The crowd screams with one voice. Hits the floor. George Hildebrandt does a flying dive and knocks Lynn off the stage. Covers her.

"Good boy, Leroy!" Mac screams. Feeling A-L-I-V-E. His blood pumping. Chugging. Heading for the breach.

"Leroy, you son of a bitch!" Shelby shouts into the microphone. The reverb bounces off all four walls. *Bitch. Bitch. Bitch. Bitch.*

Jeff Wayne is running. Racing for the door. Shelby's magic crystal in his pocket. Forty steps away.

Leroy's closing the distance to Shelby. The gap between them narrows. The gap closes.

Then suddenly Leroy stops. In the last moment, just

before he can stretch out his hand and touch Shelby
one final time, before he blows her away, he pauses
to stare at her eye's golden ring.

"I need you, Shelby," he breathes.

"Give me the gun, Leroy," she answers.

"Shoot her!" Mac screams.

*"Now,* Leroy!" Shelby barks.

Then Mac opens his mouth one last time, and his
life's blood, black as pitch, pours onto the floor.

*Kiiiiiiill her!* Rahab rages.

Jeff Wayne leads the charge against the door. Mac
whirls toward him, his gun drawn, a volcano of bile
spewing, pouring down his shirt. Jeff Wayne fires, and
Mac falls dead while the bullet's still airborne, whistling toward his heart.

"Mac!" Leroy wails. "Oh, Mac!"

Patsy Angel tears herself away from Rahab, crawls
across the stage, knocks Shelby's open purse to the
floor.

Gail watches it fall, sees Chuck's Browning automatic tumble out, glinting in the spotlight, grabs it up.

"You killed him!" Leroy shrieks, pointing his gun
at the stage. "You killed my best friend, and now I'm
going to kill you."

The three of them—Shelby, Gail, and Patsy
Angel—freeze in a tableau. A trio of girl singers, songwriters, sisters.

Leroy squeezes the trigger.

Patsy Angel dives for his bullet. Takes the slug.

Rahab roars in a fit of pique. Throws in the towel.
Stomps out. Hellishly pissed.

Gail Powell braces herself, takes aim, and fires one.
It sings, *Bye-bye, Leroy.*

The bullet cuts a swath through Leroy's golden
curls. His ice-blue eyes roll back, he keels over, and
the cops nail him to the floor.

Gail and Shelby grab each other up in the biggest-ever Nashville hug.

*But my aim is getting be-eh-ter,* Gail croons into Shelby's ear like a lullabye, rocking her.

Whereupon their song climbs into the Nashville sky of midnight blue, zooms past the stars, and spirals up up up toward a covey of country music seraphim, who nod yes, indeedy.

It has a real good groove.

And it's a hit. Oh, yes.

Gold, if not platinum, for sure.